And the
Angels Sing

And the Angels Sing

Stories by Kate Wilhelm

ST. MARTIN'S PRESS   NEW YORK

All stories copyright © Kate Wilhelm unless indicated otherwise. Grateful acknowledgment is made for permission to reprint the following:

"The Look Alike" copyright © 1988. First published in *Redbook*, October, 1988.

"O Homo; O Femina; O Tempora" copyright © 1985 by Omni Publication International, Ltd. First published in *Omni*, May, 1985.

"The Chosen" copyright © 1970. First published in *Orbit 6*, edited by Damon Knight (Putnam).

"On the Road to Honeyville" copyright © 1972. First published in *Orbit 11*, edited by Damon Knight (Putnam).

"The Great Doors of Silence" copyright © 1986. First published in *Redbook*, July, 1986, under the title "Never Tell Anyone."

"The Day of the Sharks" copyright © 1992.

"The Loiterer" copyright © 1986. First published in *Redbook*, October, 1986, under the title "Someone Is Watching."

"The Scream" copyright © 1974. First published in *Orbit 13*, edited by Damon Knight (Putnam).

"Strangeness, Charm and Spin" copyright © 1984. First published in *Light Years and Dark*, edited by Michael Bishop (Berkley).

"The Dragon Seed" copyright © 1985 by Omni Publication International, Ltd. First published in *Omni*, December, 1985.

"Forever Yours, Anna" copyright © 1987 by Omni Publication International, Ltd. First published in *Omni*, July 1987.

"And the Angels Sing" copyright © 1990 by Omni Publication International, Ltd. First published in *Omni*, April 1990.

Design by Judy Christensen

Library of Congress Cataloging-in-Publication Data

Wilhelm, Kate.
    And the angels sing : stories / by Kate Wilhelm.
        p. cm
    ISBN 0-312-06898-0
    1. Science fiction, American.   I. Title.
PS3573.I434A54 1992
813'.54—dc20   91-39003
                                                                          CIP

First Edition: February 1992

10 9 8 7 6 5 4 3 2 1

FOR DAVID AND SUSAN WRIGHT, WITH LOVE.

Contents

Foreword

I discovered the work of Kate Wilhelm in the 1970s. I was then the full-time mother of two small children. I had gone straight from graduate school into motherhood, and I was still surprised, on occasion, at the extent of my new isolation. My life was intense, exhausting, frequently joyful, but always extremely small. I was the mime in the classic sequence—the occupant of a box whose walls were collapsing.

On those days when magic touched my life in the form of two children napping simultaneously, I read. There were two or three feminist periodicals I read regularly, but they did not, in the seventies, appear much interested in mothers. The fictional work of most men struck me as essentially irrelevant to the tasks I currently faced.

I would not meet Kate Wilhelm for years and years, but she along with a number of other female writers were my chief adult companions during this period of my life. I clung to the Wilhelm heroines. They were not housewives, at least not all of them, but these women lived in the real world of increment and limitation. They shared a certain toughness, the courage to see exactly how limited their options were and to try to control their lives in spite of this. These women failed as often as they succeeded and the books sometimes ended on the failure, but the effort was the triumph. The Wilhelm heroine might be deluded about many things, but she never inflated her own importance or influence. She did the best she could in the circumstances she found.

For me, Wilhelm's work combined all the best elements of escape, in terms of its transportational drama, of exotic and lushly evoked landscapes, of past and future lives, of adventure and danger and courage, while all the while retaining an absolute relevance to the issues of my life.

My life has changed a lot since then. My children are teenagers—they no longer nap, but, given the option, they sleep till noon. And I have begun to write myself. But I have continued to turn to the work of Kate Wilhelm for companionship, for solace, for wonder, to be amazed, to be transported, to be advised.

"You can tell if it's real. You can tell. If it's there years later. If you can go to it and find it years later." These words are not mine. They come from the shattered woman in "The Day of the Sharks" and her purpose in using them is quite different from mine, but I find the words themselves irresistibly apt. There is something real that survives in the work of Kate Wilhelm.

I know of no other writer who conveys so successfully the twin truths of our lives—that the world is at once so much better and so much worse than we imagine it to be. The stories in this book range from the sharp sweetness of "The Look Alike," to the deathly quiet of "The Dragon Seed"; from the sustaining natural setting of "The Chosen," to the destroying natural setting of "The Day of the Sharks"; from the off-kilter delight of "Strangeness, Charm and Spin," to the potent politics of "The Great Doors of Silence"; from the world-opening inhalation that ends "The Scream," to the world-slamming-shut exhale of the title story "And the Angels Sing."

Kim Stanley Robinson, along with many other writers, was once a student of Kate Wilhelm's at the Clarion writing workshop in East Lansing, Michigan. Robinson told me that his class made up a game in which they ranked each other and various instructors along the three axes of strangeness, charm, and spin. Kate Wilhelm, he said, was one of only two participants to receive a perfect ten in each of the three categories.

So you'll want to read these stories with a little space between them for the full effect. You'll want to prepare yourself in advance, brace yourself, buckle yourself in. Turn to the first story. You're about to be strangely charmed. You're about to be spun.

—Karen Joy Fowler
Davis, California

The Look Alike

When Gina Crandall fell into bed Sunday night, Monday morning, actually, she had been too tired to sleep well, and now she was in the sort of twitchy, dream-laden sleep that was never refreshing. She had dropped various items of clothing on her way to bed—skirt, bra, panty hose—strewn like crumbs to guide her from the woods on awakening. As if responding to the cue, she dreamed that she was lost in a maze of department store counters, all higher than she was. Usually she switched on her answering machine, turned off the telephone bell when she was ready for bed, but she had forgotten that night, and when the bell sounded, she plummeted from dream to nightmare.

She was in the car with Stuart, laughing because the seat belt so clearly delineated the bulge of child within her. "In another few weeks, forget it," he was saying, also laughing. His laughter changed to frantic shouts abruptly; she swiveled, stared, unable to move as logs began to rain from the sky toward her in slow motion. She could make out the

1

details of bark, where the saw had bitten into the tree; one log
in particular, twenty feet long, wobbled as it fell, first one end
up, then the other, and all the while Stuart's shouts and
screams increased, became shriller, turned into a siren that
blasted her ears. The log hit the car, and suddenly she was
awake, still caught in the paralysis of the nightmare.

The telephone rang again; the sound released her muscles,
permitted her hand to move although she did not will it to do
so.

"Gina baby! That's swell! Just five rings!"

"What?"

"Wake up, sweetie. Wake up, morning time."

"Paulo?" Her voice sounded strangely muffled, even to
her; she felt a stranger to the world, in an unfamiliar place,
talking to someone she really did not know. But already the
nightmare was gone, its only trace a film of sweat that covered her entire body. "Paulo? What do you want?" She swept
her hand over her forehead, then threw off the covers.

"You awake? Want me to call back in a minute?"

"For heaven's sake, Paulo, it's the middle of the night and
I just got to bed. What do you want?"

"You're awake," he said cheerfully. "Look, sweetie, Peg
showed up at work with a fever of one oh two, and Bobby's
gone for the week, and Corinne had enough sense to put on
her robot to take her calls. That leaves you, sweetie."

She took a deep breath, ready to hang up, but he went on:
"See you over at the Riverview Mall in half an hour. And
thank me nicely, Gina. I gave you half an hour extra sleep
while we loaded the truck. I'll bring coffee and doughnuts.
See you."

She let the phone drop, lay back down and closed her eyes,
but the memory of the nightmare even though the content
was gone made sleep impossible and she knew it. She felt cold
and clammy now. After a moment she sat up, then groaned

when she looked at the clock by her bed. Five-thirty. Shower, she thought, and coffee. Let him wait, damn him.

There was a four-story Baron's Department Store in downtown Cincinnati, the one Gina usually worked in, another smaller one near the university, and this one in Riverview Mall. Yuppie heaven, Paulo called it with some justification. The mall housed a Christian Dior shop, Liz Claiborne, Tiffany, a Bloomingdale's outlet . . . The mall would be officially completed in another week or so, but as soon as the construction crews finished a section, the tenants moved in and the customers followed. It was six-thirty when Gina arrived that morning. Paulo and another display worker, Tom Gearheart, had already unloaded the truck and were fitting together the four-foot-tall Easter eggs that were to be placed throughout the store. The motif was an egg hunt, with knee-high painters hiding behind eggs with their buckets of paint, parent-mannequins looking elegant in their finery, and exquisitely dressed children-mannequins following gaudy ribbons here and there. There was also a display of Easter bonnets to be arranged—antique hats, modern hats, beautiful hats, ridiculous hats.

"And here she is," Paulo called out when she approached. "The one and only, our own incomparable Gina!"

Tom Gearheart looked embarrassed; he always looked embarrassed around her. He was a couple of years younger than her twenty-eight years, Paulo a couple of years older than she was. Gina nodded to them, scowling, and Paulo laughed with what seemed inhuman good cheer considering the hour.

Paulo Moreno was assistant manager of the display department. At their first meeting four years earlier he had asked if she dyed her hair that color, a rich auburn tending toward red, and if she would go out with him that night after work. She had not answered either question, had tried to dodge him completely for the next two weeks, which had amused him enormously. Later, she had been outraged when he explained himself. "Sweetie," he had said with mock patience, "I always try to date the new women. You'd have been a gorgeous catch."

"Don't call me sweetie!"

"But you are sweet, a dear little thing. So it didn't work with you. No harm in trying, nothing ventured, nothing gained, and whatnot. And, Gina, it gets cold out there in shadowland, you know? Cold and lonely. And you do know. Okay, let's get to work."

That was how it was with him, some of the other women had said with indulgent smiles. Gradually Gina had come to have the same indulgent affection for him, but her feeling was mixed with a touch of unease that at times came close to fear because he had an uncanny knack for saying in an offhand way things she did not want to think about. Of course, she often reminded herself, she did not believe a thing he said outside of the common ground of their work. It was not so much lying, she had decided; he simply told stories so well that he might have come to believe them himself. She had also realized that no matter how she might feel about him, no one in authority would reprimand him, because he was so very good at his job. It was generally accepted that he would not be with Baron's much longer. He was on his way up the ladder.

He had told her that at first he thought she had snubbed him because, as he put it, "I ain't exactly lily white, now am I?"

"But you're the—" She had bitten her cheek to keep from completing the sentence and he had laughed in delight, perfectly aware that she had almost said he was the most handsome man she had ever seen. Thick lustrous black hair with a deep wave, lovely melting brown eyes, the lithe body of a dancer. He said his family was from Puerto Rico, and it

might have been true. His Mama, he had said, named him
Pablo and called him Paulo because Pablos in New York
drove taxis or made deliveries. That had sounded too crazy
to be a lie. That was the problem, anything he said might
have been true and nothing he said was necessarily true.

"Okay, team," Paulo said that morning. "Gina, upstairs.
Tom, parking-lot windows. We'll have this sucker decked
out in a couple of hours. Let's do it."

And they would have finished in less than three hours if
things had gone right, Gina thought morosely at nine-thirty.
But things never went right and delays should have been
figured in at the start. She was almost done with the display
at the mall-side entrance when the security men began to
open the store for business. Already, people were appearing
in the wide corridors, window shopping, some walking with
quick purpose. Gina felt uncomfortable in her old soft jeans
and T-shirt and sneakers, good clothes for the work she did,
up and down ladders, under tables, on her knees, but the
clientele of this mall made her feel shabby, out of place.
Almost angrily she plopped an Easter basket under an azalea
in scarlet bloom; a boy-mannequin looked on blankly, a
girl-mannequin smiled a painted smile, her face tilted at an
awkward angle. Gina started to reach for that one to realign
the head, and came to a stop.

A group of children had just emerged from the bookstore
across the wide aisle from Baron's. They were laughing and
skipping, five- or six-year-olds walking in pairs, holding
hands, being led by a young woman, followed by another.
The last little girl . . . She had long smooth red hair caught
up with a green ribbon, like Tenniel's Alice. She turned toward Gina; her eyes were almost as green as the ribbon.

Gina closed her eyes hard, snapped them open again. The
little girl had stopped moving, was staring back at her with
a puzzled look. Her partner tugged on her hand, and she ran
with her, with the other children. Gina did not move as the

women herded the children toward the big glass doors, as they exited the mall, vanished outside. Then, as if in a dream, she left the display she had been working on, crossed the aisle to the bookstore, and came to a stop. A comfortable-looking, gray-haired woman glanced up from the counter.

Gina took another step. She had to moisten her lips in order to speak. "Those children . . ."

"Cute, aren't they? Riverside Kindergarten kids." She held up a paper with a childish drawing of Easter eggs. "They help decorate our windows every year. We have a contest and the winners have their pictures in the windows for a week. On Thursday they'll come back and see whose pictures are on display and they'll all get little baskets of jelly beans. If it was up to me, I'd use all the pictures, but it isn't. You working in Baron's?" She looked more sharply at Gina and started to move around the counter. "Are you all right, dear?"

"Hey, Gina, you want to buy a book, how about you do it on your time," Paulo called to her.

She turned stiffly and recrossed the aisle to Baron's where Paulo was waiting.

"Sweetie, it ain't nice to walk away and leave things— Gina, you see a ghost or something? What's wrong?"

Her mouth was too dry again. She shook her head and started to pass him to return to the display she had left. He caught her arm. "I'm all right," she mumbled finally. "I thought I saw someone . . . someone . . . I'm all right."

What could she have said, she wondered as she completed her work. She had just seen herself at age six? Even as the words formed, she denied them. Not herself as she had been, but her child as she would be now if . . . The thought refused to move beyond that.

Paulo invited her to breakfast with him and Tom, but she refused, and went home to her small apartment. Clothes were on the floor, the bed a tumbled mess, as if it were someone else's home, not hers. Ordinarily she was tidy, almost excessively neat. She started to pick up the things she had dropped, then let the garments fall again and sat on the side of the bed, staring at the opposite wall. Why had she never decorated the place, she wondered. It was almost convent-barren. No artwork hung on the walls, a bookcase was filled to overflowing, with a stack of books on each side, like unreliable bookends; movie cassettes, the television and VCR with a rocking chair before them took up most of the space; music tapes filled their own shelves, and beyond that there was little that said here is where Gina lives, this room defines Gina. She got up and went to the room where she had placed her drawing table, her paints and pencils, art books; an easel leaned against the wall. She rarely even entered that room anymore. She should have kept it as a living room, she thought distantly. Restlessly she went on to the kitchen and started to make coffee, then stopped. She did not want coffee or food or anything else.

She should try to sleep, but rejected that also. Not yet. She was off the rest of the day, all the next day, and there was nothing she wanted to do, nowhere she wanted to go, no one she wanted to see. With a chill she realized that this was exactly how she had acted six years ago; this was exactly how she had felt then, distant, removed, not interested in anything at all. Not brooding, not thinking, just not there. With determination she went back to the sink to force herself to finish making coffee, but she stared out the small window instead, seeing nothing.

She remembered how obediently she had told the psychiatrist whatever she had wanted to hear. *Tell me about the accident,* she had said. Dr. Tichenor. That was her name. Dr. Rose Tichenor. Soft curly brown hair, pale blue eyes, long elegant fingers. She remembered her fingers, how beautiful they were. *Tell me about the accident.*

"I went with Stuart to buy some special wood he needed.

A machine lifting logs broke and logs fell and smashed the car. There were sirens all around and I woke up in the hospital. The baby was stillborn."

What do you feel about it now, Gina?

"Nothing."

What do you feel about Stuart?

"Nothing."

But you plan to leave him?

"Yes."

How concerned everyone had been by her attitude—her parents, Stuart, the doctor, friends. No one had understood that she had been killed in the accident as surely as her baby; this part that was left was meaningless. And no one had understood what she meant by that; she had not understood it herself, but it was true.

Seeing that red-haired child in the mall had stirred it all up again, the uncertainties, her feelings of being half alive, a sense of waiting. She nodded. Waiting. She had spent a lifetime waiting, and she could not even name what it was she waited for. Abruptly she left the sink, went to the telephone by her bed to call the store, to ask for Sheila Lamotte, the manager of the display department, to change her day off to Thursday.

The pictures in the bookstore window that Thursday were as childish as she had expected—misshapen eggs garishly colored, funny-looking baskets. One was of a meticulously drawn basket with several round eggs that might have been traced around a quarter. There were rabbits with pink ears, and daisylike flowers in rainbow colors. Gina examined each picture carefully. She moved to the other window beyond the door, and there were more of the same. Then she drew in a sharp breath and leaned in closer. Three flowers, two eggs, all in pastel colors, and peeking over the top of a flower there was a sharp little face, slanted eyes, pointed ears: a fairy.

Gina had been a precocious reader, had fallen in love with fairies before school, had adored them until adolescence. She could remember vividly many of the illustrations in the fairy tales she had clung to beyond the age when it was altogether acceptable. She might have drawn just such an Easter picture herself at that age, she thought.

She jerked away from the window and looked for a place where she could sit down, have a cup of coffee, read for a little while. Many little girls discovered fairies at an early age. Maybe even little boys loved fairies until they were told trucks were more proper objects for their attention. It meant nothing. Nothing. Of course, she had told herself before leaving the apartment, she had no intention of waiting around all day for the child to return for her jelly beans. It might not be until late in the afternoon. She would be noticed; loitering all day was frowned upon in a mall like this one. And what was the point?

There was a coffee shop within sight of the bookstore, and she had brought a book. The first class appeared at ten. There was even a little red-haired girl among the giggling children, but her hair was coppery and so curly it frizzed. Gina watched them over the top of her book, a cup of coffee before her. Maybe that was the child she had seen, and her fatigue had tricked her into seeing a different image altogether. It was possible that her mind and eyes had betrayed her. She sipped the coffee, turned a page blindly. The next group of children arrived shortly after eleven. Involuntarily Gina rose and moved away from the table, remembered her check, returned for it and paid for her coffees.

The little girl's hair was done up in a ponytail today, tied with a white ribbon. She wore a white pinafore, white sweater, white shoes.

Gina had made no plans, had no thought of what she wanted to do, but she found herself driving, following a station wagon into a subdivision close to the mall. Her hands were wet on the steering wheel; she wiped one, then the other on her pants leg, stayed well behind the station wagon and faithfully made every turn it made, lagged when it stopped to let a child out, tried not to appear to be following. She pulled over to the curb halfway down the street when the station wagon stopped again and the little red-haired girl finally jumped out and ran up the sidewalk to a brick house. Gina drove on slowly, watching her flashing legs, the sway of her ponytail. The door opened and for a moment the sun on the glass panel of the door dazzled Gina; she caught a glimpse of the figure of a woman, her outstretched arms, a sun-blaze of red hair, and then the door closed; the stoop was empty.

She had jammed on the brakes, killed the engine. She was shaking uncontrollably. That missing part of her that she had thought dead had come violently alive; not dead, dormant only, waiting, waiting. And now it flared through her demanding recognition, demanding attention. She felt feverish from the surge, as if it were a fire storm within her. She clutched the steering wheel harder to still her hands, squeezed her eyes shut to stem the tears that had not flowed before, tried to take deep measured breaths to calm herself, but she shook and the tears burned, and her breaths were no more than gasps for air.

The part that had been quiescent, that she had thought dead, had burst into life with the certain knowledge that that child was hers. The certainty was so overwhelming, so total that she did not question it.

A mistake must have been made. Her baby had not been stillborn! In the confusion, with Stuart injured, unconscious, with her own injuries, the premature birth, a nurse, a doctor, someone had made a mistake. Her child had survived! And she had always known the child was alive, had been waiting all this time, unable to say why, unable to explain, feeling nothing, more dead than alive, waiting. She leaned her head onto the steering wheel and stopped fighting the tears; very gradually her shaking subsided, the tears came to an end.

She had the car door half open before she realized that she could not simply walk in on this family, not in the condition she was in, to bring them the shock awaiting them. The child was well cared for; obviously they loved her. They had to love her. What would it do to the child to learn her mother and father were not her real parents? Father, Gina thought then. She had to tell Stuart.

She had not been to Stuart's shop for nearly five years, and it had expanded since then. It seemed to occupy most of the block now; there was even a small showroom. She hesitated after leaving her car, then saw the office sign and went toward it, veered at the last moment toward open overhead doors that led to a shop. Stuart would be in the shop, not the office. He was an artist/craftsman who turned out beautiful handmade cabinets and furniture. They had met in art school where he was teaching because, he had said with candor, he had to support his hobby. Gradually his hobby had taken over and then supported both of them, and now it seemed to be a thriving business.

After the brilliance of the midday sun, she was blind in the dim shop, and followed a sound that led her inward although she could see little. It smelled good in here, reviving a memory as sharp and fresh as if she had inhaled the fragrance of newly sawn wood and varnish and turpentine daily all her life. Then she saw him at a bench with a lathe, holding up a piece of wood with what appeared to be an intricate curve, eyeing it, running one hand over it, exactly the way she remembered his doing. She came to a sudden stop as he turned, evidently only now aware that someone had entered.

"Gina!" He dropped the piece he had been examining; it made a melodious bell sound when it hit the concrete floor.

Oblivious, he came toward her, both hands outstretched, laughing in spontaneous delight.

The light from behind her caught his hands first and she was shaken by the suddenness, the speed of the rush of memories that were awakened. How she had loved to watch him at work, the delicacy with which he had handled fine wood, as if communicating with it, learning its secrets through his touch. She had made dozens, hundreds, of sketches of those long blunt fingers, the veins on the backs of his hands, the muscles and tendons that appeared and vanished in a way that seemed random. She looked up from his reaching hands; he was laughing the way he had then, appeared as young, boyish even, as guileless as he had always looked then. Too bony to be handsome, too craggy, with deep-set blue eyes, an oversized nose, too large a forehead; she never had been able to capture his face in a sketch. His expressions chased each other too fast, and the stillness of her sketches had made him a stranger again and again. He was so open, his face so mobile he was unable to conceal any emotion, and now the emotion was joy, happiness at seeing her, even love, although she must have been no more than a silhouette against the bright light. She flinched from his touch.

"Can we talk?" she asked.

He stopped; his hands fell to his sides in an awkward position. "Sure. My office." He wheeled about and led her through the shop that echoed with their steps. No one else was there, although it was evident that several people were now employed by the company. Lunchtime, she realized belatedly. He held the office door open, carefully placing himself so that they would not brush one another when she passed. He followed her inside and closed the door, leaned against it with his arms folded, regarding her.

Quickly she looked away. There were three drawing tables, stacks of plans, a partly completed table, extra legs, blocks of wood. On the wall there were eight beautifully framed drawings—his hands, her sketches. His desk was piled high with papers, drawings, sketches. An elaborate computer system was on a long table at a right angle to his desk. The monitor was large, expensive.

"You've been doing well," she said finally, uncertain how to begin, how to make him listen without interrupting, make him believe.

"I have a lot of time to put in here," he said.

She had kept her back to him; when she faced him now he looked startled. "You've been crying. What's wrong? What happened?" He seemed poised to move toward her; she backed up a step, up against one of the drawing tables.

"I . . . Will you hear me out? Promise? Just listen?"

He nodded.

"I saw . . . Stuart, our baby didn't die! There was a mistake in the hospital. There had to be a mistake, because she's alive. I saw her! Twice now!"

He sagged against the door. At first he looked desperately hurt, wounded in a way he could not comprehend; then he looked angry.

"Listen to me," Gina cried. "The first time I thought I was mistaken. I really did. She was with some other children in a mall. I saw her and thought I was just tired, hallucinating even. I went back and saw her again and followed her home and she's my daughter! I can't be wrong about it! She looks just like me at that age. The way she holds her head, the way she runs, everything about her."

"Gina, stop it! Stop! Our baby was born dead! My God, haven't you faced it yet? She was born dead!"

"They could have made a mistake. It happens. You read about it now and then. They made a mistake! I saw her!"

"And I saw our dead baby! They brought her to me. I kissed her. Gina, for God's sake! You know she died!"

She shook her head. "No," she said in a hoarse whisper.

"I don't know that. I've never known it. I've never believed it! You saw a dead baby, but she wasn't ours! A premature baby, that's all you saw. Admit it, Stuart, that's what you saw. Our child was in an incubator by then, and now she's a little girl with long red hair and green eyes—"

She had not realized he was moving until he began to shake her. "She's alive!" she cried. "She is alive! Why didn't they show me the dead baby? I would have known for sure then. They didn't dare!" She tried to twist away from his hands, his grip tightened on her arms.

"You were unconscious for nearly three days, that's why! You were so doped, you didn't know anything. You wouldn't go to the cemetery! You wouldn't talk about it, about our dead child, about anything. You wouldn't face the truth up and down the line. And you still won't face the truth."

She stopped struggling. "You don't know anything about it," she said dully, and could not think of a way to make him understand. All her life she had been empty, incomplete. She had thought a lover would fill the vacancy, a husband would complete her. And it hadn't happened. She could live with that, she had decided; it was all she had known, and she accepted that it was all anyone else could know—incompleteness, not finished somehow. She was like a paper doll that looks alive from one angle, but then you turn it and she's gone—nothing. She had pretended to be whole, thinking everyone else must be pretending too, that life was like that. Then she became pregnant. There was another self, separate and yet a part of her, and she knew what it was to be whole for the first time in her life.

"They should have let me die when they took her from me. I did die. I've been dead ever since. People pretend they see me as a real person, whole, but when I look I see that nothing's there. Emptiness, that's all. And yet, when I saw her today, really studied her, I came alive again. She's my daughter!"

He let his hands fall from her arms, regarding her with horror. "Gina, will you see Dr. Tichenor? Please?"

"No! You tried before to make me think I was crazy! Everyone did! Not again!"

"You were a zombie! You were killing yourself with tranquilizers! You needed help and you need it now!"

"A zombie, that's right," she said. "I won't see anyone. She tried to make me believe I felt abandoned, and that's a lie. I left my parents, they didn't leave me. I left you. They took my child. I was never abandoned! A zombie! Yes, but now I'm alive and functioning. That's my child and I want her back!"

"Where did you see her? Where does she live? What's her name?"

She started to speak, then clamped her lips, shook her head. "I won't tell you. I'm sorry I came here. You won't help me, will you? You don't care."

"Care!" His hands clenched; a muscle spasm moved along his jaw. He swung away from her, slammed a fist against the wall. When he spoke again, not looking at her now, his voice was harsh, strange. "What the hell do you think you're going to do? Force yourself on some innocent family? Try to make them adopt you? Kidnap a child? Beat her if she won't call you Mother?"

She saw again the outstretched arms, the happy child running toward them, and suddenly she was chilled through and through. A shudder passed over her, left her rigid. There was something she should remember, something . . .

"Now what?" Stuart demanded, facing her again. "What else is bugging you? What's wrong?"

She shook her head blindly and darted past him, out the door, through the shop to the sunlight. She raced to her car and got in, started in a jerky motion and sped away, shaking.

Very slowly the chill dissipated and she could breathe nor-
mally, could look around for landmarks, try to find her way
back home.

She had to think, had to think. Plan. Weigh options.
Think. She drove past her turn and kept going but no
thoughts came. Curiously blank, she continued to drive all
afternoon, now and then reminding herself that she had to
think, had to plan.

She got out of the car on a bluff overlooking the Ohio
River where mist was forming, rising. She had left the city,
left the suburbs, and had no idea where she was. Lost again,
she told herself. The hills here looked bleak, showing little
greenery yet. Too early for dogwoods and redbuds, too early
for tender leaves to unfurl and taste the air. Too late for
winter weather, although it could return on a moment's notice. In-between time, she thought. She felt immobilized,
caught in in-between time, uncertain what to do, what she
could do. Police? She almost laughed at the thought.

She flinched from the cruel words Stuart had hurled at her,
as if she could hit that child for any reason. She could recall
only two spankings from her own childhood, both adminis-
tered by her mother, both well deserved, she had had to
admit. She also remembered the times she had tried to goad
her father into hitting her, desperate attempts to force him to
acknowledge her, to actually see her. He never had taken her
misdeeds seriously enough to punish her in any way. Her role
in their family drama had been that of the invisible child.

She realized she was trying hard to find someone in her life
to help her now. With the thought, she dismissed her parents.
Not her brothers. They had a mild contempt, mild affection
for her; they had never needed her, since they had each other
and a father who adored them both. She had grown apart
from her old friends as they married, started families, moved
away, and over the past few years she had made no real

friends. She had maintained a distance between herself and everyone else. Now she had acquaintances.

She had to be careful. She already had made one serious mistake in telling Stuart what she knew. She would not make a comparable mistake a second time. Whatever she decided to do, she had to do alone, and be very discreet, or . . . She shook the unfinished idea aside. Reluctantly she returned to thinking about Stuart, the look of horror that he had not been able to conceal. He believed she was mad, just as he had believed it back then when they could still move through time. Now she was stuck in in-between time. If she couldn't count on Stuart to be her ally, then to whom could she turn? There was no one.

Dr. Tichenor? Although she knew she had been unfair to Dr. Tichenor who had never tried to make her admit any-thing, she also knew she would never be able to confide in her. She had scant memory of their sessions except for the last one. *Tell me about the accident.*

Actually Gina could remember nothing about the acci-dent; she knew only what they had told her. It had happened too fast. "Pretrauma shock," the doctor had said. "It's very common." Gina had asked her one question the last day. "Do you have children?" The doctor had said no and Gina had withdrawn once more. What was the use? Stuart couldn't understand; a childless woman couldn't understand. She had known then and knew now that there was no point in asking her mother anything personal. She stared at the mist that was hiding the river and creeping up the bluff, spreading over the lower countryside on the opposite bank. Fog. It could get bad at this time of year. Still, she did not return to her car. There was something she had to think through, something.

She remembered telling her parents she was leaving Stuart, her father's instant grunt of satisfaction over her finances. "At least you won't have to worry about money for a long time," he had said. "With the settlement and all." She had understood the words to mean she was not welcome back home as a divorced woman. Stuart had signed all the insurance money over to her and deposited it in her account, where it still remained, untouched, unwanted. Her mother had said nothing about Gina's divorce, her future; she had talked about her own job at Ohio State University where she was secretary to the provost. Her mother always talked about her job, or the garden, or Gina's two brothers. Her mother didn't quite believe in her, Gina thought then; she must have seen Gina edge-on all her life and treated her as if she were not quite real, not quite there: Gina, her invisible child. She talked rapidly with sidelong glances at Gina's father now and then, as if seeking his approval. Gina shook her head, trying to clear away the past in order to think about what she had to do. There was no reason to be going over this old and too-familiar ground again. She had long accepted that her father preferred his sons to his daughter, that she had been a disappointment to him by arriving first, that somehow he had made her mother feel guilty over having a daughter before a son. Could that be called abandonment? Openly loving one child more than another? She did not believe it. Love was never ordered up in measured doses, so much for this child, so much for that one. It happened or not, with no responsibility for its presence, no guilt for its absence.

"Sometimes," Dr. Tichenor had said that last day, "a bereaved person feels abandoned by the one she has lost."

It had not been a question, certainly not an insistent demand that Gina express such a feeling, but it had lodged in Gina's head, and she had gone over and over the brief list of people who had not abandoned her. Her parents had not. She had left home to go to school and had never returned for more than short visits. Stuart certainly had not abandoned her. He had pleaded with her to stay, to see through their grief together, to plan another pregnancy. Dr. Tichenor had meant the child, of course. Abandoned by her child?

Gina had asked, "Do you have children?" And there was no point in continuing after that. The doctor could never understand. How would she have responded if Gina had told her she was no more than a paper doll, just as she, Gina, was? She remembered standing at the window in the doctor's office, looking at the world that was obscenely, garishly brilliant with fall finery—reds that blazed, golden lights, flaring bursts of copper and bronze everywhere.

Suddenly, standing on the bluff with the fog reaching for her feet, she remembered the next thing the doctor had said that day, the last thing she had said to Gina.

"Gina, will go to the cemetery with Stuart this week?"

She had turned from the window, had not looked at the doctor for fear she would catch her edge-on; she had walked from the office and had not gone back.

How hard they had worked to convince her that her baby had died. She had not understood her own resistance then, had accepted that she was deranged by grief, had not cared if she was. She had understood that day that because she had experienced wholeness and others had not, they would never comprehend what she grieved for: not only for a child, but also for herself. It would have been as futile to try to explain as to try to describe the brilliance of the autumn day to someone who had been born blind.

They had tried to make her see their reality, and she had resisted. Stuart had stormed at her finally, "For God's sake, you can't change the fact! You have to accept it! You have to live your life, go on with it."

But his fact had been wrong, after all. His reality had been false. And she must have known even then, without a hint of proof, without a clue, without hope, she must have known her child was alive.

The fog curled around her ankles, its touch icy and cruel.

She squinted her eyes slightly and gazed out over it. It appeared to be a snowy field that stretched out forever, but it was unquiet, restless in an undulating motion, deceptive in its invitation to walk out onto it. She looked down at her legs and abruptly turned and went to the car. She was shivering with cold now, her shoes wet, her legs wet with a penetrating chill.

She had delayed too long; the drive home would be slow and difficult. There would be no thought now of what to do, what could she do; she would have to concentrate on driving. She drove too fast for the degraded visibility she encountered after leaving the bluff, but she wanted away from the fog, away from the insidious invitation to step into it. She felt so cold it was as if the fog had entered her.

Gina worked mechanically on Friday, isolated by an envelope of fog that she had taken home with her, protected by it. She was scheduled to work that weekend. Someone from Display always was on hand just in case there was an emergency. "Suppose a brat knocks over a pyramid of glasses in Housewares," Paulo had explained. "Or a dippy housewife wants the bedspread that's on a bed in Domestics. We go fix it up, sweetie." Unless a display was going up or coming down soon, usually they had very little to do on Saturday or Sunday. That week they had received a shipment of new silver mannequins, and Gina and Paulo uncrated them and put them together on Saturday with the help of a pretty, ingenuous high school student working as an intern. "You know what that means?" Paulo had asked. "Cheap labor with no benefits." This girl was called Bobby, and she had fallen in love with Paulo at first sight, she had told Gina, with deep melancholy sighs, as if aware of the hopelessness of it all.

They would take down the Easter display on Easter Sunday and put up the material for the biggest event so far this year—the grand opening sale to celebrate the official opening of Riverview Mall. A quadruple whammy of a lie, Paulo called it. "First, the mall's been open for business for nearly a year. Second, it's just another way to try to get rid of the mistakes the buyers made. Third, inventory sales were bigger. And finally, you can't even see the river from it." Actually, Display would have little to do with the sale. Their next big project was what Paulo called The Garden. Proms, weddings, the first barbecue on the patio, garden parties. He had designed that display; the new mannequins would be used for it.

Gina had not been able to make any plans Thursday night, or all through Friday night. She had not slept, but neither had she been able to think through two consecutive ideas. It was as if her brain had frozen. She had hoped that Paulo would be preoccupied with his display plans, that she would have quiet at work, no interruptions, just a corner in the workroom where she could formulate a plan. It was not happening that way.

There were a dozen of the new mannequins, silver creations, as boneless as Titian women, but reedlike and chic. The female mannequins wore size seven, the males had thirty-eight-inch chests. The heads had been packed separately and were ranged on a worktable. A fine film of white dust clouded them. As Bobby wiped each one, Paulo or Gina fitted it into the neck of one of the silver bodies.

"They don't have souls, poor things," Paulo said, holding up one of the sculpted heads. It was hairless, human shaped, without features. Even without faces, it was obvious which was male, which female. "Giordino's a genius," Paulo went on, studying the head, his own head tilted thoughtfully. "He knows the soul shapes the face, so, no soul, no face. Look at that structure, high cheekbones, proud mouth, looks like Gina, doesn't she?"

Bobby was looking at it, wide eyed. She shook her head.

"There aren't any bones, or a mouth. It doesn't look like anyone. Unless it's a robot."

"Honey bun, that's what I mean," Paulo said, and laughed.

"I'm going on my break," Gina said stiffly, and walked away.

In the lounge she studied her face in the mirror. Her lack of sleep was taking a toll; shadowed hollows under her eyes made them appear larger than ever. They looked haunted. She closed them and ran her fingers down her face, under her chin. Paulo was right; she was like the mannequins. Soulless, incomplete. She stared at her reflection again and this time she nodded. By Monday, she promised the robot in the mirror. She would know what to do by Monday, and do it.

She avoided Paulo and the high school girl all afternoon, made work for herself in Housewares until closing time, and then ducked out. She slept just as poorly Saturday night as she had all the previous nights of the week. At three in the morning, wide awake, she sat on the side of her bed and regarded the room with hatred. She had made herself a solitary-confinement cell, she realized; movies or television programming to watch, music to listen to, books to read, food in the tiny kitchen. She had no need for the outside world at all.

Her living situation would have to change when she claimed her daughter. A house in the country? She thought of the brick house in the subdivision with distaste. Nothing like that. A cottage with a fence, a garden in the back, a porch with a swing. She would quit working for the next eight or ten years at the very least. They had lost so much time together, there was so much to learn about each other, so many things to do together now. Museums, hiking, camping trips? She knew little about camping, but she could learn; they could learn together. There was more than enough money to last a long time even if she didn't work.

Abruptly she stood up. Would she have to give it back to the insurance company? She bit her lip. If she gave it back, she would have to work, there would be day care for her daughter, a sitter. She would be a lonely, latch-key child, as lonely as Gina had been as a child. In her mind she cried, No!

Aloud she repeated it. "No!" She had earned that money; it was hers and her daughter's. She would have to talk to an attorney. Then she wondered why she had not thought of that sooner. Of course, a lawyer. He would know how to go about reclaiming her child, what procedure she must go through, how to make it all legal. Her excitement mounted as the indecision of the past few days drained from her. First thing Monday morning she would call a lawyer, make an appointment for Monday afternoon, start whatever action was needed. She took a deep breath and realized it was the first satisfying breath she had managed for a long time. When she fell into bed again, she went to sleep almost instantly and did not dream.

There was a minor disturbance in Junior Sportswear the next afternoon. Two teenaged girls got into a pushing fight and knocked over a mannequin. Security ousted the girls; Gina collected the mannequin which had an arm broken off. When she reentered the display workroom, Paulo was entertaining Bobby and two women from the floor, Margo and Sue. Business was slow on that Sunday; the store was virtually empty, breaks could be prolonged without anyone paying very much attention. Gina stopped momentarily at the small group having coffee and canned soft drinks, sharing a large bag of chips. She shifted the mannequin; it was not very heavy, but it was an awkward burden, like carrying a dead person with advanced rigor mortis, she thought morosely.

"Course you can't see them by looking straight at them. They hide," Paulo was saying. "You catch a glimpse out of the corner of your eye. Ask Gina. She knows about seeing ghosts."

Gina gave him a look of cold disdain and continued on past them to an open space where she started to pull the layers of clothes off the mannequin.

"Oh, Paulo," Margo said. "How come you're an expert on everything, including ghosts?"

"Let me tell you. In Brooklyn, where I come from, we know about such things. Why, I was exorcised three times before I was twelve. Little old lady come in and Mama and her and three or four other ladies sat around drinking cherry coke or lemonade with a little rum in it and eating Oreo cookies and every time I looked up, there she was watching me. Little tiny black eyes you wouldn't think were big enough to see anything, but she saw me clean through. She'd look straight at me and then sort of cock her head like she was listening to something I sure couldn't hear. Then she'd turn just a little bit and say something to it, whatever it was. She taught me how to see it."

"See what?" Bobby asked.

"Just it. Like now, you know the silver people without souls and faces are all lined up over there waiting for someone to put their clothes on them and take them into the real world. Well, *it's* over there too, hanging out with them. Just as soulless as they are. Now you look here straight at me, not at them, and in a minute, two minutes, you'll see. You'll see."

"Paulo, stop it. You're scaring the girl to death," Sue protested.

"Why? It's not scary, not after you get used to seeing it now and then. Honey bun, you scared to death?"

"No." Her voice was wavery, though. "What do you think is scary, Paulo?"

"Hm. Not *it*. I'm too used to *it*. Vampires are pretty bad. I mean the real ones, not the movie kind."

Bobby laughed nervously. "Ghosts are scary."

"Naw," Paulo said. "Most of them are just poor lost souls who don't know how to get to where they're supposed to go next. Pathetic things, most of them."

Bobby made a noise that could have been a stifled scream.

"You caught a glimpse of it, didn't you?" Paulo said cheerfully. "Now, what you want to do next is to look directly at it and say, *shoo!* It'll go away, guarantee it."

Sue stood up and left, laughing and shaking her head.

"Honey bun, if you don't do what I tell you, it'll just hang around and you'll keep seeing it when you don't expect to see anything, and that might scare you a little. Look at it and say *shoo.*"

Gina suppressed her own smile as the girl reluctantly turned toward the soulless silver people and whispered, "Shoo."

"Now for what scares me the most," Paulo said. He glanced around, then lowered his voice, and became very serious when he spoke again. "Not ghosts, not the usual sort anyway. Not vampires or werewolves or monsters or ghouls. They're all bad, you understand, but what really scares me is the doppelganger."

Gina dropped the mannequin on the worktable where it clattered hollowly. Bobby screamed and this time did not stifle it.

With exaggerated patience Paulo said, "Now, sweetie, honey bun, if you ladies are going to go all hysterical and shrill on me, we'd better stop this discussion right here and now."

Margo snorted and finished her coffee, crumpled the Styrofoam cup. It made a nerve-chilling scritching sound.

"What's a doppelganger?" Bobby asked breathlessly.

"You sure you want to hear this?" Paulo said.

Gina left to get another teenager-mannequin from the storage area they called the People Store. She took her time, in no hurry to get back to the conversation that had taken too macabre a turn. She hated this area where the dummies stood waiting, some haughty, some smiling, some dreamy eyed, all waiting to be used, all waiting for the world to claim them. She snatched one of the young ones and went back toward the work area. She had the feeling the others not chosen were watching; from the corner of her eye she could almost catch a flutter of motion. Angry now, she stomped through the display room back to the table where she had left the clothes taken off the broken mannequin.

Margo was standing up, retouching her lipstick. "Paulo, you're too much," she said, snapping her compact closed. "Lord, Warner will have my hide if I don't get back. Doppelganger! Hah!" She walked out.

"But what is it?" Bobby demanded. "You can't just leave it there."

"Okay, honey bun. Okay. Remember, you asked. You see, a vampire doesn't much care who the victim is. Right? You, me, anyone would do. It's sort of an accident who gets nipped in the neck. Same with a werewolf, or a monster of any race, creed, or color. Right? Right. But a doppelganger's a different kettle of fish. A doppelganger's got only one person on earth to haunt. Most times no one else can even see it except for that one person. You know how those silver people got no souls, that goes for some flesh and blood people too, you see. And they got doppelgangers. Somehow that person's soul gets detached and starts to wander around. It makes itself a body, sort of, that looks just like the person the soul belonged to, and off it goes looking for that person. You see it across the street, or on a bus going away from you, or leaving a restaurant where you're eating, and that's okay because it hasn't seen you yet. Long as it's the one leaving, looking the other way, you're safe. You know what doppelganger means? Double goer. Your double's out there going somewhere else, only now and then you spot it. But if ever it starts to turn toward you, then run like hell!"

"Why? What happens then?"

"Honey bun, no two psychic forces can occupy the same ground, and sure as God made little girls to ask questions, when you and the doppelganger meet, only one walks away, and it ain't you."

Gina had not moved throughout his ridiculous story; her arms were leaden from holding the mannequin. Carefully she stood it up, adjusted the stand, each motion overcontrolled and slow; she took pains not to make any sudden noise, not to startle the girl again, make her scream again.

"That's silly," Bobby declared after a moment. "I've never seen anything like that, or heard anything like that either."

"That's because your pretty little rosy soul's all nicely tucked in and safe. Most of us ain't that lucky."

"What would a person watching them see? I mean, if they look exactly alike, how do you know which one is real and which one is the ghost?"

"Hm," Paulo said thoughtfully, "that's a real good question. I guess from the outside no one could tell, but they'd know, especially the one who gets zapped. That one would know."

"Oh, Paulo," Bobby said after a moment. "You're teasing me, aren't you? Are you really from Brooklyn? Why are you here?"

He began to tell her about his game plan: by the time he was forty he expected to be display manager of something like Bloomingdale's, or Neiman Marcus. Gina was no longer listening. She had not yet started to dress the mannequin she had brought out from the People Store. She could not remember what she had been doing when time stopped for her. In-between time, she thought distantly. Before, that had been a vague concept, distant, something to think about even if it was not quite real, but now, she thought, it was here and it was real. She had been stuck in it for days.

She knew there was something she had to think about,

something she had to think through, something. Something.
Each time she tried to consider what it could be, her mind
skittered away. Something, she told herself then. Bobby
moved into her line of vision and silently she answered the
girl's question: It's the empty one, the one without a soul who
vanishes.

She found herself walking from the display department,
heedless of Paulo's voice speaking to her, asking what? She
did not know. She walked through the store to the parking
lot and her car. A fine drizzly rain was falling. It was very
cold. She started her car and waited a minute or two for the
defroster to clear the windshield, and then began to drive.
She was seeing in her mind's eye the way the ponytail had
swayed as the child ran carrying her small basket of jelly
beans, how the sun had lighted her shining hair.

Riverview Mall was busier than the downtown district, but
she had to go there in order to follow the trail, the only way
she knew to get back to the child's house. She drove the same
route she had driven that day, as if following clearly visible
crumbs left to direct her. She hesitated on the street in the
same place where she had lingered that day watching the
station wagon come to a stop, watching the child jump out
and run across the lawn to the front door, her ponytail
swaying, her legs flashing, her white shoes brilliant in the sun.

She eased her car forward, remembering every detail about
the child, and came to an abrupt stop again, almost as sudden as her stop had been that day. A For Sale sign was on
the lawn. Had it been there before? She rubbed her eyes and
finally decided it had been; she simply had not paid much
attention to it then. She remembered starting to get out of the
car that day, how strong her impulse had been to follow the
child to the front door, to ring the bell, to make them acknowledge her. This time when she opened the car door she
did get out and stood in the drizzle looking at the house with
the brick facing. Not all brick, just a decorative finish. An-

other wrong detail. There was the stoop with a wrought-iron rail. She had forgotten that, too. Or had not noticed. It was not important.

Now she paused. The something that had eluded her all week, the something she dreaded even while she was drawn irresistibly toward it, now she would find it, she thought distantly. It was here. She felt hollow with fear and anticipation. As before, her mind refused to consider the something that compelled her, and even her head became hollow, without thought. She walked up the sidewalk toward the front door; it seemed that all around her the world had died. There was no sound, no other traffic, no children at play. Drizzly rain. Grayness. Silence. In-between time, she thought, and that was exactly right. She passed the living room windows and glanced inside. The drapes were not tightly closed; she could see the interior. It was completely empty.

The shock of the empty room jolted her from her trance-like state and she ran to the stoop, out of the drizzly rain, and pounded on the door, held her finger on the bell, pounded again frantically, whispering, begging, *please, please.* She heard a chime as if from a great distance, again and again, until finally she let her hand drop and stepped back from the door. A new tremor of shock coursed through her. The door was solid wood. There was no glass panel, no window in it. She closed her eyes hard and felt for the wrought-iron railing, or she would have fallen.

She saw again the running figure of the child, the swaying ponytail, the child entering the shade of the shallow porch, the door opening. The stoop was covered; the noonday sun could not have flashed on anything under the roof here. This was the something that she had rejected, the something her mind had refused to let her consider, the something that had haunted her all week.

The child runs up the lawn, to the stoop, laughing, her ponytail asway. The door opens and a smiling woman takes

a step forward, her arms outstretched, to welcome her child
home. She leans down to embrace her daughter; her long
auburn hair falls over the red hair of the child. She lifts the
child and turns, reenters the house. The happy, smiling
woman embracing her child is Gina.

Numb with disappointment, immobilized by fear, Gina
stood clutching the iron rail, pressed in on all sides by a
silence that seemed tangible. Finally the world began to
shape itself again, the door was just a door, time gathered
itself up, started to flow again. Her eyes focused and she
became aware of an ache in her hand from the tightness of
her grip on the railing. She loosened her fingers, each one
stabbing pain as she straightened them. Distinctly she said
under her breath, "I must be mad."

Waking dream? Hallucination? Madness. Just as Stuart
had suspected. She took the two steps down to the sidewalk
where the rain stung her with icy indifference. Walking was
a tremendous effort now; she had to think about how to
make her knees bend, how to lift one foot, the other one. Her
arms felt awkward, disconnected. She forced herself to keep
moving, afraid that if she stopped, she might not be able to
start again. She was halfway to her car when the eerie silence
was punctured by a voice almost in her ear.

"Jennifer! Didn't you hear me yelling my head off? Wait
up a minute."

She turned to see a woman holding out a package. She was
blond with a chubby round face heavily made up. She held
an umbrella.

The woman frowned as if in uncertainty, then exclaimed,
"Good Lord, you're soaked! Here, Holly left it in our house
and I found it last night." She thrust the package toward
Gina who took it automatically, without thought. "I'm glad
you came back or the poor kid might never have seen it
again, and I know she'd miss it. I stuck it in the plastic bag

to keep it dry, but that's probably as far as I would have gone to get it back to Holly. You know how I am about letters and stuff. Good intentions and all, but—"

A car horn interrupted her. She turned away from Gina and yelled, "Hold it, Stan! I'm coming. I'm coming." She grinned at Gina and tilted the umbrella against the rain that was being blown by a rising wind. "Damn man, always in a hurry. Type A, you know? That's him. You take care. Bye." She ran across the lawn toward a car in the driveway next door.

"Holly," Gina whispered, and suddenly she began to hurry. The woman had called her Jennifer. Holly's mother. She stumbled over the curb and jerked the car door open, banged her leg on it as she clambered in. She wiped her face and hands with many tissues before she opened the plastic bag and removed a book. It was a picture book of fairies beautifully painted in pastels.

She was wet to the skin; her hair was plastered to her head, clung to her cheeks. She turned on the engine and the heater and waited for the warmth to reach her. The child was real. She had not dreamed it, had not hallucinated her. Holly. The woman was real. Jennifer. And she looked enough like Gina that the neighbor had mistaken one for the other. Gradually the windshield cleared; she sat looking at the rain, falling harder now, tracking crazily down the glass.

Doppelganger, she thought, remembering Paulo's story. Double goer. Jennifer must have caught a glimpse of her; she was the one going away, running away with Holly. Double goer. *If it ever starts to turn toward you, run like hell!*

By the time she got home a howling spring storm was raging. It could continue to rain all night, or start to snow, or sleet, or clear up within an hour or so and tomorrow be sunny and seventy degrees. Spring in the Ohio River valley was like that. The wind screamed, ripped through trees in bud, denuded branches, tore weak growth apart, hurled it through the air. The horizontal rain beat against her windows with an incessant arhythmic clatter.

She pulled off her soaked clothes and filled the tub with hot water and stayed in it until she was thoroughly warm again. Then, in her warmest robe and slippers, her hair in a towel, she sat in her kitchen sipping coffee that was almost scalding, and regarded the book of fairies. She tried to determine which painting Holly had liked best, which page had the most evident wear; she examined it in search of a marked page, a pencil or crayon mark of any sort. The book remained mute.

Eventually she made herself soup and an egg sandwich and played the messages on her answering machine. Paulo had called, asked in his insolent way if she was sick, would she mind giving him a call in any case, if it was convenient. A friend from school had been in town and called. The last call was from Stuart. She listened to him a second time.

"Gina, I have to talk to you. It's very important. I'll meet you at the store at five tomorrow."

Static hissed briefly on the machine, then it became silent and the only sound was the insane beat of the driven rain on the windows. Important how? Had he changed his mind? Would he agree to help her after all? She clutched the book in indecision. Everything had changed because of the book; things that had been nebulous, maybe tricks of her imagination, had become real, and Stuart was enough of a pragmatist, enough of a realist to accept that reality even if he did not like it. She no longer thought about going to a lawyer for legal help, not now. If Jennifer had fled because she had seen Gina, that made a difference also.

She could not think of how to cope with the new situation, not yet, not until she had talked to Stuart. When she went to bed, she put the book under her pillow. Throughout the restless night she heard the maniacal wind and driving rain;

in her dreams the wind became laughter that always arose from a place behind her. When she spun around to locate the source, there was no more than a suggestion of movement, as if a diabolical fairy were hiding in the flowers, taunting her.

As soon as she saw Paulo at work the next morning, she remembered his message to call, the first time she had thought of it again. She began to take off her dripping raincoat, and said, "I'm sorry I didn't call. I forgot."

He shrugged his slender shoulders. "It's okay, sweetie. What I get for worrying about you. You all right?"

She nodded.

"Sweetie, if you're all right, I don't never want to see no dying person."

"Don't call me sweetie!" She nearly ran to report in to Sheila Lamotte, the manager of the department, aware of Paulo's gaze following her. All around, in every corner, in the People Store, behind the rows of worktables, the shelves and hangers of clothing and accessories, she could almost detect a multitude of undefined figures in motion. Here, there, everywhere except where she was looking.

Sheila Lamotte was very handsome, gray haired, regal in her bearing, in her fifties, very sure of herself, of the value of her work, her position in life generally. Gina was envious of her and admired her sincerely.

"I'm assigning you to work with Paulo on The Garden until it's done. He has carte blanche, you know. As long as he stays within budget, anyway." She stopped and regarded Gina thoughtfully. "Do you want to make a formal complaint about him?"

Gina flushed, shook her head. She had not been aware that anyone else realized how much Paulo distressed her at times.

"If you do," Sheila Lamotte said, "I'll take it, of course. But it would be better for both of you if you can work it out. Gina, The Garden is very important to Paulo, and could be important for you, too. It will attract attention, I'm certain.

And Paulo specifically asked for you to assist him. He thinks,
and I agree, that you're the best we have."

"After him," Gina muttered.

"Of course. After him."

The brief interview was over, the subliminal signal given
that Gina understood perfectly. She turned to leave, hesitated at the door, then said, "Thanks, Sheila. Actually Paulo
and I work extremely well together."

Sheila nodded. "I know."

"Okay," Paulo said in his office that was separated from the
larger workroom by a makeshift plywood partition. "We'll
have three steps, in white wrought iron. Bride, bridesmaid,
matron of honor, or mother of the bride. Flower girl. No
more than six figures. And masses of flowers. Here are the
colors."

His sketches were the simplest line drawings flooded with
the colors he wanted. He had an unerring eye for balance, for
placement, for color. Gina could visualize the tableau perfectly.

"Dutch iris," she said. "Shirley poppies, baby's breath—"

"Irises are too big."

"Not the Dutch irises. I'll round up some pictures . . ." She
was drawn into the work, became absorbed, and was surprised when he announced lunchtime.

"How's about I order a couple of sandwiches from The
Gallery?" Paulo asked. "That way The Garden picks up the
tab, one of the little perks." The Gallery was the department
store restaurant.

"And we work through lunch," she said, but she nodded
her agreement. "Chicken salad on whole wheat."

"So we talk about work. You sure don't want to talk
about what's bothering you, now do you?" He picked up the
phone and waved her away. "Go wash your hands, sweetie.
Sure wish they understood about pastrami around here."

* * *

Late that afternoon, during a coffee break, Gina took the book of fairies from her purse and leafed through it once again. Had Holly missed it yet? Would she remember when she had last seen it, where she had left it? She became aware of Paulo looking over her shoulder and snapped the book shut.

"You ever wonder why modern artists draw fairies with such pink cheeks and golden hair?" he asked mockingly. "The answer, Mr. Bones, is that they are playing the game of pretend. Pretend fairies are sweet little things, sell them to all the pink little girls out there who aren't ready yet for the real world, and most likely never will be ready for it."

Gina slipped the book inside her purse. "And you, of course, know all about fairies."

"Well, I know they aren't dear little things. You know the Pied Piper was a fairy, don't you? With his silver flute. That's the dark side of the dear little things, the side that pipes away the children into the hill and they don't never come out again. A fairy takes a fancy to a baby, and bingo, she takes it, leaves a changeling in its place and one day that changeling flies away home, laughing like a fiend. That's the dark side, too. A fairy tempts you with a bit of ambrosia that you can't resist and you wake up old and alone twenty years later. That's the dark side."

Her hands were trembling. In a shaky voice she said, "Stop it, Paulo. Please, just stop it." She stood up.

"Sure, sweetie. Whatever you say."

She bowed her head, held the table with both hands. "Why do you do that, call me that? Why do you have so much contempt for me?"

There was a long silence. Finally she looked at him and saw anger on his face, in his eyes. No more playfulness, no more amusement, just anger. It made him look very old and bitter even.

"Gina, women like you live in a dream world of fairy tales and Prince Charmings and happy endings. You remind me of a cat that got singed by a fire and ain't never going to warm up by a flame again, no matter how cold it gets. You're so unreal you're like a guy's sweet dream of a woman. One touch and poof, you're gone. And the poor dude twitches and turns and wonders what happened, what did he do. Sometimes I want to put out a finger and touch you, just to see if anything's really there."

"You don't know anything about me," she whispered.

"Sweetie, I know everything about you. I have an appointment with Sheila in a couple of minutes. See you in the morning."

Alone behind the partition in the workroom, she finally sank back down into her chair. Now she could hear the other display crew members coming and going, a burst of laughter, something being dragged across the floor, voices drawing near, receding. It must have been going on all day, but she had not noticed earlier; she had been too preoccupied with the project. He never called Sheila anything but her name, she thought, and nodded. That was right. Sheila demanded respect, deserved respect. She realized that she had folded her hands on the table, the way a child who was determined to be good might do. Carefully she loosened her fingers, separated her hands. Someone was whispering on the other side of the partition; a second person laughed quietly. Peg? Tom? Maybe the silver people were moving about. She shook her head and pushed her chair back, scraping it louder than necessary, just so they would know she was here, someone was here. The quiet voices were stilled.

No more fantasies, she told herself. No more dreams. No more fairy tales. He was wrong about Prince Charming. She had not believed in that myth for many years, but there was a little girl named Holly. She was real. She had a mother who looked exactly like Gina; that was real. No ghosts, no doppelgangers, no hallucinations; they both were real. She felt a muscle tighten in her chest, and repeated the words silently, "They are both real."

Jerkily she began to straighten up the table, to put Paulo's notebooks and sketches together, gather up her notes and sketches and slide them into her folder. She felt almost as if she were watching her own awkward movements from a distant vantage point; all her motions were jerky and graceless. She could just leave it all for tomorrow, she thought, and remembered that tomorrow was her day off. She continued to put her things away. Wednesday she would work with Paulo again, and she knew that neither of them would mention this little incident. He would call her sweetie and she would ignore it. She did not know anything else she could do. She would never tell anyone why he called her that. Never.

Stuart was waiting for her outside the entrance to Baron's. "Hello, Gina. Where are you parked?"

"In the Parkade on Fourth."

"Let's take your car. I left mine at Maggio's Bar and walked over."

He was wearing the same old jacket he used to wear most of the time, a tan all-weather jacket that looked frayed and shabby now. The pockets bulged, just as they always had. He never would shop for himself unless she went too, she recalled; she had bought his shirts and socks and sweaters. Once she had tried to make him shop for slacks and he had protested, saying he had a pair of slacks; when and if they wore out, he would get another pair.

They walked the three blocks to the parking garage in silence, and up the elevator to the fifth floor where she parked every day. He did not touch her, did not take her arm, or offer to drive. He waited patiently until she unlocked the passenger door to let him in, but he watched her as she started the engine and drove.

"You look awfully tired," he said, then turned to stare out the windshield, as if he had committed an indiscretion.

Maggio's catered to business lunches and after-theater crowds; at this time of day it was not crowded, not even noisy. She was relieved that they could get a booth with a lot of space to keep them well apart.

She waited until he ordered wine for her, bourbon for himself, and a bowl of nachos. When the waitress left, Gina asked, "Why did you call? You said it was important."

"It is important."

He was too watchful, too quiet. She had seen him become this still in the past at times when he knew he had a fight coming and was prepared to go all the way with it. It was not that he deliberately composed his face, made his features reveal little; he was incapable of doing that. It was rather as if all his energy were concentrated on what he was thinking, what he was planning, none was left over to move his facial muscles. She tensed, waiting for him to begin.

"The other day," he said slowly, "after you left, I went to see a detective. I hired him. I asked him if there was any way to prove, really prove, what happened six years ago in the hospital. He treated me as if I was a nincompoop and assured me there was. I have his report, Gina, certified documents, proof."

She started to rise, and his voice sharpened, his face became tight and hard. "Sit still and listen to me. You owe me that much."

The waitress brought their order. They remained silent until she was gone again.

Gina's hand rested on her purse. Under the soft leather she could feel the outline of the book of fairies, Holly's book. She raised her glass with her other hand and sipped the wine. "Go on," she said then.

He pulled a thick envelope from his pocket and placed it on the table. "The report's in there, along with a couple of documents, copies of birth certificates, names, children's and their parents'. There's a list of the emergency room staff, and another of the operating room staff. There's a detailed summary of exactly the procedures they used. Two other babies were born in that hospital the night our daughter died, both normal, full-term births, both accounted for. It's all in there, Gina."

She made no motion toward the envelope. "Why did you hire him?"

"I fell in love with you the first night we sat and drank cokes and talked about art. Remember?"

"Don't do this, Stuart. Please."

"I have to," he said doggedly. "Just listen. I fell in love with a beautiful, gay, happy, wonderful girl whose eyes flashed green fire now and then, as green as emeralds when she was happy or excited. I saw that girl die and a stranger take her place. I told Rose then, and I'm telling you now, if there's anything on earth I can do to bring back that girl, I'll do it. Anything, Gina."

"You saw Rose Tichenor?"

"Yes, for months after you walked out. You lost a child and threw away a husband, but I lost a child, too, and I lost my wife and didn't understand why, unless I was to blame for the accident. I wanted to kill myself for causing our child to die, for hurting you so desperately. I needed help, too."

His candor was unnerving. On their third date he had declared his love and she had laughed and said, don't play games, okay? He had looked puzzled, almost childish. "I don't play games with people," he had said. "I don't know how." His honesty was still unsettling. He had not been able to hide his spontaneous joy at seeing her in his shop; he could not hide his pain and unhappiness now, or his determination to say what he had to say to her. She pressed her hand tighter on the book in her purse.

"I didn't blame you. I never did. I knew it was an accident."

He nodded. "I know that too now. One of the things I learned from Rose is that if you can't live with the truth, you can't really live at all. I hoped and even prayed that you'd come to accept the truth, that you'd come back to life. If you're ready to do it, I want to be around." He leaned back then, as if he had come to the end of all the things he had been compelled to say to her. For the first time he lifted his glass, drank deeply.

She drank her wine then. Stuart pushed the nachos toward her; she shook her head.

"You never could drink on an empty stomach," he said.

"This is all I want. I have to go now."

"You won't talk about it? Won't even look at the reports?" He nudged the envelope in her direction. She did not touch it.

"There's no point in it. You know what you believe. I know something different."

"You can't deny the facts, damn it! Those are facts!"

She traced the outline of the book with her finger.

"There's one more thing," Stuart said then with a touch of weariness. "I asked Rose to join us for a drink."

"I told you I won't see her!"

"I don't give a damn if you see her or not! I thought maybe you wouldn't feel so threatened now, that you were coming to your senses finally, that you'd admit at last that you need to talk to someone. She agreed to come over only if I promised to tell you in time for you to run and hide if you're still scared to death of her. Scared of the truth."

"You don't have a clue about what the truth is," she cried furiously. "I know that child's name—Holly. I know her mother's name—Jennifer. I know what her mother looks like. Exactly like me. Exactly. Her neighbor mistook me for her! That's the real truth, not whatever paper is in there." She took a long breath and exhaled through her mouth. "And I'm not afraid of Rose Tichenor. Neither of you can touch me. I don't care if you think I'm stark, raving, you can't do a thing about it!"

"Oh my God!" he groaned. "What in God's name do you think you're doing?"

"I'm looking for the real truth! And here comes your tame psychiatrist!"

Gina felt as awkward as a schoolgirl and braced herself as if for a reprimand. She felt unkempt after her day in the workroom of the department store. Rose Tichenor had always been elegantly dressed, beautifully groomed. That day she wore a dark silk dress with a matching jacket, and her fingers were as long and tapered as Gina remembered. She appeared perfectly at ease as she held out her hand and greeted Gina as if she were a colleague. She sat down by Stuart and began to eat the nachos. She had too much sense to ask how Gina was; she might have been a casual acquaintance who happened by, but her eyes missed little, Gina knew.

The waitress appeared and Rose Tichenor ordered wine, Stuart nodded toward his glass and Gina's. She did not protest. She wanted another glass of wine suddenly.

"Tell her what you just told me," Stuart said after the waitress was gone once more.

She told it stiffly and badly, and heard it as a ridiculous story as the words came out. When she reached the part about recognizing Jennifer belatedly, after the family had moved away, Stuart snorted in disbelief.

"You didn't mention that part the other day."

"I forgot. My eyes played a trick on me and I had to close them because I thought the sun flashed on a glass door." She watched Rose Tichenor who was listening with the same quietude she remembered from before. She gave the impression that she was listening harder than most people did, that she was hearing more than most people heard. Gina moistened her lips. "That happens. I've read about it. You see without being aware of what you've seen until later." She sounded belligerent to her own ears.

"It happens rather frequently," the doctor agreed.

"First the child looks like you and then it's the child and her mother," Stuart said impatiently. "How about the neighbor? People down the street. Damn it, Gina . . ."

Rose Tichenor smiled at Gina. "Did you know that several hundred people turned out for an Elvis Presley look-alike contest recently? I saw it on television. Some of them looked exactly like him. And Marilyn Monroe look-alikes number closer to a thousand, I understand. It happens."

"And the kid?" Stuart snapped. "That doesn't explain the child."

"That's a problem," Rose Tichenor admitted. "Is it possible that you have family members you don't know? A cousin perhaps?"

Gina shook her head.

"It would have to be her mother's side," Stuart said with resignation. "Gina looks exactly like her mother. Or how her mother must have looked at her age." He regarded the thick envelope, touched it with his fingertips.

He wanted the doctor to take his side, Gina knew. He wanted the doctor to insist that Gina study the contents of the envelope, that she admit she had been mistaken in the face of his evidence. She stopped looking at him, and for the next few minutes she and the doctor talked about her family. No cousins that she didn't know. No aunt or uncle hidden away on her mother's side of the family. No family skeletons. But did she really know that, or was it simply an assumption, she asked herself suddenly, and she had no answer. She said she would go talk to her mother the next day.

"What for?" Stuart demanded.

"If nothing else, then to eliminate the obvious possibilities," Gina snapped back at him, and glanced swiftly at Rose

Tichenor to see if there was a glint of satisfaction in her expression. There was nothing that she could read.

"Several possibilities exist," Rose Tichenor said pleasantly. "The cousin theory. Another genetic link along the line. Coincidence. Gina might have been mistaken, but it's a little hard to say the same for the neighbor who returned Holly's book to her." When Gina produced the book, Stuart ignored it, but Rose Tichenor examined it with interest. She returned it to Gina and stood up. "I really must go. Gina, if you learn anything, will you give me a call? I'd like to know the ending of the story."

Gina said she would and watched the woman leave the bar. Rose Tichenor believed her, she thought with a rush of gratitude toward her. She had not made the automatic assumption that Gina was crazy, that she had been hallucinating. Neither had she admitted to possibilities stranger than a blood relative or coincidence. But she was right. The obvious things had to be ruled out first. She wondered briefly if Rose Tichenor had planted that idea in her head, made her somehow see that it was a reasonable thing to do. She dismissed her suspicions quickly. It did not matter one way or the other; it was a good idea, and it gave her a starting place. First rule out the obvious explanations.

"At least take the reports with you," Stuart said tiredly. "I kept a copy of everything. Chuck it when you're done with it."

Reluctantly she put the envelope in her purse, along with the book of fairies that made a lie of everything in it.

Late that night, driven by restlessness, sleeplessness, Gina opened the envelope and read the report, examined the documentation the detective had assembled. Enough for any reasonable person, she admitted, and began to stuff it all back, then stopped. A detective! She could hire the detective to trace Jennifer and Holly.

And, she thought with defiance, if her mother would not

really talk to her about the past, about the family, she would have the same detective investigate her own relatives. She started digging through a box of papers looking for her birth certificate, something for the investigator to start with, but also a lever, she thought, to make her mother realize how serious she was about learning the truth about herself. She found the birth certificate and sat back on her heels on the floor regarding it with dismay. It was totally worthless.

It was not certified, not notarized. She took it to the table under a better light and studied it. Now she could see that more than likely all the signatures on it had been written by the same heavy black pen, in the same handwriting even. How had she got by with this all her life? The answer to that was easy; who ever bothered to check? Once anyone got into the system, there was a paper trail forever—transcripts, immunization records, diplomas . . . She studied the signatures: Carol Hennings Crandall, and her father's, Harvey Crandall, the doctor's name, all in her mother's handwriting, she realized, with just a suggestion of an attempt to change the script from one signature to the next.

Gina blinked nervously. Her left hand began to creep up her right arm, feeling, poking, testing, testing. She had a strong impulse to run to the bathroom and study her face in the mirror, to hold the hand mirror and study her profile, the back of her hair, her shoulders . . . She jerked her hand away from the arm and pounded the table with both fists. "No," she moaned.

That night she dreamed that she encountered a pillar in a desert. It was eerie because it was wreathed in mist that did not evaporate in the heat of the sun. The mist swirled and reformed and swirled again, always hiding the pillar that appeared to be black. She circled it trying to see it more clearly and it changed. Not a pillar, but a statue, a faceless, boneless female form. She was on fire, she thought, too hot to bear the sun any longer; she yearned for the cooling mist, and finally she reached through it to touch the statue, to see if it was cool. At her touch it changed again, began to shrink inward, to collapse into itself. The mist roiled around it like a miniature storm cloud. The pillar/statue vanished, and the mist began to sink into the sand. Feverishly she tried to gather it into her hands, and then she understood that she had to take the place of the statue. She took a step, another, positioned her feet where the statue's feet had been, and instantly the mist swirled about her, immobilized her. In the distance she could see someone approaching, and she knew that person would be drawn here, just as she had been, that that person would be compelled to reach out and touch her. She knew when that happened, she would vanish into the desert floor. She squinted, trying to see through the enveloping mist, trying to identify the approaching figure. The mist parted momentarily and she saw that it was Gina drawing near.

Carol Crandall was ten pounds heavier than her daughter; she used a hair brightener to maintain that same auburn luster, wore the same colors that were so becoming to them both—greens, tans, cream colors. She had yielded with reluctance to Gina's insistent demand that she get home half an hour before anyone else was due. When she opened the door, however, she was smiling.

"Gina! How wonderful to see you. Come in! Come in. You look marvelous. I was so surprised by your call. And of course you'll stay for dinner. Bobby and Dave will be so disappointed if you don't. You'll want to hear about Dave's job offer—"

"Mother, stop! I have to talk to you before they get here. Before Father gets home. Please, let's sit down and talk."

Carol started to move through the living room toward the kitchen. The house was bright and cheerful, furnished with antiques, rich looking. "Come along and we'll talk while I see what's in the freezer. I love having you, of course, but with a little more warning, I would have planned—"

"Why is my birth certificate a fake?"

Her mother stopped moving, nearly at the door to the hall and the kitchen beyond. After a moment she reached out and straightened a lampshade, an authentic Tiffany, she liked to tell people. Then she turned and looked at Gina with an astonished expression. "What a crazy thing to say! What in the world do you mean?"

"Just tell me," Gina said, very tired suddenly. "It's not something that can be kept hidden, whatever it is. I can have a detective look into it, if I have to. It's a fake. Why?"

Her mother aged visibly as she and Gina stood unmoving. Not just separated by the room, Gina thought with despair, but by all the years of her life, by the lie that had lain between them like an invisible barrier that neither had been able to breach.

"Leave it alone," Carol said finally. "Go back to Stuart, live your life."

"I have to know."

"An identity crisis? At your age?" She attempted another smile, but it was a forced grimace. "Gina, it isn't important now. That's the distant past, and whatever happened back then had nothing to do with you, not really. You and Stuart had everything going for you. Go back to him, start over again." She was very pale and stiff.

"Just tell me, for God's sake!"

"All right! You'll see, it's nothing. Harvey isn't your father. I was married before and it was a terrible mistake. I was eighteen; he was nineteen. We did nothing but fight, and after four months we were ready to call it quits, but I was pregnant, and we put off the divorce until after you were born. Then he walked out on us. I wanted to save you some hurt. I wanted to protect you from knowing that your real father had abandoned you, had never seen you again after he left.

Harvey agreed to become your father. It just seemed the best way to handle it."

"No one else knew? Uncle Ralph, Aunt Judith?"

"No. I didn't tell them anything. They knew I had run off with your father, of course, but nothing else. By the time I was married to Harvey and we all were seeing each other again, it was past history. There was no point in telling anyone."

"Are they all, Uncle Ralph and Aunt Judith?"

"Are they all what? I don't understand."

"The family I know on your side, your brother and sister, their children, are they all your family? Did you have aunts, uncles?"

"Gina! For heaven's sake! I was afraid you'd be devastated by finding out about your father, and you want a family tree? Is that what you're after?"

"Yes," Gina said stiffly. "That's what I want. And my father's name."

The color had come back to Carol's face. She looked infinitely relieved. "Gina, I'm sorry. His name was Garrick Ryan. I should have told you. I see now that I never should have misled you."

"Lied to me, you mean. My whole life is a lie and always has been."

"I said I'm sorry," Carol snapped. "It can't be undone. The old family Bible's in the study. Just be careful with it. It has all the names and dates, everything. I was the only one who had any interest in it when my mother died . . ."

Gina walked past her to the study as she continued to talk. Abruptly her voice became silent, and a second later Gina heard the kitchen door squeak open and closed again, just as it had always done when she lived in this house. She went to the study and examined the family history recorded in the large old Bible. There were no surprises; her birth had been entered, as the daughter of Carol and Harvey Crandall. As

soon as she was finished, she left her mother's house without
speaking to her again. They would have to talk, but not yet.
How relieved her mother had been to get rid of that particular secret, she thought, driving once more. How mean Harvey had been to hold it over her all those years. But she felt
dissatisfied, as if she had missed something after all.

On the interstate it was a two-hour drive between Columbus
and Cincinnati; she had driven that way to see her mother,
but her return was on the old Columbus Road. She no longer
was in a hurry. She stopped somewhere to eat and later could
not have said where, or what she had.

Everything was being stripped away from her, including
her father, she thought without any particular emotion, as if
thinking about someone else whom she did not know very
well. There was so little left of her now that it would not take
much more whittling for her to vanish altogether. Even her
birthday never had been hers. She had been born the day
after her mother was nineteen; they had always shared a
cake, shared the celebration. She had been the invisible child
who did not even have her own birthday. Suddenly she realized that she had been looking at her hands on the steering
wheel, not at the road. Frightened, she pulled off at the next
chance and found a coffee shop where she drank bitter black
coffee.

She had expected to learn nothing from her mother, and
instead her whole past had changed. It was not true then that
history was unalterable. People believed in so many things
they never questioned. Stuart believed in the paper trail the
detective had laid for him. She had talked to that same
detective this morning, had neither trusted nor distrusted
him, but had gone there simply because she had his name. He
had asked how she came to find him and she had admitted
he had worked for her ex-husband, Stuart Marsh.

"Bad time for you and Mr. Marsh," he had said sympathetically. "He said he wanted real proof, and that's what I dug out for him. It'll hold up in court or anywhere else."

He believed in his paper evidence also, she thought, sipping a second cup of coffee. She had hired him to find Jennifer and Holly. He believed Jennifer was Holly's mother. She had not known what else to tell him.

"Shouldn't take long," he had said. "Maybe by tomorrow."

She had given him her work number as well as her home number. Maybe tomorrow, she thought, and found that she was staring at her hand holding the cup. She shuddered.

The next morning, Paulo asked in exasperation, "Gina, you sick or something? You gone deaf on me?"

"Or something," she replied. She felt as if she were on the desert walking with leaden feet toward a pillar wreathed in mist, and she knew that when she reached it, she would be compelled to touch it, to take its place when it vanished, only to be dissipated herself.

The phone rang; he snatched up the phone and muttered, "Display, Moreno." He listened, scowled at Gina, and said, "To tell you the honest-to-God truth, man, I don't know if she's here or not. My bet's on not." He thrust the phone toward her.

"Some joker you got there," the detective said when she identified herself. "Got the information for you. You have a refund coming, too. Didn't take any time at all to speak of. I asked the neighbor." He laughed.

"Tell me," she said, nearly whispering, her mouth gone dry. The desert, she thought distantly.

"You want to drop in for the written report and the refund?"

"No. Just tell me. Wait a second. I'll write it down." She pulled a pad closer, one of the carbonless copy pads they used.

"Suit yourself. I'll mail you a check. Here goes: Jennifer Hawkins . . ."

Her hand was shaking almost too hard to write the name and address; outside of Atlanta, Georgia, he said. As soon as he hung up, she called the in-store travel agency and asked for the first flight out for Atlanta. Then she leaned back and closed her eyes, taking deep breaths, trying to get enough air to ease the tightness in her chest.

"Gina, you in bad trouble?" Paulo asked. "You need some help?"

She shook her head, opened her eyes, and stood up. She ripped off the top sheet from the pad and started to walk.

"Gina!"

She stopped at the end of the plywood partition and looked at the long worktable, looked at the fluorescent lights overhead, at the plank flooring where two sheets of paper had fallen. Wherever she did not look directly, she was aware of the flurry of motion. The soulless silver people were astir, she thought. She looked at Paulo, and for a moment she was drenched with terror. If he said *shoo* to her, she would be gone, vanish. Not now, she pleaded silently, desperately. Not when she had come this far. She had to take the next step and then the next. She felt pinned by his stare; he was the one who understood that she was soulless, incomplete. He knew things, had always known things that no one should know. She was the paper doll, she remembered; seen full on she looked normal, but if she turned he would no longer see her. Then he couldn't touch her, make her vanish before she finished what she had to do. As Paulo started to move toward her, she turned and fled.

On the plane she promised herself that if Stuart was right, if this woman, Jennifer, just resembled her a little, or even a lot, if that was all it was, a coincidence, then she would go back to Rose Tichenor and do whatever the doctor wanted her to do. Anything. She would accept that she was mad. She would have to accept it, she knew, because all her actions since she first saw Holly were those of a mad woman unable to resist a compulsion. A mad woman who no longer could distinguish between reality and fantasy and keep them separate. That defined madness. She would accept that she needed treatment, whatever Rose Tichenor prescribed.

She bowed her head over the book of fairies. But she knew. She knew that she and Jennifer were identical, the same in every way. She knew that Holly should be her daughter. She knew she was the empty one, the incomplete one.

"Yes, ma'am," the taxi driver said to her on the way to Jennifer's house, "this is about the prettiest place on earth this time of year."

She made herself see the suburb they were passing: azaleas in bloom, camellias, roses . . . He kept driving, talking cheerfully, apparently not at all perturbed that she remained silent.

"That's pretty far out in the boonies," he had said when she showed him the address. He had looked at her dubiously and she had remembered that she was in the clothes she had worn to work that morning—jeans, a T-shirt, sneakers. Madness, she had thought in despair, and paid him in advance.

Red earth, brilliant greens of new leaves and young grass—Holly's colors, her colors. Yellow irises and fire-engine-red tulips. White pasture fence. Everything was in technicolor under the spotlight of sun. She had a sudden memory of how it used to be when her family went to the seaside for vacations, how she had always known when they were getting near the ocean. Long before they were close enough to smell the sea, to feel the changed, charged sea air, she had sensed its presence, its immensity. She had that feeling now;

she could sense the end of the journey, the immensity that lay ahead.

"That's it," the driver said finally, stopping at a two-story house. No longer in the suburbs here, the houses were well separated, with small farms, acreage. Here an orchard, there a plowed garden plot, horses . . .

"Want me to wait?"

The question surprised her. She shook her head, and started to walk to the deep porch, and forget him instantly. There was no hesitation now, no glances about to examine the house, to look for anyone. She felt as if a part of herself, the part that time could trick so easily, had started this walk eons ago, longer ago than she could remember, that she had always been on this journey for as long as she had lived. She climbed the four steps and walked to the door, rang the bell, and waited.

When Jennifer Hawkins opened the door, a look of expectancy on her face, it was like looking into a mirror. She stared; her face turned ashen and she swayed, clutching the door.

Gina's hand reached out, stopped short of touching her. "I'm Gina Ryan," Gina said faintly.

"He told me you were dead! Father said you died at birth!"

Each took a tentative step forward at the same instant, and then they fell into each other's arms, laughing and weeping.

They compared past histories, scars, even impacted wisdom teeth. They laughed together and wept together again and again.

"I always knew I had a twin sister who died at birth. I've missed you all my life."

"I thought Harvey was my father. There was this great big hollow feeling, emptiness. I decided I must be crazy."

"Father said my mother ran out on us when I was two months old. He couldn't find her again. What terrible guilt they must have, both of them giving away a child. Community property, that's what we were. One for him, one for her."

"When I saw Holly, everything fell apart. I was so sure she was my child, that the fairies must have spirited her away somehow."

Gina looked at the book and smiled; Paulo had been wrong. The fairies had brought them together.

"Holly would have died if it hadn't been for Dr. Spencer. He's a genius with premature babies. They said she was born dead, he revived her and kept her alive."

"To think we were in the same city and only an accident made me start looking for you."

"We were just there for a year. Steven worked on the mall where you first saw Holly. He was there to oversee the completion of the detail work and I was tired of being alone. I insisted that we all go for the year. We rented out this house, rented a house there. We must have moved the day after you followed Holly home. What if you hadn't!"

"There was no way I could do anything else. From that second, I didn't have any choice."

They talked until the day turned into twilight. Holly was with her father at a birthday party; they would not be back until seven. At one point Jennifer said soberly, "I read every book I could find about twins. Father used to say it was morbid to dwell on it. Then Steven . . . He couldn't understand. No one could. I had him, a beautiful child, everything, and still now and then a terrible feeling of loss, of sadness would overcome me. Something was missing and I couldn't explain it to anyone because I didn't understand it myself."

Gina was nodding, also somber now. "I tried to tell Stuart there was another self, separate and yet a part of me, that without it I was incomplete. I couldn't explain it either. But I knew, even if we haven't invented words for what it was that I knew."

The doorbell rang and Gina watched her sister leave to see

who was there. The vacuum was gone; the paper doll was gone; the doppelganger gone, the aching emptiness, fear of madness . . . Not just gone, but even the memories of them were receding, dwindling. She was startled to hear Stuart's voice at the front door.

"Gina, for God's sake, you're scaring everyone out of their wits. Paulo Moreno called me, gave me this address. I couldn't believe—"

Gina walked into the foyer. As if acting independently, her hand and her sister's hand reached for each other. Stuart looked dumbfounded. She took his hand gently, turned to Jennifer and said, "This is my husband, Stuart."

O Homo; O Femina; O Tempora

udson Rowe stared at the screen where black lines and numbers and symbols chased one another over the green background like football players over Astro-turf. The final equation appeared and the dance ended. He groaned. There had been no mistake. He pressed the Print button and continued to gaze dully at the equation that had the beauty and elegance of truth. When the printing was finished, he collected his disks and the printout, turned off the terminal, and stood up, realizing belatedly that he was stiff and hungry, and tired enough to assume that he had not slept for several nights.

Dazed with fatigue he left the laboratory, walked down the silent hall of the Mathematics Building and out into the cold. He stopped abruptly. There was a bare tree breaking up the light from a corner street lamp; no person was in sight. He heard footsteps and turned, saw a watchman approaching.

"How long has that tree been there?" he asked.

"What tree's that?"

"That one!"

The watchman glanced at the tree, at Judson, back to the tree that was being singled out. "Longer than either of us has been around, I'd say."

"I guess I never noticed it before," Judson muttered.

"Yeah. When the leaves go, it changes, doesn't it?"

Judson started to ask what month it was, but he bit the question back and said good night instead, and tried not to run to his car. In it he looked at his watch: two-thirty. No wonder the campus was empty. He drove home, looking at everything as if he never had seen it before, the winding campus streets, the intersection that was barren of traffic now, the all-night hamburger stand, empty. He drove without thinking of which streets he wanted, where he was to turn, which house was his. He felt as if he had been away a long time.

When he let himself into his house, he heard the television and followed the sound through the kitchen to the living room where Millie was on the couch covered with an afghan.

"I'm home," he said staring at her. She was prettier than he remembered. Her hair was turning from gold to a light brown, nicer this way, and her eyes were bluer than he remembered, larger, and now, at least, meaner.

"Me too," she said, and turned back to the television.

"How's everything?"

"Fine."

"Are you mad at me?"

"Of course not. Last week I told you I was leaving, running away with another man, and you know what you said? 'That's fine, honey. Whatever you want.' And you haven't said a real thing to me since. You haven't asked about our daughter, or the lawsuit, or the mortgage payments, or the leak in the bathroom."

"Good God! What daughter?"

She sighed and stood up. "Have you eaten these last few days? Have you slept?"

"I don't know. I don't remember. Millie, you're kidding me, aren't you?"

"I'm kidding. Scrambled eggs? Are you finished with the new theory? Is that why I'm visible again?"

"Millie, it's . . . I have to call the President or someone."

"Like Chicken Little?"

"But the sky *is falling!*"

"With or without cheese and onions?"

He followed her into the kitchen; she took his hand and led him to a stool at the counter, pushed him down onto it. When she put a glass of milk before him, he tasted it as if he never had seen anything like it before.

"Time's slowing down, Millie."

She broke an egg into a bowl.

"I couldn't believe it at first. I've checked everything a dozen times. It's slowing down."

She broke another egg. "There is no such thing as time." She cracked the third egg. "Did you leave your coat at school?"

He looked down at himself. That's why he had been so cold. "It's slowing down at an accelerating rate and there's nothing we can do about it."

She stirred the eggs gently. "Time is an abstract concept that we invented in order to talk about change and duration." She added cheese and onions to the eggs, put butter in the skillet and watched until it started to sizzle, then added the egg mixture. "Time," she said then, "has no independent existence of its own. Change can happen faster or slower, but there is no such thing as time that can change its own rate of passage."

"And when it slows down enough," Judson said glumly, "it's going to stop altogether."

She put bread in the toaster and got out jam. "We invented time in order to talk about seasons, physical change, growing old and dying."

The eggs were done at the same time the toast popped. It always amazed him that she knew to the second how long things took to get done. She never even glanced at a clock when she cooked. Instinct, he thought uneasily; it had nothing to do with real time.

She put the food before him. "If there are no events, there is no time," she continued. "It's inconceivable without events that change, that evolve. It doesn't exist except as a figure of speech. Like time is of the essence. Essence of what? Another figure of speech."

"With the mainframe I'll be able to predict exactly when it will stop," he said and began to eat.

"Darling, just tell me one thing. Did you use the square root of minus one to get your results?"

He nodded, his mouth too full to speak.

She smiled, broke off a piece of his toast and nibbled it.

"You shouldn't have waited up," he said stiffly as soon as he could speak.

"I wanted to. I knew you'd come home eventually, hungry, tired, cold. Besides, I can sleep in tomorrow. Saturday, you know. No classes." She taught medieval English literature.

"I know that," he said, and wondered which Saturday, which month. He glanced over his shoulder at the calendar and saw that October was the month displayed.

"The twenty-eighth," she said kindly. "This is the weekend that we change time. Do we set the clocks back, or forward. I never remember. When you lose an hour," she mused, "where do you suppose it goes?"

"You don't have to make fun of me," he said bitterly.

She put her arms around him and kissed his cheek. "I love you," she said.

Icy rains came, then snow, and more ice, then warmer rain that washed it all away. The trees were enveloped in a pale green haze that turned into a dense canopy that filtered the light, turned it green, then golden and red, and once more became bare limbs that broke up the pale illumination of the street lamps.

"You're going to be bored," Judson said as he settled down next to Millie in the auditorium of the conference center. "Dukweiler's a bore even to me."

"I wouldn't have missed this for anything."

"Did you really listen when I gave my paper?"

"You know I did. You talked about epsilon and alpha and omega and there were those infinity signs here and there on the blackboard, and then you multiplied everything by the square root of minus one and the audience applauded. You were magnificent."

"I've had good comments already. They're going over the figures with everything from hand calculators to the mainframe."

"I told you not to worry. Of course, they'll take notice."

Dukweiler was introduced and started to read his paper. He wrote down numbers and symbols on the board as he talked. He was an arid speaker, obviously too nervous even to glance at the audience. His presentation was too fast for Judson to follow and do the equations at the same time.

Judson felt a chill midway through and leaned forward intently. When Dukweiler finished, Judson turned to Millie. "Did you hear that? Do you know what that idiot is claiming?"

"It sounded a lot like your paper. All those epsilons and alphas and omegas, and then he multiplied—"

"I know what he did! The idiot! He's got it all backward!"

"He thinks time is speeding up?"

"I can refute his findings!"

She picked up her knitting again. "I think those men are coming to talk to you. I'll wait here."

He left her and walked to the rear of the auditorium. A surge of attendees rushed for the podium and another group of people moved slowly in his direction, some speaking in low voices, some frowning in thought, a few working their calculators methodically as they walked. Half and half, he thought with satisfaction, and tried to see who had lined up in the enemy camp. He nodded to Whitcombe who was the first to reach him. As others drew near, they spoke in measured tones, choosing words carefully, and they were solidly on his side; they had been convinced by his proofs, by his rigorous logic. It was an inescapable conclusion, they agreed; time was certainly slowing down and a situation was developing that would prove to be of the utmost gravity.

Finally the two groups began to disperse; it was cocktail time, happy-hour time. The gang at the podium led the way to the bar in a near stampede; the other group followed more leisurely. When Judson freed himself, he looked at Millie, calmly knitting with a slight smile on her face. It was just as well that she did not understand the seriousness of the time problem, he thought as a wave of tenderness passed over him.

"Will we experience anything differently?" she had asked.

"Relative to what?"

"Ah well," she had said. "Nine months will still seem like nine months." And just like that she had dismissed one of the great mysteries of the universe.

"Judson," Whitcombe drawled at his elbow, "we'll be sending you an invitation to speak down at Texas A and M. Have to get together about the best time before all this breaks up."

Judson nodded. A life's work lay ahead of him. More than one lifetime. He smiled at Whitcombe. "Happy to come down," he said, "if I can find the time."

The Chosen

"Lorin, where are you?" He heard Jan's call and wished she hadn't come out. She called again, closer. Reluctantly he left the tree trunk he had been leaning against and answered.

"I'm here, Jan. I'm coming."

He knew she couldn't see him in the dark under the mammoth trees, but she was plainly visible in the clearing at the edge of the woods: a slender, spectral figure with loose white-blond hair blowing in the wind, gleaming under the full moon. She had a long wrap about her, and it too was luminous in the silvery light. He hurried a bit; probably she was cold, and he sensed her fear. It had been in her voice; it was in her stance, her refusal to enter the woods to find him. She saw him then and took a step toward him, but again stopped and waited. When he reached her she threw her arms about him and clung for a moment.

"I was so worried," she said. "You were gone for hours."

"Honey, I'm sorry. I thought you were asleep." He turned so that he could see the forest over her head. The smooth trees at the edge of the woods reflected the pale moonlight, and behind them there was a solid black wall. No wind stirred under the trees; no sound was there. High above, hundreds of feet over them, the tops of the trees made whisper-soft rustlings. He remembered how it had been walking under the black canopy, and he yearned to return to it, with Jan at his side sharing his awe. She was pulling him back toward the ship, and he put his arm about her waist and turned his gaze from the forest.

She was saying, "I was asleep, but when I woke up and found you gone, I couldn't go back to sleep. It was too quiet. I waited over an hour before I came out . . . I didn't tell any of the others."

He tensed with a flash of anger. It died rapidly. He was acting erratically; she was loyal and wouldn't report him. Simple as that. And she had shown courage in waiting alone, going out alone. He said nothing and they walked toward the dome-shaped tents at the side of the ship. The tents were all dark and silent. He paused once more and glanced back at the still woods, then they went inside their tent.

"I made coffee. It's so late . . . Maybe we should just go to bed."

"Jan, don't talk around it. We've never done that with each other. Not this time either. Okay? There's nothing wrong with my taking a walk in the night. I do it a lot."

"Yes, but that's different. People in the city wait until night but this is so . . . I just wish you wouldn't do it here."

He laughed and caught her to him, hugging her hard. She shivered and he realized how cold she was. "Honey, I'm sorry. You're freezing." He rubbed her arms and back briskly, then put her to bed, pulling the cover to her chin. He sat on the edge of the bed with his coffee. "Come out with me tomorrow. Let me show you the forest and the clearing I found."

"I did go for a walk with you, remember? Miles and miles

of walking." She snuggled down lower in the bed and yawned.

"But that was with the group . . ." Jan had closed her eyes already, and her face had softened with relaxation. Lorin kissed her forehead, then walked to the tent flap and stood looking out until the moon was hidden by clouds and there was only darkness. He put down the cold coffee and got into bed beside her. She fitted herself to his body without waking and with his arms around her he listened to the silence.

"It's such a lonely world," Jan had said the first night, staring at the dense blackness that was the forest. "It is so still that it is nightmarelike. Nothing but wind, sighing like ghosts through the trees. Whispering. Don't you feel it, Lorin, the whisper, too faint to catch the words?" She had cocked her head with an abstracted look on her pale face, and Lorin had caught her arm roughly.

"Jan, snap out of it! It's just silence. For the first time in your life you know what silence is like. The stuff we prayed for night after night."

"Never again," she had said, with a stiff, set look on her face, a look of fright denied, of anger at the causeless fear.

Lincoln Doyle, the leader of the expedition, worked them all unmercifully, but even with the full schedule there was not enough work to shut out the world that surrounded them. All the others seemed to share Jan's reaction to the silent world. There were twelve of them, all with sunup-to-dusk tasks to complete, and all with the same listening look when there was a pause in their own noise. Doyle turned on the recorder, blasting music through the valley, and that helped. But at night the silence returned, deeper, more ominous.

At first no one had believed Lorin's report that there was no animal life, but they had come to accept that, as they had come to accept the mammoth conifers that grew where oak and maple and birch trees had stood. The trees were giants, three hundred feet or higher, with tops that met and tangled in an impenetrable web of needled branches. Their trunks were from ten to thirty feet through. There was scant undergrowth in the pervasive gloom of the forests, but at the river's edge where the ship stood, and in the clearings, there were bushes and vines and a vivid green, mossy ground cover. Other places had waist-high grasses, and he had seen a grove of deciduous trees in the distance on one of his exploratory trips. But no animal life. No birds. No insects. No fish. And stillness everywhere. As he was falling asleep the silence became an entity, a being with cradling arms and soothing fingers that penetrated him, searching out and healing bruised and torn nerves.

They had breakfast with the others in the group. The music blared so that talk was in shouts. Doyle looked especially grim that morning. He was a small, thin, intense man. Lorin could imagine him on a high stool frowning over a ledger after hours in a musty office.

"Steve tells me we can expect a storm tonight or in the morning," Doyle said precisely, clipping off each word, as if he had to pay for them in cash. "We have to get as many of our samples in today as possible. When the cold front comes through with the storm, we could get snow, and that would upset our schedule. Barring that, I am confident that we can finish here within a week, as planned."

Since there was no work for a biologist in this lifeless time, Lorin's daily tasks varied with the requests for assistance from the others. Today he was to accompany Lucas Tryoll to the coast, follow it south to the tip of Florida, go inland, and return over the area of the Mississippi River taking pictures of the land. He was pleased and excited by the assignment.

They flew due east to the coast where New York City once had been. Manhattan was gone, as was Long Island. There was only a bay that reached far inland, and was twenty miles across. Most of the New Jersey coast had been swallowed by the ocean, and Delaware Bay was indistinguishable from the rest of the sea. A solid green roof of treetops hid the land almost to the edge of the ocean. There were no offshore islands.

"Spooky, isn't it?" Tryoll said after several hours. "I still say we should have settled for the last time."

Lorin looked at him quickly, but there was no humor on the man's brooding face. Lorin remembered the last time they had arrived to find people turned savage, and animals even more savage. They had all been in the last stages of severe malnutrition and radiation sickness. He tried to recall a time that he preferred to this, and failed. Sickness, or overcrowding, or a wasteland of radioactivity, or glaciation . . . He touched Tryoll on the arm and pointed: there was no Florida, no islands as far as they could see, hundreds of miles out of unbroken deep blue-green water.

Tryoll turned the plane and followed the coast to the delta of the gargantuan river that emptied into the gulf. From their height they could see the brown water-swirl pattern as the river flowed into and finally became part of the pale blue of the sea. The Mississippi was miles wide here, shallow, and brown with silt. They followed it north, and the scenery below them was the same as everywhere else: forests, no signs of life. There was a great, shallow inland sea over what had been Nebraska, Kansas, or Iowa. Lorin couldn't tell where they were. Clouds were forming to the north of them when Tryoll turned eastward again, coming to mountains, and then heading north. There were only clouds under them now, gray concrete, rolling plains, but still the cameras worked, taking infrared movies through the dense layer, mapping the land that lay invisible under them. Once Tryoll said that they would have to land, and Lorin felt his heart thump with excitement. But Tryoll flew on grimly and Lorin knew that he'd risk crashing into the mountains or being iced by the storm rather than land and spend the night here in the silent forests.

When they put down at the campsite a hard rain was driving in, cold and stinging against their faces as they raced back to the ship. Lorin showered and changed into warm clothing, then went to dinner with Jan.

"We're all going to sleep inside tonight," she said. "Steve predicts an all-night rain, and possibly snow by morning."

"Inside? But we have heat in the tent."

"But if it snows . . . It will be more comfortable inside the ship on a night like this."

Lorin put down his fork and took her hand between his. "Jan, please come back to the tent with me. Have you ever slept where you could hear rain in the night right over your head? Have you ever seen fresh white snow falling, covering everything with dazzling white?"

"You know I haven't."

"When we get back home we'll be on the sixty-third floor again, with forty-seven floors over us. All we'll ever see of rain is a dirty suspension of grime running off our windows, or down our clothes. Can you imagine what this rain will be like?"

"It might be 'hot.' "

"You know it isn't." He resisted the pull of her hand as she tried to free it. "Jan, we've been through a lot together. Remember the wild cats?"

She nodded. "I still don't see how domestic cats could change like that. But don't you see the difference? You know I'm not a coward. I just don't like the silence. I keep listening harder and harder for something, anything. It's as if I know that something is out there, but I haven't been able to listen hard enough to catch it yet, and I have to keep straining . . ."

He had tried and failed to understand how it was with them, the ones who found it eerie and alien. He said, "Jan, we have only one more week here, then back to make our reports and wait for reassignment. It could be months, or years before we're alone like this again. Pretend we're on vacation. Pretend it's a vacation zone, will you."

She made a derisive sound. Her hand in his yielded and relaxed though, and she said, "You're playing dirty. You pushed that button on purpose, didn't you?"

He laughed with her. He had done it deliberately. They had met in upper New York State Vacation Zone Number Eighty-two. He remembered the long lines of people, antlike on the concrete mountain paths, bunched at the overlooks, spread twenty-five feet apart everywhere else. They had met at one of the view spots—Lookout Nineteen.

Arm in arm they left the ship and ran to the little tent in the blinding rain. After changing from his wet things Lorin stood in the tent opening, watching the storm. "This will reinforce the cyclic theory. Back to the forest primeval. Doyle is bound to recommend this zone for exploitation. You can tell he's eager to get back and report this find. An army of men will come and mine and timber and raise animals for meat. Let's come back with them, Jan. There are things we could do. . . ."

"What? I'm a bacteriologist, and you're a biologist. Can you locate ores, or handle cattle, or build a slaughterhouse? It will be mostly automated anyway. There won't be any research done beyond what we do now in the preliminary probe. Lorin, do close the flap now. It's getting cold in here."

He knew it wasn't, but he pulled the flap partially closed, and continued to look out toward the black trees blowing in the wind. Racing sheets of rain obscured everything, thinned to allow a view of the forest, and then came back redoubled in strength.

"We could learn to do something that would be useful here," he said softly. Behind him he could hear Jan making the bed. The aroma of coffee filled the tent: she had been keeping herself busy, trying not to see out, trying to shut out the storm noises, and the feeling of aloneness. For a moment

Lorin almost wished that he had not pressed her to stay out with him, wished that he had come back alone. The moment passed and he let the flap close the rest of the way and went to sit by her and sip coffee with her.

"Jan, try to see what I mean. We could have a good life here. You could have children who would have room to run and play in the forests, swim in the river . . ." She was staring at him wide-eyed, her face very pale. "You would get used to the quiet . . ." She shook her head.

"I would go mad," she said finally. "Always listening for something that isn't there. Later, after they get the town built, maybe after they get the town built, maybe then we could come back. . . ."

"How many other places like this have they already found? Five, ten? We don't even know. Are we allowed to go to them?" His voice became bitter. "No one goes to them except the workers who get paid a bonus for 'extraordinary conditions' in the environment. No other people go. Too costly. It will always be like that, Jan. Always. The only way we can come back is as workers who really hate the place. We'd have to pretend. . . ."

"They'll find a way around the energy exchange," she said, but without belief.

"Never. There has to be an equal mass-energy exchange or the ship doesn't make it. Period."

"You're not being reasonable," Jan said, with a show of temper. "They wouldn't let you abandon your profession now. You are doing valuable work. Anyone can come and do the rest after we locate the zones and check them out. Besides, we won't go back to our old apartment. This trip qualifies us for one of the garden apartments, and a raise. What's got into you, Lorin? You never talked like this before."

"I never saw a zone like this before. I didn't know there could be one like this. I thought all that talk was only talk.

Why else give the men that kind of bonus for working in a place like this? Bonus! They should be charged for the privilege. Garden apartments! Two windows instead of one."

"Lorin, not now, please. I'm too tired to argue with you. Even if you don't have work to do every day, I do. That's your trouble, no work of your own." She crawled into the bed and pulled the cover up to her chin. "Are you coming?"

"In a minute. Just a minute."

The rain and wind were abating. The storm was over. He went again to the flap and was struck by an icy blast of air when he opened it. He adjusted the pressure inside the tent, making an invisible wall between him and the cold air outside. A fine freezing mist was falling; he put his hand out and felt the needlelike sting. Suddenly he wished they hadn't found this time zone at all. Earlier he had said there was a cyclic pattern, but not now, not since the Bok-Gressler-Harney Temporal Mass-Energy Exchange Theory had been proven empirically. The theory stated in mathematical terms that a body could move forward in time, giving the formula for the energy demanded for such a displacement. It was like being at the end of a rubber band, Lorin thought, standing with his hand out in the freezing mist. They were at the end of it and with every passing minute it was stretching farther, growing tauter. At the end of a preset interval it would snap back into place, and they'd be back there. Doyle could change the duration of their stay; he could shorten it as much as he chose, but he could not lengthen the interval in the future by even one second.

That was the first drawback. The second was that the mass had to be exactly the same for both directions. If there was any difference in mass when the snap came, the ship vanished. Finis. No one knew where it went. Some said a dimensional transference took place, but no accepted theory had been advanced yet.

The cost was beyond comprehension, but not so great that

trips couldn't be made in the endless search for raw materials that sustained the world, and food to keep the people on the right side of starvation. Doyle's team had trained together for three years before their first probe, and there had now been seven probes for them, each one costing upward of five hundred million dollars. With an estimated four billion years in Earth's future to explore, an infinite reserve seemed available to mankind. Even as he had talked to Jan about returning to work in this time zone, Lorin had known that he was talking nonsense. His training made him valuable only where he was now. Economics dictated that he would never see this world again once he had left it. He pulled his hand inside the tent and pressed it to his cheek. His fingers tingled and started to hurt. Slowly he got into bed beside Jan.

The next morning the trees were sheathed in silver. Emerging from the tent, Lorin caught his breath and stared at them. They were like intricately wrought silver columns reflecting the milky sunlight. At the breakfast meeting when Doyle checked their assignments, he asked to be allowed to take soil samples from deep in the woods. He would bring out cores for testing. Permission was granted and he slung his pack over his shoulder as soon as he could leave the meeting and tramped through the mossy ground cover that was brittle with ice. Inside the woods, the trees were convex, obsidian wall sections topped with etched glass branches that gleamed and sparkled and became prisms where the sun shone through them. The tangle of vines and shrubs was a fantastic exhibition of twisted glassware bent into impossible designs, with impossible joinings. As Lorin worked collecting his soil samples, the ice broke and fell; the ice from the shrubs and vines hit with soft tinkles of melody; the upper branches of the trees dropped their sheaths with crashes of thunder that reverberated throughout the forest.

And there was another sound, a soft plop, plop on all sides of him. The needles of the giant evergreen trees developed in clusters of fives, and at the base of each fan a nut had grown and ripened. The needle clusters had been pointed slightly upward before the freeze; now they drooped and the nuts rolled loose and fell to the ground.

Lorin picked up one of the nuts and found it surprisingly heavy. It was a rich, golden tan, about as big as a golf ball, and the covering was suedelike, soft, slightly rough, indented to form five sections. He peeled one of the sections back, exposing snow-white meat. He finished peeling it, saving the skin for testing, and saw that the meat was in five wedges, not divided, but clearly marked. Probably as it dried and shrank, there would be oil, and the sections would be separated. He cut a thin slice off, smelled it, and finally bit into it. The meat was crisp and tender, slightly salty, completely satisfying. He ate it and gathered more of them.

He didn't return for lunch, but worked through until it began to grow dark under the dense trees. All about him the tinkle of dropping ice, the less frequent explosions of thunderous sheets crashing to ground, and the ceaseless plop, plop of nuts falling was like an orchestra heard in rehearsal. When he went back, his step was light, and his face peaceful. He approached the ship in darkness and outside the door he paused for one last look at the deeper shadow of the woods behind him. He could hear Doyle's voice from the other side of the ship's doorway; the door was open.

"No need to delay any longer. Further testing and probing would merely confirm what we all know now. . . ." There was the less forceful voice of Tryoll, his words indecipherable. Doyle said, "Tomorrow night, at the latest. Just long enough to finish the tests that have been started. . . ."

Lorin felt rooted for a long time. One more day only. Slowly he entered the ship where Doyle met him. He made his weight exchange carefully, and watched as Doyle checked it and checked and okayed the specimens he took inside. Lorin took the discarded material to the side of the ship and left it there with the rest: a growing pile of trash, boxes of junk that couldn't be used any longer for any purpose, some of it poisonous, radioactive, indestructible. He felt a surge of anger at the pile of refuse, and wished they could at least bury it. But that was no answer. Buried, it would still be poisonous, obscenely out of place on this pristine world.

Jan refused to stay outside with him again. "I keep waking up and listening," she said. "In here, at least, there are the sounds of machinery, and other people. Something. I don't like it out there, Lorin. I simply can't get used to it. I am frightened, cut off . . ." She shrugged helplessly and he didn't urge her. He decided to sleep in the tent alone. The others looked at him uneasily; no one understood his behavior. They would all be glad when they were away from this silent, dead world, back making their reports, sleeping in their beds again, getting ready for another probe. Lorin waved and walked to the tent.

The weather had turned quite cold following the storm, and snow was expected that night. He made coffee and drank it, waiting for the snow to begin. When it came he stood watching it for an hour, then pulled on his outer clothing and went outside. The silence of the world was deepened by the snow; it was a black and white silent scene, like a pastoral charcoal drawing come to life. The snow fell straight down, it changed the landscape, made the forests more alien, hid the tent from view almost instantly, and softened the outlines of the ship, making it appear dreamlike and hazy.

He walked along the edge of the woods, lifting his face from time to time to catch the falling snow on his cheeks, feel it stinging his eyes. From time to time he looked back at the ship, growing dimmer and dimmer, until finally it was gone. He took a deep breath, but there was an ache deep within him at the thought of Jan sleeping apart from him. He walked for an hour before he turned back, going into the woods for the return trip. There was little snow under the trees; it had been captured by the roof of green that was fifty, one hundred feet thick in spots. There was only an occasional plop of a falling nut now; that phase was over. The quiet of the forest was deeper than he had known before, a sleeping forest under a snow featherbed. When he listened for the river he could hear the rushing water splashing over rocks off to his left. He guided himself by the sound of the river, drifting out of range now and then, only to veer to his left until it was there again.

The pure, cold river, the meat of the nuts, oil for burning, for candles, mushrooms, roots, the strange waist-high grasses with cornlike ears on them. It was a bountiful time on Earth, more so than he had known.

When he finally got back to his tent, he felt his exhaustion as a weight pulling him down on the bed still fully clothed. He fell asleep instantly, and his sleep was deep and restful.

Before breakfast he called Jan to the tent and showed her the nuts he had found, and when he finished telling her of his day's work, he knew that Doyle must have had time to make his announcement about departure.

"Honey, get some sample bags together, will you?" he said to Jan. "I'll go check the day's assignments for us."

She nodded and started to check the contents of his bag. Lorin met Doyle at the ship door.

"Where's Jan? I want her to hear this, too," Doyle said.

"I'll fill her in. She's busy right now checking our stuff for today. I found a swamp yesterday that is exuding heat and fumes. I think she should get samples from it. If you don't have other plans for us."

"That's okay," Doyle said uninterestedly. "But get back before dark. We're going back immediately after dinner." He turned away without waiting for an answer. Lorin took a tray with coffee and biscuits for Jan and went back to the tent. She looked surprised at the service, and he said quickly, "Big day for us, honey. Doyle wants samples from a swamp

I stumbled over yesterday. We're to eat and start right away. It's a long walk."

She stiffened and he added, "I had to argue with him to let me go with you, and he isn't happy about it. He might still change his mind and send me out with Tryoll again, so we'd better hurry."

Jan reached for the biscuits and coffee. They finished quickly and he led her straight into the woods, not giving her a chance to stop and talk with any of the others, and not until they were a mile from camp did he start to relax. He whistled then and presently she joined him, whistling harmony.

There was no trace of the snow remaining, and the ground under the trees was dry and springy. A pungent odor filled the air. Lorin detoured from his planned route and pointed out the reason for the smell. Where the snows had fallen through the treetops and melted, thousands of mushrooms had sprung up overnight. Looking at them spread like a carpet Lorin was reminded of a painting he had seen once of a courtyard of white cobblestones. The shiny white caps touched one another, were packed into an area twenty-five feet by forty. They skirted them. There was a look of wonder on Jan's face.

"They are all edible," she said. "That's the same kind that we found down nearer the river. Do you know how much they cost back home?"

"Everything here is edible, and free," Lorin said happily. "Not a poisonous plant, or spore, or virus, or bacterium. It's a lovely world now, Jan."

She squeezed his hand in reply, and he noticed that some of the stiffness had left her, and that she no longer was listening quite so hard. After a while she complained of tiredness and asked how much farther it was.

"Let's have some lunch and rest," Lorin said. They had been walking for over four hours. He lowered his pack and took out a plastic cover that he spread out for her to sit on.

She rested with her back against one of the trees while he prepared their food: he boiled water over a tiny fire of nut skins, and to the pan of boiling water he added mushrooms and sliced needle nuts and a handful of the green moss. Jan watched without speaking. When he handed her a cup of the soup she stared at it for several seconds, then said, "Didn't you bring any of our dri-freeze food? Why this?"

"For fun," Lorin said. "Try it." He lifted his cup and sipped the broth and found it even better than he had expected. After a moment Jan tasted hers. They smiled at each other and finished the pot of soup without speaking again. For dessert Lorin peeled raw needle nuts and cut the sections apart. "All things to all men," he said solemnly. "Fried in their own oil, they are better than potatoes; ground, they make a dandy flour . . ."

Jan looked troubled, and he stopped talking and took her hand. "You are having fun, aren't you, honey? It isn't so bad now, is it?"

She shrugged and glanced about her at the trees and the deepening gloom that filled the spaces between them. "I don't like it; I don't feel safe here, but as long as I don't think about where we are, just remember that we are here together, then I'm all right. If you went away even for two minutes I might start screaming."

"I won't go away even for one minute," he said. He turned her around and pointed to the tree that had been her back-rest. "Look at the pattern it makes, honey. Like great scales overlapping, climbing up the tree in a spiral, getting smaller and smaller as they get near the top." He rubbed his hand over the smooth glossy tree, and when Jan moved slightly away without touching it, he didn't force the issue. There would be time. She began to roll up the plastic cover, not looking at him. "We'd better be getting on. Is it much farther?"

"Not much now," he said. He repacked and they walked

again. After another hour Jan began glancing at her watch from time to time, and a worried pucker appeared on her forehead.

"Lorin, do you remember exactly where the place is? Are you sure?"

"I think so," he said. "It can't be much farther now. Tired?"

"No, of course not, but we have to get back before dark. . . . Maybe we should start back now. I don't think we'll have time before it gets too dark in here."

"Half an hour more, then if we don't find the swamp, we'll go back. I was sure I could go straight to it again."

After the half hour was up Jan insisted they turn back. An hour later they both knew they couldn't get out of the woods before night fell.

"Lorin, we can't stay out here overnight. I won't. I can't!"

"Honey, it's all right. There's nothing here at night that wasn't here in the daylight. I'll be with you. I even have a tent we can pitch."

Jan whirled about and stared at him unbelievingly. "You did it on purpose! You deliberately brought me out here too far to get back before dark! What will Doyle say? And the directors when he reports it?"

"We got lost, that's all. Who can say anything about that? We got lost." Lorin caught her to him and pressed his face against her hair for a moment. He said softly, "I had to come out for one night, Jan. I had to bring you with me. I couldn't help myself." She didn't relax in his arms, however, and he kissed her forehead, then got busy with the tent. He made a fire before the tent, and there was the light inside it. He started to cook their meal and presently Jan came out to help him; they sat before the crackling fire and ate, and Jan kept her gaze on the flames and didn't look beyond the light at all. Later he made love to her, and after she was asleep, he left her side and stood in the dark forest for a long time, simply feeling happy.

The next day Lorin increased their distance from the ship, knowing instinctively which direction he wanted, not able to tell how he knew from hour to hour when he couldn't see shadows or the sun's position. But he knew. And slowly Jan grew to understand what he was doing.

When she balked, Lorin put his pack down and caught her arms. "You can't help yourself, Jan. Don't you see that? I love you too much to leave you behind, and I can't go back again. Not now."

She said, "We have three more days here. Then we have to go back, Lorin. You know that?"

"I know."

She nodded; looking at his face, studying his eyes, his mouth, she said, "All right. I'm with you. I wouldn't have come if you'd told me what you planned, but I am here, and I won't spoil it for you."

Arm in arm they walked again, whistling, singing, stopping to gaze in awe at a waterfall they found, laughing at each other's clumsiness in crossing the brook that formed the falls. They found a cave and stepped inside it, and Lorin said thoughtfully, "It would make a good home when the tent wears out, or if it gets too small."

Jan stiffened again at his words, and her tension stayed with her for the next hour, fading gradually as the cave was left behind. Lorin didn't refer to it again, but he made a mental map, locating the cave on it for future reference.

On the third day Jan knew he wasn't going to take her back at all. She sat down on a boulder and kicked the deep mat of needles and nuts. "I won't go any farther. You could kill them all by this, and you know it. If we turn back right now, and don't waste any time, we can make it before the snap takes them back." She kicked a nut viciously. "You would murder them all without a thought?"

"I left a complete list with weights on it for Doyle to substitute," Lorin said. "He's no fool. He'll be careful when he knows he has to make substitutions. They'll be all right."

"And if they die, won't that be even better for you? Then no one would ever discover this time zone. You know they never double-check if they lose a ship. They assume that it was a bad time and let it go at that. Is that what you hope for?"

He hadn't thought of it consciously, but with her words, he knew that the thought had been there. He jerked the pack up and slung it over his shoulder. "All right, so that's what I hope for. You know who will get to come to a zone like this? Those who hate it. Like Doyle, and you. They'll come here and sweat out the minutes until they can leave again, living only for the bonus that's waiting for them, afraid all the time, wishing the zone would burn up, or sink into the ocean, dumping filth here, taking what's good and clean, leaving their filth behind. Can you imagine what this place right here will look like in ten years? When they finish with it, it'll be as bad as the fire-bombed ruins we found on the third probe. I don't care if Doyle and the others live or die. If they're careful they'll get back. But are they alive, will they ever be again? Alive in hell?"

He started to walk. She had to follow; she had no choice but to follow, and he would make her forget the other world, the other time that was like a fading nightmare.

A searing pain hit the back of his head, and he clutched it, staggering, thinking she had thrown something. The pain deepened and he fell, and abruptly there was only blackness.

He heard, from a great distance, "He's okay. He'll wake up in a moment. Negative."

He waited without moving, trying to remember, and there was a blank. Hands were fumbling about the back of his head and he opened his eyes warily. A nurse smiled at him.

"I'm just removing the electrode wires. Relax a few minutes, and then you can get up."

"The test is over?"

"That's right." She finished, and wheeled a portable psych machine away to the corner of the room. She returned and placed coolly professional fingers on his wrist for a moment. "You can sit up now, if you want."

"How did I do?"

"Dr. Doyle will be in in a moment. He's talking to your wife now, I think."

Lorin sat up and the pain in his head made him blink. He touched the back of his scalp gingerly. The nurse laughed. "The electrodes are still there. Just below the skin. We don't take them out, so if you ever need a good psychoanalysis, you're all set. Compliments of the house." She laughed to show that she joked, and after a bad moment he grinned back at her. Although he couldn't find the thin platinum wires with his fingertips, he would be wired the rest of his life, ready to be plugged into a psych machine and played like a record. He stood up carefully, but there was no dizziness, and the headache was fading. He looked at the clock over the door. He had been there four hours.

Dr. Doyle came in and shook his hand enthusiastically. "You go home and get some rest now, Lorin. We'll call you in a day or two, after we analyze the results. If you don't hear by Monday, report back to your regular job and wait. We never know what kind of bugs we're going to find that will delay us." He shook Lorin's hand again and was gone before Lorin had a chance to ask him a single question.

The nurse ushered him from the room to another room where more nurses were busy at desks. He went to a desk with an information sign over it and asked for his wife.

"I really couldn't say," the nurse said, without looking up.

"But we both took the tests. She should be through now too. . . ."

"Not my department. You'd better go on home and wait
for her." The nurse opened a ledger and started to run her
finger down columns of figures.

Lorin tried to get back inside the test room, but the door
was locked now. None of the nurses knew anything about the
tests, and finally he went to the door marked "Exit." It
opened only halfway and he squeezed through into an ante-
room that was a bedlam of confusion and noise. He tried to
open the door again, but it wouldn't open at all from this
side. Someone caught his arm: "My husband, tall, heavy,
bald, did you see him? Is he in there? He went in two weeks
ago. . . ." Lorin shook his head. "Is Dr. Doyle in there?"
someone else yelled. Someone else was holding a snapshot
before his eyes; he thought it was of a woman. The press of
people was so thick that he couldn't go straight to the street
door, but had to squeeze through openings, to be forced
backward, to inch forward again painfully. He saw an opening and stepped into it, relieved at the lessening of the pressure of bodies. Then he saw why there was the open space.
A psycho in the telltale yellow coverall. Revolted, he turned
back to the crowd. The psycho followed him. It was a
woman. She screamed at him, "Stop! Tell me what happens
in there! What do they do? What did they do to me?"

The crowd gave ground before her and he knew that the
look of disgust that was on everyone else's face was also on
his. He managed to get people between himself and the yel-
low-clad woman. The noise was deafening. Every time the
door to the inside offices opened, there was a surge toward it,
and the cacophony increased. His headache returned,
stronger than before.

He finally got to the outside door, but hesitated again. He
took a deep breath; the fetid air in the room was better than
the air out in the street would be. He went outside and was
caught up immediately in the swell of people on the sidewalk.
Three hours later he arrived at his own building, exhausted

and panting. The elevators that went to his level were out of order, so he rode to the fiftieth floor and walked up the next thirteen flights of stairs, stumbling over the gray children who played there. Jan was not in the one-room apartment.

He waited for her all afternoon, listening to the neighbors above and below and on both sides of his small room. Children screamed and shrieked in play through the halls and on the stairs. Women shrilled and men cursed. Radios played out of synch, on different stations; airplanes overhead and traffic below competed with rising decibels; sirens, the blare of advertising trucks, the screech of the elevator again in service. He pressed his hands over his ears; his headache was blinding. Why didn't she come home? The lights came on: neons, streetlights, traffic lights; haze descended and haloed the lights. He fell asleep toward dawn.

That day he returned to the test center and waited along with all the others in the anterooms. Jan didn't come through the doors from the inner rooms. On the third day he returned to work.

He was stopped at the door of the biology lab by his supervisor, who handed him an envelope and hurried away without speaking. Lorin opened it with shaking fingers, his heart thumping wildly. He was certain it was his test confirmation, and orders to report back to the test center. . . . He stared at the curt message: *Report for analysis 9 A.M. Mon. Thurs. Fri., Rm. 1902 Psych Bldg.*

He didn't enter the lab. He knew his bench would be occupied by someone else. He went to the psych center and was issued his yellow coverall, and shown his iron frame cot. The other men in the ward didn't stir as he entered, no one looked up at him. He felt his cheeks burn with shame and he sat on the edge of his cot and waited for 9 A.M. Thursday to come. He knew why Jan hadn't returned, would never come back to him. He ground his hands into his eyes and tried to remember the test, what he had done wrong, how he had revealed insanity. When a sonic boom shook the building, he covered his ears and pushed hard against them, trying to think. He wished he could go for a walk, but the thought of walking in the center of a circle that moved with him everywhere he went, of seeing the disgust and loathing on the faces of those he approached . . . He sat on the edge of the cot and waited, and tried to remember, and when night came he lay down wearily and stared at the ceiling, trying to remember what he had done wrong, and he listened to the clamor of the city that never was still: traffic; voices singing, shouting, cursing, screaming; sirens; jets; foghorns; elevators; sound trucks; televisions; phonographs; buses; elevated trains . . . Nearby a jackhammer started, and an alarm went off. Lorin stuffed his fist into his mouth to keep from screaming, and lay staring at the ceiling trying to remember.

On the Road to Honeyville

*F*ather died in April. In July Mother said, "We're going home."

Like that. We're going home. Over the next four weeks, through the packing and sorting and getting rid of, and real estate people, and prospective buyers, through it all I kept coming back to those words. Montauk was home, the only one I'd known, although Eleanor said she remembered a city apartment, and Rob insisted he did too, lying, because he was only a baby when they bought the Montauk house.

"You mean Lexington?" Rob asked.

Horses, rolling pastures, the old Widmer farm where Grandma still lived.

"No. I mean Salyerville."

I was washing dishes. Eleanor was dashing around getting ready for a date and Rob was fixing the stereo, across the counter in the family room. There was a long quiet waiting time after Mother said Salyerville. Eleanor broke it. "Why? I thought you'd have to be carried back there, words to that effect."

"Things change."

"Well, not me. I have to be in Ithaca by the end of August, and . . ."

"Of course," Mother said. "We'll get you settled in school first."

"Are we broke?" Rob asked.

"Not completely. Near enough. Too broke to keep this house. I'll work, but even so . . ."

He had a wreck the first day of March and died April 6, and in between he had two operations and never left the hospital. I saw myself on the starched sheet, pale, hovering between life and death, the doctors thick around me, the first such case they'd ever seen. And such a pretty girl, so brave.

"I won't go either. Those hick schools!"

"Rob!"

"I won't!"

I turned from the sink to see her standing at the table looking at me. I knew that if I said no, too, we wouldn't go. I knew that. She was waiting, not moving. Maybe not even breathing. And I thought, I can't decide. I'm not old enough. I don't understand enough. She waited, and I knew that I was afraid, not like in the movies, or from reading a horror story, not like anything I'd ever felt before. I nodded.

So Eleanor went to college and Rob went to live with our uncle and Mother and I began the long drive home. I took a test once, along with some of the girls. It was a scientific personality survey to gauge the chances of your having a happy marriage. Joanne found it in a true love magazine. One of the questions was, "Are your parents (1) ecstatic together, (2) happy, (3) neutral, (4) unhappy, (5) miserable?" I checked number one. My score showed that I would have a much better than average marriage. They never fought, and it seemed natural to walk into a room where they were and see his arms about her, or see them kissing, or something like that. I couldn't really believe they'd still be interested in sex, he was already forty and she was nearly there. At that time I thought they'd had sexual intercourse in the past because they had wanted a family, and I forgave them for it.

It rained almost every day in April. Toward the end of the month on a day when the sun finally came out I knelt on the big red chair with my chin on the back, not thinking, not really looking out even. And suddenly I was crying, and I hated the day for being sunny and the air for being warm, and Rob for having band practice and Eleanor for having a part-time job.

"Elizabeth, honey." She put her arm around my shoulder and I hated her because she wasn't crying.

I pulled away, but I couldn't stop crying. That night I woke up and went to the kitchen for a drink. As I went by the living room, I saw her, in the same chair, the same position, and beyond her the moon was lighting up the back yard. I kept thinking of that afternoon and night on our way to Salyerville. I hadn't gone to her because I had known she'd pull away from me just exactly the same way I had pulled away from her. We had both cried in his chair, hopelessly, unable to stop or be consoled. And now we were going to do something about it. I didn't know what. But I felt certain we were on our way to do something about it.

I wouldn't go to church or Sunday school after he died. The minister came out to talk to us all, and he kept saying things like God's ways are mysterious, and death is but a transition from this life to a better one, and Jesus would save us all from damnation, if we would admit him to our hearts and not be bitter over God's will being done on earth. Rob kept saying "Yeah," and "I guess so," to his questions. Eleanor treated him like special company. "Wouldn't you like more coffee, or another piece of cake?" Mother didn't say much. She was knitting Eleanor a vest, and she watched her needles and the yarn, although her hands could do it alone.

I glanced at her once or twice, then away again, afraid she'd see me looking. I was embarrassed for her.

"Elizabeth, won't you come back to us Sunday? Let us help you in this difficult time. Let God help you."

I stared at the cake I was holding.

"Elizabeth!" Eleanor's voice, the voice she used if I tagged along when she didn't want me. The voice she used when I mimicked one of her boyfriends.

I shook my head.

"Elizabeth, God will help you."

I looked at the minister then. He was sincere, his eyes were bulging a little and his cheeks were very pink and moist. I shook my head again. He reached out for me and I drew back. I didn't want him to hold my hand while he prayed God to comfort me. Eleanor had held still for it, I wouldn't. I drew back and stood up, holding the dessert plate very carefully. "Daddy didn't believe in God. I don't either. And if I did, I'd hate Him!"

Rob wanted to belt me. Another hour, he must have been thinking. Later, his glance threatened. I'll fix you later. Eleanor was humiliated and ashamed of me. She'd want to fix me later too. Mother put the vest on the table and stood up. "Excuse us, will you please. Come along, Elizabeth." And she took me out, down the hall to my door, and gave me enough of a nudge to get me started inside. I was still carrying the cake, but now I was shaking. She reached out and took the dish and put it down on my dresser. No one ever mentioned the incident to me again. The minister didn't come back.

After the interstate highway the state road we took was like something you might see a stagecoach on at any time. Originally built too narrow, it was trimmed even more by eroding shoulders. We were in hills that became steeper as we drove. The road twisted and turned to conform to the valleys as much as possible and although it was September each valley was a heat trap, holding moist heavy air.

I glanced at Mother from time to time. She was wearing a little white head scarf to keep her hair from blowing, but strands of hair had pulled loose and they were curling about her face. I thought what a pretty profile she had. I had always simply accepted her prettiness without thinking about it, this appreciation of her profile and the curling bits of hair below her ear and against her cheek wasn't like that. I studied her face, examined it closely for flaws and good points, the same way I'd do a new girl at school, or one of Eleanor's new boyfriends. My mother was very pretty.

"What's the matter, honey?"

"Is it always this hot?"

"Of course not. Feels like a storm might come up."

The sky was deep blue, cloudless. I stared at the road. She was humming, very low, probably didn't even know she was doing it. I got out the road map and began adding up the miles from the highway to Salyerville. We were only doing about forty. One hundred ten miles, about.

"I don't think it's very accurate," she said. "See how far it is to Honeyville, will you?"

"This road?"

She swerved around a pothole and for the next few minutes was too preoccupied to answer. Our speed dropped to thirty.

"I guess no one goes there from the north anymore," she said finally, when we made a sharp curve and came out on a straight road that was relatively smooth.

We had been on the road for two hours, it was almost five. There was a break in the hills westward, and through the gap I saw the sky. It was gray on black, and moving. Mother looked at the sky and braked hard; for what seemed like a long time we watched the roiling clouds through the opening in the hills, like looking at a fight through a keyhole. There

was a tension in Mother that hadn't been there before, not
even when a passing truck swung in ahead of us and nearly
forced us off the road early in the day. She stared at the
clouds, then turned to look at the road we'd come over, and
then squinted at the long valley before us. It was a narrow
valley, the road went over a couple of bridges, then seemed
to end at the base of a steep rocky hill. I knew that was just
another of the sharp turns, that after it the road might continue at the base of the hills that had become mountains, or
we might start climbing yet another chilling mountain road,
potholed, with no guardrails. I didn't want to be on a road
like that when the storm broke. There was no sound in the
valley, and with the thought I knew I was wrong. Water. A
stream off to the right, hidden by bushes and low trees, but
now I could hear it faintly. The clouds had completely filled
the gap. It was like watching the creation of a new mountain
range, the upward thrust of darkness. The air was as hot and
heavy as ever, more so since we weren't making our own
breeze, but suddenly I shivered.

Mother lighted a cigarette, and that added to my fear; she
smoked very seldom. Being afraid when you don't know why
is the worst kind of fear, I thought, and tried to find a reason.

"Well, we can't go back. Can't turn around here, and I
don't have nerve enough to back up over that last stretch.
And we can't stay here. So, onward. Right?"

"Why can't we just wait for it to storm and be done with
it?"

She started the car and accelerated to sixty, then had to
brake hard for the first of the bridges. "Look at it, honey. If
there's a downpour, that little stream will almost fill this
valley." The bridge was like many others we had crossed,
posted "Narrow Bridge. 10 M.P.H." Rickety, ancient, its
sides close enough to brush us, four, five, six times the width
of the tiny stream it crossed. I glanced toward the west and

now it looked as if a gray-black mountain range had grown up to the sky and was advancing eastward.

"That was pretty dumb of them," I muttered, looking at the crumbling road ahead, obviously much flooded in the past. "Why'd they make the road so low? Why didn't they raise it or something?"

She concentrated on driving and I watched the road and bridges also. It wasn't that the bridges were so ancient, I decided. It was their design; they had been built for a different kind of traffic, not wide swift automobiles. We got out of the valley only minutes before the storm broke and we stopped on the road that began to climb into the mountains again. I twisted to watch the streams turn into torrents; the water swirled and boiled over the road in several places. It became very hot in the car quickly, and it seemed that the rain was from all directions at once. There was no window that we could open without having rain blow in, and in spurts it came down so hard that it was like being parked under a waterfall, and only the pounding roar of water could be heard. Then a lightning streak would illuminate everything, the hills, the blowing trees, the rocks that appeared turned to glass under the sheen of water, all would flash into sight with painful intensity followed by the equally painful blast of thunder.

After the storm, night came suddenly. Driving was even more treacherous because all the holes had been filled with water. I searched the map for a turnoff, another road, anyplace to spend the night. Nothing. Sometimes we passed other roads, deeply rutted gravel or dirt roads that intersected ours, vanished among the rocks of the hills. We didn't turn onto any of them. It would have been stupid to exchange bad for worse. Occasionally we smelled wood smoke. Cooking stoves, Mother said. She was smoking a lot now, more than I'd ever seen before. Our road got worse, the surface was crushed rock, and it was narrower.

I dozed and dreamed of being in bed, warm and comfortable, listening to the light murmur of Mother's voice, and the deeper growly tone of Father's. I woke with a jerk. "Are you all right?" I asked her, as if she had been the one to doze.

"I'm fine." Her voice was tight.

"Maybe we should just stop and sleep in the car."

"The mosquitoes would eat us up." She pushed in the cigarette lighter and groped in her bag for her cigarettes. "We surely will get to Honeyville before long now."

I found the cigarette pack for her, a new one. It was after eight and I was getting hungrier and hungrier. "I hope there's a restaurant there." This was part of it, I thought, glancing at her as the tip of her cigarette brightened. There had to be a better way to get to Salyerville. A better road, even if it meant going out of the way a bit. We should have been there by six, according to our pretrip estimate. Seven at the latest. I didn't fall asleep again, but everything got more and more dreamlike. A mist lay low in the valleys and that was right too. It had to be hard and dangerous and seemingly endless. It couldn't be just another trip. Orange eyes hung above the mist straight ahead.

"Betty, flick your dimmers, tap the horn. It's paralyzed, hypnotized by the headlights."

I hit the floor hard and my fingers clenched, ready to whip the car around the animal. The mist swallowed it. I wet my lips and opened my hands and looked at her. She was too rigid, as frightened as I was. If we had a wreck, no one would find us. No one would know. There hadn't been another car, truck, nothing. I stretched my legs to ease a cramp in my right foot, my braking foot. I tried to imagine how cramped she must be feeling, the soreness of her calf, her shoulders, the stiffness in her neck. She reached up and rubbed the back of her neck.

"Remember that time we were on our way back from

Canada?" she said, almost shrilly. "Your father . . . We saw a deer on the road that night too. He said . . ."

"I remember."

It had been a long time since our road had crossed another road. I strained to see the map under the dash light, but it didn't help. I had no idea where we were any longer. "Mother, why Honeyville? I can't even find it."

"It's on a side road. I can't remember the number. It was just the road to Honeyville." She pushed herself back in the seat, stretching. "I know some people there. We could spend the night. My cousin and I used to exchange visits. Aunt Tattie lived there."

Before I could ask who she was, Mother said, "Not really my aunt. Or anyone else's, far as I know. She could take off warts."

I couldn't stop my left hand from jerking, as if trying to hide all by itself. The warts on my little finger and ring finger felt larger than ever. "Will we see her?" I had read about people like that who could do things.

"Oh, honey, she was an old woman when I saw her the last time, twenty-five years ago." We came to a crossroad then. She hesitated a moment, then shook her head and drove on. It was ten-thirty. The fog or mist was denser now. We were creeping along in a white cylinder that grew higher and more solid as I watched. Beyond the walls the world was strange and unknown here, and invisible. It might have been nonexistent, and only the fog cylinder and the car real.

"Was Aunt Tattie a healer?"

"No. Oh, warts, and some said other kinds of skin blemishes, birthmarks, and the like. My father didn't believe in such things. We weren't really allowed to talk about her, or to see her. But we all did at one time or another."

Like Father and my Tarot cards, I thought, and the magazine horoscopes and the palmist who put up a sign at the beach a few years ago. I tried to imagine Mother twenty-five years ago. Long hair? Like mine? Father always said I looked like her, same red-brown hair, same size and shape. "I just hope someone has something to eat," I said and studied the fog.

We turned at the next intersection. It had to be wrong, I thought. We bounced along on a dirt road that went up and down and back and forth. Mother's hands were very tight on the steering wheel and she stared straight ahead. She wasn't smoking at all now. Suddenly I was jolted out of the dream-like state that I kept slipping into by her voice. I thought she had cried out. She laughed harshly. "I'm sorry, honey. I yawned. You'd better talk to me, I'm getting pretty sleepy."

The road was worse, but the fog was lifting, and off to the right I could see the dim shape of a barn. Farmland here. Maybe here the radio would pick up a station. There'd been nothing but static since leaving the interstate highway that morning. I gave it up after a minute or two. Still nothing.

"Nothing has changed here at all," Mother said, adroitly skirting a hole. "Did I mention to you after this year, after the insurance is settled and everything is straightened out, I'm going back to the university for my Ph.D.?"

"What for?" I stared at her, but she was still looking straight ahead, only now I thought her lips were curved in a faint smile.

"You know that I was just two credits short of my master's degree. Then Eleanor came along, and . . . well, I always thought that some day I'd finish up and go into research psychology. There are so many things . . ."

I clenched my hands, wanting to scream at her, No! That isn't what we're coming back for! But I didn't know why we were coming back, so I didn't say anything, and then I saw the first lights. Honeyville.

Much of the town was dark. There were three dim street-lights, and a few old cars parked along the street, but it seemed that almost everyone was in bed already. Then

Mother said, in an excited voice, "For heaven's sake! There's Aunt Tattie's house!" She slowed down, then stopped. "She'll know if Emma is still here. Come on." We got out of the car and went up the sidewalk to the frame house with a wide porch. A bare light bulb hung from a chain on the porch. Mother had started up before me, but she stopped and I caught up with her. She turned back toward the car. "You go on and knock. I left my purse in the car."

I took several more steps toward the door; it was open and I tried to see inside without entering. Then I heard a grumbling voice. "Don't hold the screen open. Mosquitoes thick as dust in here." I went inside. An old woman was sitting at a small table. She beckoned to me without looking up. "Don't be skittish, girl. I don't eat young'uns." She was unbelievably old, her skin was brown and thin, transparent on her hands. She reached out and took my left hand, then rubbed her thumb over the warts, mumbling in a barely audible monotone. "Rub a seed potato over them, then bury it where the moon will shine on it and when the potato rots the warts will be gone." She raised her head and the brilliant blue eyes that studied me were young eyes with dancing lights in them. I don't know how long I stood with my hand in that ancient hand, staring at those young eyes. Emma's voice roused me, broke the tableau. I pulled my hand away.

"What did she tell you?" Emma asked, walking home. "I heard the part about a better than average marriage, and three kids. What else?"

I looked up and down the quiet dirt road, and the dark little town. There was nothing to see. "I don't remember," I said. Then I did. "She said that I'd become a famous scientist, or something." We giggled over that for a long time after we went to bed, until Aunt Janie told Emma she'd send her Pa in if she heard anything else out of us.

I didn't go to sleep. I stared at the ceiling and felt a fear that I couldn't explain or rid myself of as if somehow the world had shifted and nothing was what I had thought it was. But I couldn't describe why it frightened me so. And under the fear, waiting for it to ease, there was an overwhelming sadness that finally seized me and I buried my face in the pillow and wept, and didn't know why.

The Great Doors of Silence

*C*ass Mercer is alone, driving the long distance from San Francisco to Phoenix. She is not yet thirty, slender, dark haired, the kind of woman younger girls envy for her freedom, her self-assurance. She does have an enviable job; she is an architectural landscape designer for a major firm in Seattle. She has brought along some of her work on this trip. In the motel later she will add azaleas or rhododendrons to the drawing, and perhaps several dogwood trees. And tomorrow and the following few days in Phoenix she will absent herself now and then from the family reunion pleading work. In truth, the job could wait, but she planned it this way so that she will have an excuse to withdraw when she wants to. She used the work as her reason for excluding Dan from the family get-together.

Dan wants to marry her. He is a computer systems analyst, probably a genius, she thinks. They have lived together for a year, and during this time her life has been exciting, exhilarating, serene, good in all ways, but she is not certain it would continue idyllic if they were married. She has been slow to respond to his proposal.

The Nevada desert speeds past; she is driving twenty miles over the limit. She usually does. Now and then she edges up to eighty and when she notices, she makes an effort to slow down and hold the speed nearer the limit, but that never lasts more than a few minutes. There is nothing to see except the desert fringed with indistinct hills and mountains, too far away to register as peaks and chasms and abysses. The distant range is no more than an irregular skyline with streamers of clouds. The road is straight with nothing on it as far as she can see ahead and through the rearview mirror.

On their way from Seattle to San Francisco where Dan has business to take care of, he asked if she was ashamed of him. They were not using the air conditioner then; the wind, whipping her hair, whipped the words past her almost before she could catch them. Now the windows are closed and the air conditioner is blowing cool air on her legs, and against her midsection. No matter how she adjusts it, the stream of air hits her like an assault.

"Have you told them about us yet?" he asked.

"No. I will when I'm down there."

"I should come meet your family. Are you ashamed of me?"

"Dan!"

"Well, solid middle class family, lawyers, Episcopalians, southerners—they might not like a nice Jewish boy like me."

"They're not bigots! I hadn't even given that a thought!"

She really had not. She does not know if he believed her.

If she were keeping a travel journal, she thinks the next day, she would start it: *And on the fourth day we entered the state of Arizona, having traveled through rain forests of the northwest, the arid California valleys, across mountains and the high plateau . . .*

She told her father she could stay for no more than three days; distances in the west were too great for a longer visit.

"You can fly down," he answered reasonably. "It would be cheaper in the long run."

She agrees. It would have been. Now the heat assails her each time she leaves the car; the glare of the sun on the road, on the cactus spines, on the hood of the car stuns her eyes through her dark glasses. From time to time she adds pomade to her lips and nose; her skin is an incompetent barrier against the withering aridity.

She rounds a bend in the mountainous road and nods at the new vista, almost as if she has been expecting something this strange. Grotesquely shaped Joshua trees appear like an alien army in random disarray, frozen in time, shepherded by a few tall seguaro guards, caught, paralyzed as they came over the crest of a hill, marched down the long slope toward a valley. Has anyone ever put up markers, kept watch day and night, month after month to make certain they are really motionless? She can imagine them moving at some infinitesimally slow rate, but only when no one is looking, during periods of the dark moon, or the black hours between moonset and sunrise. They flash by, stiffly pious and proper, pillars of the desert, arms outspread under the glaring light as if to demonstrate there is nothing to hide, and, she feels, they are aware of her. When no one can see, they move; only her presence now on the road compels them to stillness.

She has not seen her father for seven years, since her graduation from college. She has not seen her brother Eric for even longer than that, and she has not seen her younger sister in five years. Her family lived in a pod under pressure for all their lives, and when a rent appeared, when it split apart, the children were expelled with such force that if they never had met again, it would have been reasonable. Eric lives in Texas, she in Seattle, and Rebecca in New York, and now for the first time since they left adolescence, they will be together for a few days. To measure growth against the wall, leaving tangible marks behind to prove they have been there?

To compare school experiences, job experiences, childhood reminiscences? Not that, she is certain.

"If it weren't for my grandparents," she said to Dan on their way to San Francisco, "it would be different. But they're too old to accept our living together. They wouldn't understand." Her grandparents will celebrate their sixtieth wedding anniversary in three days.

She loves to watch the transformation that changes Dan's face from a dark, brooding, rather solemn mask to a lighted, open look of happiness when he searches a restaurant and finally finds her. She loves the way his hand touches her now and then throughout the night, as if to reassure himself that she is there. She loves his surprises: a catered dinner once in their apartment; his own cooking on Sundays; a cluster of helium-filled mylar balloons that stayed aloft for weeks, were named, became pets.

Dan loves her, but Dan wants to buy property, wants his own house with a fireplace, and woods edging up to the backyard, wants her at his side on rainy nights. Dan wants a family. They could afford house help, help with a child, with children. He does not want her to stop working; he is proud of her work, of her promising future.

She drives through the Joshua Tree National Forest, and it is so foreign to anything she has ever seen before, she could be in another solar system, on another planet. Speeding toward her alien family.

How much Eric's voice sounds like her father's, she thinks that night, sitting on the wide, covered terrace behind her father's house. It is not cool outside, but they have come out to sit almost as if it were a ritual: the clan gathered before the immense swimming pool, the most telling symbol of affluence, gazing at it instead of each other. They are not in darkness—too much light spills from the various floor-to-ceiling glass doors and windows on this side of the house—

but decently shadowed, revealing little that is meant to be hidden.

Eric has put on twenty pounds, a tall, stout man now, with a deep voice, a good lawyer's voice, with the same rhythms and cadences that her father always used. How did he learn to do that? she wonders, listening to the sound of the words, not their meaning.

Rita, Eric's wife, strikes Cass as a mistake, not a Texas woman. She is untanned, delicate looking, tall but somehow frail.

Their three-year-old child, Jason, is as brown as a walnut and incredibly busy. Cass never realized how busy such a small child could be. He dashes in and out of the house, chases runaway balls and electric cars and building blocks that mysteriously sail through the air.

Cass is suffering the déjà vu effect of seeing her father and simultaneously her grandfather in him, seeing another evening. Her mother was there, making it an incident from her very early childhood, before she was five. Her mother died when Cass was six, and for the year before her death, she had been ill. But the night Cass is remembering included her mother, alive, well, but quiet. She was always quiet. They were back from a visit to . . . she cannot remember what, only that they were returning and it was dark; the grandparents were with them, visiting them? Rebecca was running back and forth, manic with excitement. *For God's sake!* her father exclaimed suddenly in his good lawyer's voice, deep, vibrant, resonating. *Put her to bed!* And her grandfather's voice followed, equally rich, deep, *These kids are running wild!*

There is no more of the memory. It is as if her father and Eric moved up the game board to assume new roles, and a new player, Jason, has joined in the game.

"Put him to bed!" Eric says suddenly. "He's driving me crazy!"

Rita stands up and calls to Jason that it is bedtime, but he cries and clings to Florence until Eric takes him inside himself. They can hear Jason screaming.

No one speaks until Eric returns and resumes his seat, lifts his glass and drinks deeply. Father continues where he left off, talking about the real estate market in Arizona.

The automatic cleaning system is like a snake in the pool, in constant motion, searching for something, coiling, uncoiling, lashing out, even flipping above the water now and again, splashing water on the walk around the pool. The spilled water dries rapidly, sucked up into the dry air, lost forever.

"I wish Rebecca had come today," Florence says to Rita softly, not interrupting the men. They are onto wills now. Arizona is Mecca for a lawyer who specializes in estate planning, trust funds, wills. That is Father's specialty. "Rebecca is the real scholar of the family," Florence goes on. "Already a Ph.D. in literature, and only twenty-seven. She was at Oxford for a year, you know."

Cass lived with Florence from the time she was ten until she went away to school at seventeen and never said anything to her or heard anything from her that was not one of the social phrases that allow people to inhabit the same house without open hatred poisoning the air.

Florence is fifty now, and putting on fat around her hips and waist, giving her a tubular shape. Her legs are very good, and her face is youthful, unlined. She avoids the sun through most of the day, swims before ten, shops late in the afternoon. Every day she takes a nap. She always did. Cass remembers how puzzled she was as a child when an adult who obviously was not sick went to bed every single day in the middle of the day. She and Florence have been exceptionally polite to each other this evening.

Cass realizes with a start that Rita is talking about her next baby; she is pregnant again, three months apparently. They want a girl next time.

Abruptly Cass stands up. "I'll get more coffee," she says. "Anyone else want anything?"

No one does and she escapes inside the house where she can hear Jason crying. From the kitchen window she can see the group on the terrace and she stares at her father. Years and years ago he reached his peak, but he has not started down the other side.

He is fifty-nine, as rich as he chooses to be, drives a Lincoln Continental, plays golf, serves on committees, is generous with his checkbook and his time for worthy causes. Does he know that he is edging into his own father's shadow day by day, that Eric is drawing closer to his space all the time? Does he see Eric in the child Jason, who is still crying in a distant bedroom? She felt a shock on her arrival at how large her father is. It seemed strange to be embraced by him; she had thought she remembered his largeness only because she had been a small child, but her memory is correct after all: he is very tall and heavy without being fat.

She adds a dash of bourbon to her coffee and returns to the terrace, allowing herself another half hour before she will plead the pressure of work and go to her room. Perhaps by then Jason will be asleep.

"Hey, Cassie," Eric says, "want to go to Vegas tomorrow?"

"Thanks, but no. I'm driven out for the time being."

"I'm driving," Father says. "Plenty of room. Becky's not due until sometime after dinner. Her fault if no one's here to meet her."

Cass remembers the quarters she dropped into her purse. In the lobby of her motel last night there was a row of slot machines. She put in two quarters and walked away with both hands full of coins. She has not even counted them. She shakes her head. "I'll get some work done." How strange, she is thinking; she did not care if she won or lost. Losing meant nothing; winning twenty, thirty quarters meant nothing either.

"Do they dress up much?" Rita asks, and the talk goes on to the Vegas style of clothes and Cass is not listening. Ten more minutes. She drinks her bourbon and coffee.

She was so tired when she went to bed that it was a long time before she could relax enough to sleep; at six-thirty Jason wakes her. Irritably she pulls the pillow over her head and drifts back to sleep, this time to dream.

She is very small, lost in an unfamiliar place with menacing trees and shrubs. Far in the distance she can see the edges of gigantic doors coming together in slow motion. She is desperate to reach the doors before they meet because she knows she is too small to open them again, and she has to get through, out of this place. She runs, dodges around bushes, bumps into trees, darts this way and that, and all the time the doors are closing at the same steady rate. She stumbles and falls, runs again, is bruised and sore, and finally she reaches the clearing before the doors only to see them come together. They are so high she cannot see the top of them. There is no handle, no doorknob, her fists make no sound as she beats on them in misery and frustration.

She wakes up again, feeling suffocated. Her hair is wet with sweat from being under the pillow. She decides to swim before breakfast, swim until she is able to shake the aftereffects of a dream that already is fading from memory, but leaving an unpleasant sense of dread.

"You won't actually be baby-sitting," Eric says at the table later, finished with his own breakfast. "Mildred will be here, and she'll stay until we get home if you want her to."

"That would be silly. Don't worry about him. Between us Mildred and I will take care of him. I'll be here all night."

"Just don't let him out by the pool alone," Rita says,

worried that they actually will be leaving him apparently. "He isn't used to a pool without a fence."

"We never fenced kids out of anything," Father says. "You can't fence off every danger. You've got to train the child, not try to protect him that way."

"It was already there when we bought the house."

"Jason, come here!" Eric calls brusquely, obviously impatient to be starting, impatient with the last-minute anxieties that have Rita looking hesitant.

Jason comes to the doorway and stops. Eric waits for him to approach the group at the table and then says sternly, "You stay away from that pool, you hear me? And you be good today or you know what I'll do when I come home?"

Jason says nothing. His face is twisting as if he is going to cry.

"Don't you start that again! We'll be back after a while. Aunt Cassie will stay with you. And Mildred. And you better be good!"

Jason mumbles something and looks at Rita and does start to cry. Eric pushes his chair back angrily, but before he can reach Jason, Cass lifts him and carries him from the room.

"Just go on," she says. "He'll be fine as soon as you're all gone." Jason is arching his back, screaming, kicking with both feet. He is very strong to be so little.

He does stop howling as soon as they leave and she puts him down. His eyes are red and swollen and he is soaked with perspiration.

"That was some show, kid," Cass says, regarding him gloomily. What do you do with a three-year-old, she is wondering, trying to remember what Rebecca used to do. She has not been with a child since then. "Want to show me your toys?"

There are battery-operated cars, the building blocks, wooden beads to string, several balls, and a few stuffed animals. He shows her the toys one by one silently.

"Can you talk?"

He nods.

"What do you want from the toy store?"

"Bicycle."

"Okay. Let's go see what we can find." She tosses a fluffy pig back into the toy box and stands up. "First you have to wash your face."

She tells Mildred, the cook/housekeeper, that they will be back before lunch, and gets directions from her about the nearest shopping center with a toy store, and they leave. Jason won't sit down in the car and finally she makes him get in the backseat where he can kneel if he wants to, or stand on the floor. She is beginning to feel sympathy for Eric, she realizes, driving slowly, afraid of bouncing the child off the seat altogether. He is on it and off it endlessly. Hyperactive? She hopes not, hopes no one will suggest that they start him on speed to calm him down.

In the toy store she buys him a tricycle, oversized crayons, a large pad of newsprint, a few books, and a swim board. When he starts to cry for a fire engine, she says coolly, "Would you rather have a horn or a bell for your bicycle?"

He stops crying immediately and tries out the horn and the bell, back and forth, and finally picks the bell. Terrific, she thinks. Father will love it! He doesn't want it wrapped, and he rings it all the way home, standing on the floor in the back, the bell on the seat, ringing, ringing, over and over.

He won't sit on the tricycle, but wants to push it from behind and Cass knows this is dangerous. It could get away from him, make him fall on his face.

"That isn't how to do it," she says. "You have to sit on the seat and put your feet on the pedals and push them. That's how it works."

She picks him up and tries to position him on the trike; he screams until she puts him down again. "Okay! You win! We'll do it your way. Put your foot here. You have to hold

both handles, Jason." Slowly, laboriously she teaches him
how to stand on the foot rest and push until he can go for a
short distance alone on it. At least he can't ring the bell this
way. She realizes that he has wet himself and she leaves him
with Mildred while she checks her car for a puddle. When she
returns Jason backs away from her.

"Don't spank! No spank!"

She stops at the look of terror on his face. "I'm not going
to spank you, Jason." There is a sudden sickness in the pit of
her stomach as she stares at the child. She looks up from him
to Mildred, a stolid, heavy-set Chicano. Mildred turns away.

"I'll have his lunch ready in a minute, Miss." She leaves.

"Let's get some clean clothes on, honey," Cass says. "You
have to wash your hands for lunch. After you eat, I'll read
you a story. Okay?"

When she strips him, she tries not to see the bruises on his
buttocks, tries to believe he fell down, tries not to remember
Rebecca's buttocks with the same pattern of bruises, all the
times when she herself chose not to sit down, chose to wear
long sleeves, refused to go swimming, afraid others would see
the marks, the ugly blue-turning-to-green-and-purple marks.

She examines him carefully, pretending to be wiping his
sweaty body, trying not to show her revulsion and sickness.
There is a slight discoloration on his left shoulder, almost
faded completely. On his right upper arm is another bruise,
old, but plainly visible. How incredibly small his fingers are,
his wrist bones.

After his lunch, she reads to him and then he naps for two
hours. Later they play in the breakfast room, drawing silly
animals on the newsprint, coloring them, making up stories
as they create life. Very late in the day she takes him into the
pool and shows him how to use the swim board, how to
propel himself around the pool. She chases him through the
water, never quite able to catch up, and they both laugh a lot.
He splashes water in her face whenever she draws near him,

then, arms working furiously, paddles himself away from her. It is a lovely game with him.

Mildred comes out to tell her there is a phone call, and for a moment Jason's face wrinkles up to cry when she says they have to get out of the pool. He regards her intently, then starts to splash his way to the end where the steps are. She swims at his side, holds the board while he gets off, and they leave the water together. Mildred takes him inside for a bath and Cass sits in the shade to use the terrace phone. The caller is her sister.

"I'm not coming," Rebecca says without preliminary. "Just tell them something came up, will you?"

"Sure. How are you?"

"I'm okay, same as always. You?"

"Same as always."

There is a long pause and then Rebecca asks, "Is it awful?"

"Worse than that. Becky . . . do you really want to know?"

"No. I have to go, Cass. If you ever get to New York . . ."

"And you, if you ever get to Seattle."

She watches the water snake whip around the pool for several minutes after hanging up.

"Ancassie, will you eat with me?" Jason asks at her elbow.

"Sure. Who else would I eat with? The chair? A goat? A pig? The tree?"

He giggles and takes her hand, pulls her toward the dining room doors.

"I have to dress, monkey. I can't eat in a wet bathing suit."

When they sit down to eat, she sends Mildred home. After Jason has finished his dinner she asks, as casually as she can manage, "How did you get such a sore fanny?"

She can see the change that comes over his face but cannot immediately identify what it means. It is almost as if he is gone, the face is empty with no one behind it.

"I fell down," he says looking straight at her, and she

remembers. Tell me you know I'm lying, that is what that look means. Make me confess I'm lying to you, make me tell you the truth; that is what that look signals.

She nods. "You know someone has to do the dishes now, don't you?" He comes back from where he has been.

"The dishwasher does it," he says seriously.

"Hey, dishwasher, get out here and do these dishes!" she yells, then looks at him with dismay. "It can't hear, I guess."

"You have to carry them to it," he says. "I'll show you how."

Jason sleeps like an infant, knees drawn up under him, his butt sticking up in the air, his thumb in his mouth. She leaves his door open in order to hear him if he cries out, but he sleeps quietly.

She keeps thinking of her Aunt Edie, her mother's only sister. Aunt Edie drank, she remembers. Father detested her; he still hates for women to drink anything stronger than a little wine with meals. Aunt Edie suspected—knew—and was helpless because everyone lied to her. *I fell down. I crashed my bike. Eric and I were fighting.* She wanted to help. If she had been able to find a way, perhaps she would have helped. But the real problem, Cass admits, was not Aunt Edie, or even Florence, but Mother. Why did she tolerate it? That was the real problem for as far back as she can remember. Why didn't she make him stop? Suddenly she is overwhelmed with despair and guilt, the way she always is when she tries to make sense of her own past.

"We didn't kill our mother!" she says aloud and starts at the sound of her voice. Saying it does not make her believe it. He had to punish them for hurting their mother, for making too much noise, for lying, for fighting among themselves, for all the terrible things they did that worried their mother and finally killed her. Mother didn't stop him because he was right. They deserved their punishment.

She paces the silent house, goes to the terrace and back inside, and finally opens the sliding glass door and leaves it open, so that she can sit on the terrace and still hear Jason if he wakes up. The house will get hot and humid, she thinks angrily. Let it! She wishes her father were home so she could repeat that to him.

She is remembering the last time her father beat Eric. He was fourteen, had not spurted upward yet the way he would in the next year. Rebecca sobbing in her bed, beaten for something or other; Cass nursing a sore arm where he had yanked her away from her sister, thrown her against the wall so that he could get to Rebecca, and Eric . . . Walking into the house, yelling something, unaware that Father was home. He took off his belt with deliberate care, moving slowly, his eyes fastened on Eric who was transfixed with fear. Eric forced to take off his pants in front of his sisters, turn around, bend over . . . And later, whispering, praying for his death, plotting his death.

The intensity of the memory is terrifying. This is the first time she has ever examined that particular memory; she is shaking violently as she remembers her own words, her own prayers that night.

Then Florence came and she thought it was all over. For Eric it truly was over. He grew, made the high school football team, planned to become a lawyer, became a model son, and stopped talking to his sisters, especially Cass. It worked, she thinks dully. For Eric it worked. Father molded him into the perfect son. He never took his belt to her. He never had to. His hands were enough. Why didn't she run away? She can't remember now why she didn't run away. Because of Rebecca? She knows that is not the reason, although there was a time when she said it was. She was too afraid. If he caught her, and he would have, he would have used his belt. That was reason enough.

The memories are making her stomach spasm, making her

head ache with a dull pounding beat. Her hands are wet as it gets closer to midnight. They will be back soon and she has no idea of what she will do, what she can do. There is no one to talk to, no one to whom she can explain how it was. Who would even believe her? Eric is the president of the junior chamber of commerce, or something like that, a pillar of society, an up and coming attorney with impeccable manners, married to the daughter of someone equally upright and highly regarded. Who would believe her? Who would have believed it of her father?

You don't tell them because you're so ashamed, she thinks, feeling the fire on her cheeks at the thought of telling anyone that her father beat her regularly until she was sixteen years old. She feels a sudden bitter jealousy of Rebecca who has chosen not to know, not to come back, and she cannot think why she came back. It has something to do with Dan.

Stop hating, she thought a long time ago when Dan asked her to marry him. First she had to stop hating, stop being afraid. Then, the hatred and fear were deep; neither had any effect on her from day to day. Now she is under assault by waves of fear and the hatred is thick in her throat; it makes her heart thump painfully.

She finds herself pacing again until she ends up at the telephone in her father's study. She sits at his desk, looks up the Houston area code, and dials information, her fingers trembling so hard she has to start over twice. There is a children's services division with an emergency number. She writes down the number and puts the slip of paper in her pocket, leaves the study, feeling feverish and light-headed. She wants a drink but knows she must not have alcohol on her breath when she confronts her brother. That was how her father always discredited Aunt Edie, calling her boozy, a wino, a common drunk . . . She has ice water.

It is nearly one when the car drives into the garage and

they come into the house with Eric in boisterous good spirits. Father looks tired and for the first time he looks old.

"Cassie, you should have come along!" Eric cries. "Everything I touched turned into money. I won over six hundred!"

"I have to talk to you."

"Did something happen with Jason?" Rita asks. She looks tired also, and very pale.

"He's fine. No problems. Eric, I do have to talk to you."

"For God's sake, not tonight!" Father says roughly. "We've had a strenuous day, even if you didn't. It'll keep until morning. Is Becky here?"

"No, she called. Something came up." His face tightens in a familiar way and she turns to look again at Eric. "Let's go out to the terrace."

Florence leaves the room quickly with a mumbled good night. No one pays any attention. Now Rita hurries out.

"I'll check Jason," she says.

"Cass, go to bed," Father orders. "Eric, you want a drink? I sure do."

"I'll get some ice," Eric says and goes to the kitchen, leaving Cass with her father in the living room.

"I told you to go to bed!"

She watches him go to the bar and pour bourbon into two glasses. He should have been a trial lawyer, she thinks: he is handsome and physically attractive in the way he moves, the way he holds his head. His hair is silvery gray and thick, with a touch of wave. He could have been a politician. Eric may yet go into politics, he said earlier. He will look like Father in a few more years; he will be a good politician.

Father turns from the bar and appears surprised that she is standing there. "In my house," he says icily, "I am still the master. I expect a guest in my house to conform to my wishes."

"I'll leave as soon as I talk to Eric."

"You'll either go on to your room and go to bed, or you'll leave now, this minute."

She shakes her head, not trusting her voice again. Is that what she meant, that she would leave the house, not just the room? She is not certain. When he takes a step toward her, fear races through her body, brings out sweat on her face, churns her stomach. He knows she is afraid. She feels a deep humiliation and shame.

"You still up? Look, Cass, give me a break. Okay?" Eric reenters with a jug of water and a bowl of ice cubes. "Honestly, I'll spend as much time as you want tomorrow talking it out, whatever it is."

"Now. Tonight. And I don't want to talk with you and Father. I want to talk to you alone."

"There's nothing you have to say to him that I can't hear. Spit it out, Cass. You've been spoiling for a fight ever since you got here, sitting back, watching everyone else all the time. Let's have it and get it over with." Father turns his back on her again to put ice and water in his drink. "Say when, son." He adds a little water to the second glass and stops when Eric motions. "Well, cheers. It's been a hell of a day!"

It's hopeless, Cass thinks with despair. "Don't you remember how it was?" she whispers desperately. "You must remember!"

There is no answering flicker in Eric's eyes. He hardly glances at her, crosses the room to a deep chair and lowers himself into it tiredly. "It's after one," he says. "I'm having a nightcap and then I'm going to bed. Is that what you had to say?"

"You can't do it to Jason. For God's sake, Eric! Don't do it to him."

"Has he been lying to you? He knows I won't put up with that."

"I'll report you," she says, hardly audible now.

"You'll report nothing," Father says brusquely. "Eric dis-

ciplines his son only to the extent that he needs it. I can testify
to that. So can Florence. You came into this house hating
your brother and jealous of him and his family. You've
always been jealous of Eric. Always a troublemaker. You'll
report nothing. You'll not bring disgrace to this family! You
hear me?"

She backs away from him, sees Rita in the doorway, her
eyes bulging, terrified at the scene.

"Tell her, honey," Eric says, leaning back in his chair,
swirling the ice in his drink, watching it. "Doesn't Jason fall
down a lot?"

She nods, moistens her lips. "He's forever falling down.
I . . . I don't feel well. I'm going to bed." She flees.

"Cass," Eric says, watching the ice, "think about it. My
parents, her parents, my grandparents. They're my witnesses,
you know. How much of your life do you want dragged out
into the open?"

"Why do you do it? He's a baby! You need therapy . . ."

Her father is moving toward her; he is going to hit her, she
realizes, and suddenly she turns and runs from the room,
runs to her bedroom and slams the door, leans against it
shaking. When she is able to move, she throws her things into
her suitcase. She has unpacked very little; it does not take
long. She washes her face and forgets to put on lipstick
although she is holding it. When she is ready to leave, she
goes quietly through the hall to the living room. He is there
waiting. She does not enter, but backs up soundlessly to the
dining room, out to the terrace through the glass doors, and
lets herself out the backyard through a high wooden gate.

For a long time she drives aimlessly in circles, afraid to go
out on the desert at this time of night, too tired to know
where she is going. Do they know what they do? Do they
really think it's discipline? She has to know the answer, she
thinks fiercely, or she can do nothing. If they really, honestly
believe they are right . . . There is no way to end the thought.

He gave them good food, a good house, clothes, allowances, sent them to good schools . . . You can't weigh that against the other, she tells herself. It isn't possible to weigh the good things against the hell they had to live in.

She can't marry Dan now. She has to cleanse herself of the hatred and the cowardice and fear that dominate her. What if Dan changed? What if his gentleness turned into brutality? What if he beat their child? What if she did? Maybe this is the secret everyone carries around and no one talks about.

She is lost and the street signs are blurred; she runs a red light before she can even think about stopping. Finally she sees a motel with a vacancy sign and she checks in, finds her room, locks the door, and then falls across the bed into a restless sleep. She dreams of the terror-filled, strange place where the trees and shrubs make it impossible for her to reach the great doors as they silently draw together. She beats on them and wakes up drenched with sweat, weeping.

She fumbles in her pocket for the slip of paper with the emergency number for the children's services division of the Houston city government, and, weeping, she dials. She thinks no one is going to answer, but at last a pleasant voice says hello, and Cass begins to talk.

The Day of the Sharks

*H*er tranquilizer is wearing off, Gary thinks, when Veronica begins to tell him about it again. He stops listening almost immediately, and watches the road.

". . . that thin voice coming in my ears, hour after hour. You know, he doesn't dictate it like that. He pauses and goes out, has coffee, sees other patients, but day after day, having that box talk to me . . ."

The road is a glare, the sun straight ahead, centered in the dazzling whiteness of the concrete; the bay they are skirting is without a ripple, an endless mirror of eye-hurting brilliance. It will be beautiful when the sun is actually setting, he thinks, but now his eyes burn, and the damn air-conditioning in the rented car is malfunctioning, alternately shocking them with random cold blasts, or leaving them sweltering in the airless machine that smells of deodorizers and cleaning fluids.

". . . and they weren't people. Not after a while. They were gall bladders and thyroids and kidney stones. I began to wonder if there were any people even connected to them. You know? Free-floating kidney stones."

A flight of birds catches his attention; they just clear the water, almost touching the surface with their broad wings that look tattered, old, as if they have been at war, are flak-torn.

". . . system's supposed to help with the filing, for the computers, or something. Everything by number, not even parts of the anatomy any longer. Just numbers and prices. Case histories of numbers."

Her voice is getting high, tight, the way it does these days. Her posture has become rigid, her gaze fixed on a point straight ahead; she can stay this way for hours, unmoving, seeing what? He can't imagine what she sees. He grasps the steering wheel harder, wishes she would take another damn tranquilizer and be done with it. She will eventually. But she is afraid of them throughout the day until after dinner when it doesn't matter if she falls asleep. She took two at breakfast and dozed on the flight from Chicago to Tampa; it was a peaceful flight.

Ahead, a squat, ugly complex comes into view, black against the glaring sky, his next landmark. He slows to make the turn off the highway over a bridge onto a narrower road. Now, with the sun to his right, he can drive faster. The islands have nothing on them, a few palm trees, some dunes, scrub that looks like felled palm trees, more birds. Sea gulls, he thinks, with near triumph. At least he knows sea gulls. Six miles farther.

His thoughts turn to Bill Hendrix and his wife Shar. And then he is thinking only of Shar. For the first time after she and Bill moved down here she pleaded with him to come visit. He could fake a business trip. He could meet her in Tallahassee, or Miami, or somewhere. Then no more begging, no more anything, until the call from Bill. "If you're going to the Bahamas, hell, man, you've got to come for the weekend, at least. You can fly on from Tampa on Monday."

"We should have gone straight on to Grand Bahama," Veronica mumbles, facing the arrowlike road that seems to plunge into the blue water in the distance. A low dense clump of green rises on the left. The greenery expands, becomes pine trees, motionless in the still, late afternoon. "Turn again just after the pines," Bill's instructions went on. There is only one way to turn, left. They enter the subdivision under construction.

Unfinished houses are ugly, Gary thinks, obscenely ugly, naked, no illusions about them, the land around the buildings cluttered with junk that will be hidden away by the bulldozers, but there, always there. The landfill is dazzling white: sand, shells, the detritus dredged from the bay to create land, brought up long enough ago to have bleached to snow white.

"We should have gone straight on to Grand Bahama," Veronica says again, louder, still not looking at him.

"I told you, I have this business with Bill. We'll leave first thing Monday morning."

They wind through the subdivision, following instructions. A short causeway, to the end of the street, on to the point. There is Bill's house, with a yard fully landscaped, green and flowering. Gary's eyes narrow as he looks at it. The house is almost hidden from the street, but what shows is expensive, and the landscaping cost a fortune.

Bill said only three houses were finished, and that one is still vacant. The buyers will move in on the first of the month. They have not passed the other completed houses.

"I hardly even know them," Veronica says, not quite whining although a petulant tone has entered her voice. Gary doesn't know what that is supposed to mean. They were friends for more than five years. Gary wonders if she ever suspected Shar, if Bill ever did. He is almost certain no one did, but still, there is the possibility. Veronica knows there was someone. She always knows.

He parks in the driveway, but before they can get out of the car, they are suddenly chilled by a last effort of the air conditioner. He feels goose bumps rise; Veronica's skin takes on a bluish cast. Bill and Shar are coming out to meet them.

She has a beautiful tan, the same dark gold all over her legs, her arms, her face. Her hair is blonder than it was before; she might have been a little thinner before, but otherwise she looks exactly the same. There is a sheen on her skin, as if she has been polished. She is tall and strong, a Viking type, she calls herself. Nothing willowy about her, nothing fat or slack. She has long, smooth muscles in her legs; her stomach is as firm and flat as a boy's. She wears white briefs and a halter, and rubber thongs on her feet. Bill is a bit shorter than she is, thickly built, very powerful, with thick wrists and a thick neck. Size seventeen. They are both so tanned that Gary feels he and Veronica must both look like invalids.

"My God! Ghosts!" Shar cries, as Gary and Veronica get out of the car. She embraces them with too much enthusiasm and warmth, and Gary can sense Veronica's withdrawal. Next to Shar, Veronica appears used up, old. She is only thirty-one, but she looks ill, as she is, and she looks frightened and suspicious, and very tired. There are circles under her eyes; he feels guilty that he has not seen them before, that only now, contrasting her with Shar does he recognize the signs of illness, remember that this isn't simply a vacation.

"Hey, it's good to see you," Bill says, putting his arm across Gary's back. "Come on in. A drink is what you people need. And tomorrow we'll get out in the sun and put some color in your cheeks."

It should be warm and friendly, but it isn't. It is like walking into a scenario where every line has been rehearsed, the stage sets done by art majors; even the sky has been given an extra touch of the brush. It is gaudy now with sunset, the ambient light peach colored, and out back, visible through a wall of sliding glass doors, the bay is brilliant, touched with gold.

"Two hundred sixty-five thou," Bill says, waving his hand as they enter the house where the furniture is either white or sleek, shiny black. He goes to a bar and pours martinis already made up, and they sit down where they can watch the lights on the bay. Between them and the golden water are red and yellow flowering bushes, an Olympic-size swimming pool, a terrace with enough seating and tables to serve as a cafe. "Too much, isn't it?" Bill says, grinning. "Just too goddam much."

"Are you hungry?" Shar asks. "Dinner won't be until pretty late. We're having a little party, buffet about ten. How about a sandwich, something to tide you over?"

"Oh, Gary," Veronica says, stricken.

"No sweat," Bill says. "It's a business party. You know, people I owe. Just happened to coincide. Don't feel you're interrupting anything."

Still, Veronica looks at Gary as if pleading with him; he shrugs. "It'll be all right," he says, trying to make his impatience sound like patience. "She hasn't been feeling very well," he adds, glancing at Shar.

"It won't be too much of a drag, I hope," Shar says lightly. "Wind us up and watch us entertain. Isn't that right, Bill?"

He laughs and pours more drinks. "You'll fit right in, Gary. Just watch how their eyes gleam when I tell them you're an investment counselor." He laughs again.

The party is little more than an excuse to get loud and drunk, Gary admits to himself later, wandering on the terrace with a drink in his hand, tired from the over-long day, bored with people he doesn't know, doesn't want to know. He knows their types, he thinks, watching a heavy-set man in a flowered shirt mock-push a nearly bare-breasted woman into the pool, laughing, leering, lusting. Shar touches his arm.

"Dance?"

They dance, his hand warmed by her golden back that is almost too smooth to be human. "Can I see you alone later?"

She smiles and doesn't answer.

He dances her to the end of the terrace, more discreetly lighted than the other areas, and kisses her. "Later?"

"Don't be an idiot. With your wife and my husband on the scene?"

"Veronica will be knocked out with tranquilizers, and Bill's on his way to passing out."

"What's wrong with Veronica?"

"Nerves, I guess. She flipped out at work. Tried to burn down the office or something."

"Good God! Did she really?"

"She says she was only burning the files, but the whole place would have gone up if it hadn't been caught when it was."

"What did they do to her?"

He is tired of talking about Veronica, tired of thinking about her. "Hospital. Two weeks. Now a vacation, and then into analysis, I guess. She's under a shrink's care."

"Poor Gary," Shar says, her voice amused.

He can't see her features, but can feel the warmth of her skin, smell the elusive scent that she wears, that she always wore. When he starts to kiss her again, she moves away and walks back toward the house. "Later," he says, this time not asking.

She smiles over her shoulder and stops to chat with a group of men standing at the sliding door to the Florida room.

Finally, Gary spots Veronica at a table by a man, clutching her glass tightly, her eyes glazed in the way they do when she drinks more than a glass of wine. He curses silently and turns to see Bill approaching with another man in tow. Bill is red faced, perspiring heavily, and the grace that he displays when sober is gone. He lumbers, stumbles into things, loses coordination in a way that seems to suggest that his limbs have different reaction times. He wards off a table before he is within reach, then hits it with his thigh, and belatedly clutches a chair to steady himself. Gary moves closer to Veronica and the unknown man; he doesn't want to talk to a drunken Bill.

". . . density ratio so fouled up that no one knows what the hell they're going to do. Six hundred units per acre. Now I ask you, does that sound too terrible to you, a city girl? You know Chicago can handle that many people, what's the difference?"

Veronica shakes her head helplessly. "Units?"

"Yep. They're saying no more than two fifty per acre. Two hundred fifty! What kind of condo can you put up with only two fifty?"

Veronica looks almost desperate; relief relaxes her face when Gary draws near. "Have you eaten yet?" he asks.

She stands up, nods to the man, and takes Gary's arm. Her fingers dig in convulsively. "How long will this go on?" she whispers, as they walk toward the buffet.

She looks and sounds terrible; she should go to bed. Her tension is almost a palpable thing, electric. He feels that he could touch it, be burned by it.

Bill blocks their way, still with the tall man. "Gary, want you to meet Dwight Scanlon, president of the development company I was telling you about. My good friend, Gary Ingalls, and Veronica."

"Hear you're on your way to Grand Bahama," Dwight Scanlon says, taking Gary's hand. "Lovely place. We've got a hotel over there, in fact. You have your rooms reserved? Look, cancel them, why don't you? I've got this suite, nobody in it, nobody scheduled for it until June. Yours for the taking."

Before Gary can refuse, Scanlon has turned to Veronica. "Have you seen the moon coming up over that bay yet? What a sight!" He offers his arm; she puts her hand on it tentatively, and they walk out together.

Bill downs his drink and runs his hand over his face. "Gotta turn on that air conditioner pretty soon."

The air conditioner is on, but the house is jammed with guests, and waiters and caterers. The sliding doors to the terrace have been open all evening. Gary wanders back out-side where he sits down at a wrought-iron table. His head is buzzing, not unpleasantly, and there is a lightness in his legs and arms, also not unpleasant. He watches a sinuous woman work her way through a cluster of people to approach his table with evident purpose.

"I'm Audrey Scanlon," she says, and sits down after pull-ing a tiny chair very close to his. "You're Gary, aren't you?"

He nods.

"Perhaps you'd like to help us launch our boat Sunday," she says. She does not touch him, but he has the feeling that she is all over him.

"No way," Shar says coolly, suddenly at Gary's side. "He's ours until Monday morning; aren't you, Gary, dar-ling?"

Audrey stands up. "Maybe we'll see you in Grand Ba-hama," she whispers and now she does touch him. Her hand lingers a moment on his arm, and when she moves away, she doesn't lift it, but lets her fingers trail over his skin very lightly.

"Bitch," Shar says, when she is gone.

"No doubt, they just happen to have this little company that they would love to have recommended to prospective buyers." He sounds bitter even to his ears. Shar pats his arm. Someone calls her and she leaves him.

Soon Veronica returns from the dock; her eyes are shining. "I've been propositioned, I think."

"Scanlon?"

She nods. She looks very happy.

"His wife just did the same with me. They must be fresh in from the swamps."

"Don't make it sound like that," Veronica cries. "Maybe he just found me attractive! Wouldn't it occur to you that someone else might still find me attractive?"

"He wants me to list his company," Gary says. "And he has as much finesse about it as a hippo humping a hippo."

"I wouldn't have done it." Her face twitches and settles into the newly familiar rigid lines. "I wouldn't have done anything," she says woodenly. "Why couldn't you let me have my little fantasy?"

"You should go to bed. You're so tired, you're ready to keel over."

She walks away unsteadily.

Someone falls into the pool; within minutes there are a number of rescuers in the water. After that it seems almost spontaneous, although it never really is, he knows, for others to begin shedding their clothes to jump in. Gary swims naked, as do Shar and Audrey, and a dozen others. All laughing and playing and then huddling in towels and drinking again.

Guests are leaving now, and presently there are only three or four remaining, drinking with Bill, nostalgic about old times, before the islands were bought. Veronica has vanished, possibly to go to bed. Gary takes Shar's hand and leads her to the terrace, beyond it to the velvet lawn where he spreads his towel and hers to make a bed. He lowers her to the ground; she doesn't resist.

Immediately afterward she draws away. "I have to go in," she murmurs. "I can't stay out here." She stands over him; he sits up and puts his arms around her hips, pulls her to him, presses his face into her pubic hair and bites softly. She moans and sways, but then pushes him away. "No more. Not now."

She runs, naked, gleaming in the patio lights briefly, then vanishes into one of the rooms that open to the terrace.

Gary swims again, but he knows he is too drunk to be in the water alone; he climbs out shivering, with exhaustion as much as from the cold. The guest room has an outside door, he remembers; he finds it and goes in to shower and dry himself and dress again. Veronica is not in the room. When he returns to the living room, all the guests are gone. Bill has brought out champagne that he, Veronica, and Shar are drinking.

They drink until dawn flames the sky and then they go to bed. It is eleven when Gary awakens with a pounding headache; Veronica is already up and out.

"Take this," Bill says when he enters the dining room. "Don't ask questions, just drink it." It is a juice drink, heavily spiked with bourbon. For a moment Gary feels his stomach churn, then it settles down again. The drink is very good.

Veronica looks awful; her eyes are red rimmed and bloodshot, sunken in her face. "Why don't you try to sleep some more?" he says, too miserable to care one way or the other.

From the kitchen come sounds of things being banged about. Bill winces. "Caterers' clean-up crew," he says. "Let's go out to the dock until they finish."

"I'll bring the cart," Shar says. "God knows we all need something to eat, and coffee, lots of coffee."

The sun is hot, but the breeze is refreshing. The bay is about a mile wide; there are no signs of civilization, as long as they face away from this subdivision. Now and again a jumping fish makes ripples that undulate in the water as the tide flows in like a river.

"Twelve feet deep here," Bill says. "It's shallow up in the

fingers. Point's the place to be." His boat is thirty-five feet, two-forty horsepower Westinghouse . . .

Gary gazes at the gently moving water and doesn't listen to Bill cataloguing his treasures. Objects and wielders, he thinks. They all were objects and wielders of objects last night. Changing roles as easily as they changed their clothes. Even his too-brief contact with Shar was object and wielder, and he does not know who played which part.

Suddenly he recalls the scene when he first visited Veronica in the hospital. She was stupefied from Thorazine, or something they gave her. Her voice was singsong. "I don't think there are any people, Gary. Nowhere. They're all gone, and I don't know where they went. I'm so afraid." She did not sound afraid, only dull and drug-stupid.

Later, Bill will make his pitch, Gary knows. *Hit a little snag, old buddy. You know how it goes.* He knows. He drinks the strong black coffee, thinking how distant his head has become, throbbing like drums not quite heard, but felt as pressure. Across the bay the land has not been developed yet and shows a low green, irregular skyline, a fitting place for the drums to originate from. He watches a boat sail up the channel, nearly all the way across the bay.

"We'll just rest up this afternoon," Bill says. "Take life easy, that's the motto down here. Not like your big city, eh?"

No one replies. Veronica is nibbling on a piece of toast; some color has come back to her face, but it is probably only the beginning of a sunburn. Shar's gaze meets Gary's and she lets her eyes close slightly, a very faint smile on her mouth.

"And tomorrow, bright and early, we'll take the boat out," Bill says. "Do a little fishing out in the gulf." He pours more coffee and lights a cigarette.

"What's that?" Veronica says suddenly, sitting upright. She points. "A shark, or something."

They all look as a dark form breaks the smooth surface of

the water, arches up, and vanishes again. It is on their side of the channel, several hundred yards out.

"I'll be damned," Bill says. "One of those whales. I thought they all died." He watches and when it breaks the water again, he nods in satisfaction. "It's a false killer whale."

"Killer whale? Here?" Gary asks.

"*False* killer whale. Harmless, just looks like the real thing. Listen, let me tell you what I saw a few weeks ago. Damnedest thing I ever saw in my life. Over near Fort Myers. I was driving along, heard this report on the car radio about whales beaching themselves. So I thought, what the hell, I'd go have a look. Beach was crowded with people by the time I got there, but nothing was happening. I keep binoculars in the car, you know? So I got them out, and watched. There was a line of those animals out there in the water, quarter of a mile offshore, just laying there in the water. Not moving a muscle. No surf, no wind, as calm as that bay is right now. I kept watching, beginning to get bored with the whole thing, you know? They weren't doing a damn thing. Just laying there. Then, by God, they started to move in. All at once, all together, like a goddam chorus line. And they kept coming, and kept coming until they were in water too shallow to swim in and they began to roll. People were jumping in from everywhere, yanking on them, trying to get them turned around, headed back out. Some people had rowboats, a couple of motorboats, people in the water up to their necks, just trying to get those things back out to sea. And while they're working with this bunch, another bunch was starting in, the females and young. They'd been waiting half a mile offshore for some kind of a damn signal, or something, and now they were coming in. People kept getting the first ones turned around, and those whales would just sort of swerve a couple of feet to one side or the other and back they'd come in to shore. It went on for hours. Some of the boats towed a couple of the big males out to sea again, I guess hoping that the others would follow them. They didn't."

His voice is low, awed, his gaze following the movements of the whale in the bay. "They got a lot of them out to sea again, but a dozen of them made it in. They died on the beach. Mass suicide. The damnedest thing I ever saw."

No one speaks for several moments, then Veronica says, "Why?" Her voice is tight and high. "Were they sick?"

"Marine biologists couldn't find anything wrong. No sharks in the water. No storms to mix them up, and it was too deliberate to think they just made a mistake, misjudged the depth of the water. No one knows why."

"That's crazy!" Veronica cries, jumping up. "There has to be a reason. There's always a reason!" The shrillness of her voice is startling. She clamps her lips and runs up the dock, back inside the house.

"God, I'm sorry," Bill says, his big face contrite. "I shouldn't have told that story. It . . . it haunts me."

"Forget it," Gary says. "What happened to the rest of the whales? You thought they all died?"

"That's the worst part," Bill says soberly. "The next day they found them down in the Keys. Beached on one of the islands down there."

Shar stands up. "I'll go do something about lunch. The caterers must be gone by now."

The whale continues to swim in great circles out in the bay, close in, then farther out again. Bill begins to tell Gary about the financial problems his company has encountered, through no fault of their own. Gary promises nothing. He will study the financial statements, the local restrictions, and so on. Bill understands. He lays his hand on Gary's arm and assures him that he understands.

Veronica doesn't come out for lunch, and after the others eat, Shar and Bill withdraw to nap. Gary puts on his trunks and swims in the pool, then stretches out under a cluster of

palm trees, something *Reclinatus,* Bill said. You can transplant full-grown palm trees, instant garden, Gary thinks,
listening to the wind in the fronds, a soothing rainlike sound.
You dredge up the bay bottom, smooth it out, cover it with
a carpet of sod, plants trees, flowers, shrubs, plant a house,
plant people. Instant paradise. And there are no insects in the
ground. Barren, pseudodirt. Not real.

Veronica said, after her hospitalization, "Sometimes I
wonder, if I reach out to touch you when you're not looking,
not thinking about me, not concentrating on being you, will
my hand go through you?"

"Meaning?"

"I don't know. Nothing you do is real. You work with
money—bits of paper that have no meaning. You don't even
see the money. It isn't real, just figures on paper, symbols in
the computer. You don't make anything, or fix anything.
After you finish for the day, does the office lose its shape,
melt down to nothing until you get back and give it a pseudo-
reality again?"

"Veronica! For heaven's sake!" He reached for her and she
drew away sharply, in recoil almost.

"No! That isn't real either. A touch, a kiss, a fuck. Pseudoreal."

"I don't know what the hell you're talking about."

"You can tell if it's real. You can tell. If it's there years
later. If you can go to it and find it years later." Her voice
became a whisper, her gaze on something he could not see.
"Money becomes figures on paper. Patients become organs
that become numbers in the computer. Pseudoreal."

After she is well again, they will separate. He has already
decided. She is young, pretty until she became ill. She will
marry again, maybe even have children. She wants children;
he said later, after we're established, a little money saved.
Later. And he will find someone new, someone with gaiety in

her laugh, who isn't sick. Someone who will bring fun into his life again.

He dozes in the shade and awakens to find that the sun is burning his legs. The distant throbbing has entered his head; it is his head, but there is another noise, screeching and screaming.

"Hey, old buddy, you want a gin and tonic?" Bill calls from the doorway.

"I sure as hell want something," Gary says. He feels worse than he did that morning.

Bill steps out to the terrace, shielding his eyes with his hand, looking at gulls screaming, diving, shrieking, just off the end of the dock. "Must be a school running," he says, and starts to walk toward the commotion.

Gary follows him slowly. They stop halfway up the dock. The whale is alongside the structure, the entire animal clearly visible in the quiet water. Blood is flowing from under it. The gulls wheel and scream overhead; now and then one of them dips to the surface of the water, darts up again.

"I will be God damned!" Bill says in wonder. "She's going to give birth. For Christ's sake!"

The whale pays no attention to the men on the dock. Now and then a long shudder passes through her, rippling from her great black head down to her tail. She is gleaming black, nine feet long, sleek; her blowhole opens and closes convulsively. She shudders; her body twists. She sinks, surfaces again.

"She's in trouble," Gary says.

Bill looks at him blankly.

"It shouldn't take more than a minute or so. I read that somewhere. And she's bleeding too much."

The stain rises in the water, spreads like a cloud. It seems to rise like smoke signals.

"There must be someone who knows what to do," Gary says, staring at the helpless animal. "The university?"

"It's after five, Saturday," Bill says. "The Coast Guard. I'll call them. Someone there will know."

Gary stands on the dock, his hands clenched, watching the animal and the distress signals dispersing through the water. He doesn't hear the others until Shar says, "Oh, my God!" He turns to see her and Veronica staring at the whale.

"They'll find someone to send," Bill says, hurrying across the yard. "It might take a while, though."

The animal doesn't have a while, Gary knows. He doesn't say it. They continue to watch in horrified fascination as the ripples that are pain reactions spread throughout the animal regularly.

Suddenly Shar draws her breath in. "Oh, no!" she cries. She is staring out at the bay. "Sharks!"

Gary sees them, two fins moving through the water almost leisurely, as if they know there is no need to hurry. Bill turns and runs to the house. He comes back moments later with a rifle. He puts a handful of shells on the dock and loads a clip.

"Where are they?" His voice is hoarse, the words slurred. Shar points. He doesn't raise the rifle. "Too far," he says in his strange voice.

It is excitement, Gary realizes; his own mouth is dry and he feels prickly with sweat and goose bumps, as if something loathsome has touched him.

"It won't do any good," Veronica says, and her voice is different, too, high and clear, but steady. "As soon as the baby is born, she'll want to go out to sea, won't she? They'll be waiting for her."

She is looking out at the channel. There are more fins. A pack then. They must have followed the trail of blood from out in the gulf. Veronica appears transfixed, as if in a trance.

"You'd better go inside," he says. She does not give any sign that she heard him. He touches her arm and she twitches with a convulsive shudder, like the whale's. She does not look at him. "Get inside, damn it!" His hand falls from her arm and he turns away. She wants to see the blood fest, he real-izes, sickened. The near rapture on her face makes her look like a transcendent Joan at the moment when the torch touches the faggots. He takes a few long steps away from her, but then comes back; he can't leave, neither can he stand still and watch. He hunches his shoulders and paces back and forth, back and forth.

Suddenly the rifle goes off and the sound is a shock that hurts. It rolls over the water, echoing.

"You can't kill them from here!" Shar cries.

"Only wanted to nick one," Bill says, aiming again. "They'll turn on one that's wounded, maybe leave her alone." The sharks move in a great semicircle, not coming directly toward the dock. They are swimming faster. He fires again.

"The bastards! The bastards!" Bill says over and over, nearly sobbing. "The bastards!"

Without warning the false killer whale moves away from the dock. She swims for about ten feet and rolls to her side. A cloud of blood spreads over the water. The gulls screech in a frenzy. They swoop down on the water, hiding the whale from view. She jerks and makes a great splash; they rise, screaming.

The baby is being expelled. Gary can see the body, the curled tail already straightening, and now the head is free. With what must have been an agony of effort the mother whale rolls suddenly, away from the infant, making a complete turn in the water in one swift, sharp movement. She has broken the cord. As she finishes the turn she comes up under the infant and nudges it to the surface. It rolls to one side and does not move. It is white underneath, three feet long, and it is dead. It starts to sink and again the mother whale nudges it to the surface of the water. And again. And again. Gary turns away.

He hears Shar being sick over the rail of the dock.

"They're coming!" Veronica screams.

Gary swings around in time to see Veronica snatch the rifle from Bill's limp hands; Bill is staring at the whale as if in a daze. Veronica points the rifle and begins to fire very fast, not at the sharks, but downward. The sleek black whale thrashes in the water, she tries to jump, but doesn't clear the surface, and then a paroxysm of jerks overtake her; finally she rolls over. The sharks begin to hit her.

Veronica turns toward the house; the rifle in her hands is pointed directly at Gary. He does not move. Her face is closed and hard, a stranger's face. She opens her hands and the rifle falls, clatters on the shells still on the dock. She walks past him without another glance at the sharks, at him, at anyone.

The water churns and froths; it is all red. Shar staggers away from the rail. She reaches for Gary's arm to steady herself and he jerks away involuntarily. Her hand would go through him, he thinks; she begins to run toward the house.

"She's afraid your wife will burn it down," Bill says in a thick, dull voice. For a moment his face is naked; he knows. "I might burn it down myself one day. Just might do that." He walks away, his shoulders bowed, his head lowered.

The frenzied gulls, the boiling water, the heat of the sun, all that's real, Gary thinks. Veronica firing the rifle, that was real. He remains on the dock until the Coast Guard cutter comes into sight, speeding toward the dock. The water is calm again; there is nothing for them to see, nothing for them to do. He doesn't even bother to wave to them. One of the men is standing in the boat scanning the water, and suddenly he points. The sharks are still in the channel. The boat veers, makes waves as it swings around and heads out away from the dock.

They didn't even see him, Gary knows. He is not surprised. Slowly he lifts his hands and looks at them, and then lets them drop to his sides. In his mind is an image of a raging inferno.

The Loiterer

I turned my back for what seemed just a few minutes and everything from my childhood had changed. Most of the houses had shrunk; the trees were not the giants they had been; the distances had diminished. My mother's house was smaller, the yard nothing like what I remembered. It had been spacious, a magic place: a woods, a jungle, a meadow, even an ocean. Now it was a forlorn backyard with closely sheared grass that had become brown already in the summer heat. I had forgotten the heat. Sullen, windless heat that was so heavy with moisture that nothing felt dry: skin, clothes, my hair, the furniture inside, bedding, all felt clammy, and a musty odor hung in the air. I had lived in this house until I was nearly thirteen; we had moved, and when I came back this time, another thirteen years had gone by. After leaving here, the first thirteen years had become dreamlike, years that belonged to someone else; now the second group of thirteen years had that quality.

The night we arrived, Mother waited until I put Lissie to bed in the sweltering upstairs room that once had been my room, and then she said, "We'd better have a talk, don't you think?"

"Yes, Mother."

"You and Lissie can stay here as long as you need to, or want to," she said. "But he is not welcome. If he turns up, he can't stay in this house. I just want to make that clear."

"Yes, Mother. But he won't be coming." I was so tired that she seemed to be surging forward and receding as I looked at her. She was not yet fifty, very handsome, younger looking that night than I, I was certain. She had on a sleeveless dress, no hose, sandals. I remembered later how red her toenails were that night; I had not painted my nails, fingers or toes, since I was sixteen. She did not seem at all hot. I was sweating, and deep inside me something was clenched hard and tight.

"Do you know where he is? Will he support his child?"

"He doesn't have any money. He said he'd write when he has an address."

Her mouth tightened, the way it always did when she was angry, but her voice remained calm. "When you called you said you didn't know what you'd do. Have you had time to think of anything yet?"

"Yes. I'll get a loan and finish school, and I'll get a part-time job. Next week I'll start looking. We'll move to an apartment as soon as I find something."

There was nothing I could have said that night that would not have made her more angry. She stood up and went to the front door, checked the locks, her motions stiff and unnatural, her back almost rigid, like someone wearing a metal brace. Facing the door, fooling with a lock, she asked, "Did he hurt you or Lissie? She's so small and thin. And you. You're skin and bones. Have you been sick?"

"No. I'm all right, and Lissie's fine. Mother, he loves us both. He wouldn't hurt us."

"Just abandon you," she snapped. "Well, you can stay.

You failed me as a daughter when I needed you, but I will do what has to be done."

"I couldn't come," I whispered. "You know I was due. Lissie was born that week."

"Thank God, I had Harry Lee," she said. "I'm going to bed. I have to leave at seven-thirty in the morning. There's milk and cereal for Lissie. I get home at a quarter to five. Good night, Beth."

My father was killed in an accident at work, inspecting a bridge. The day he died, Harry Lee called to tell me. "Mother needs you," he had said. When I told him I was expecting any minute, he had hung up. I called her; she had wept and screamed over the phone, and then she hung up. We were so scattered; I was in Vermont expecting a child, Mother was in San Diego, and Harry Lee was in Atlanta. Tenants were living in the Louisville house. As soon as Lissie was six weeks old, I borrowed money for airfare and called Mother to say I would arrive in two days and she said not to bother. She was on her way to Harry Lee's house in Atlanta where she planned to stay a month or two, and after that she was going back home to Louisville, to this house I had come home to.

There were two bedrooms and a bath upstairs, another bedroom and bath downstairs, the living room, kitchen with dinette space, a family room with a large color television. Everything was neat and shiny clean. There were porcelain figures on end tables, covered candy bowls with peppermints, hard candies, and jelly beans. Everything looked fragile or forbidden, not meant for children. Even the kitchen floor was not meant for children; it had been done over in white vinyl. The day we arrived, when I examined the house, and again that night talking to Mother, I knew I had made a mistake.

"Mommy, can we go home now?" Lissie asked on the second day. Her hair was plastered to her forehead, a heat rash had erupted in the crooks of her arms, behind her knees, around her waist and neck.

"Not yet, baby," I told her.

I took her for a walk that afternoon to show her some of the neighborhood where I had played and roamed as a child. I was shocked by the changes. The streets that I remembered as broad and tree lined, playgrounds for hide-and-seek, places where I had skated, now carried swift traffic in four lanes, forbidden to Lissie. The traffic was so close to the fence, to our gate, that even the sidewalk now seemed dangerous with no room for error, for a misstep. It was as if the sidewalks had crept into the yards, usurped the lawns, pushed them aside, crowded almost against the houses that once had stood far back and deeply shaded. The church on the corner where I used to turn to go to the library was tiny and dilapidated, the steps leading to the double doors sagged; time had eroded the sanctity, the mystery. It was just a sad little frame building in need of paint. We visited the library, cramped and darker than I recalled, and borrowed many books, then started back, completing a circle. This was the way home from school. The candy store was a convenience store now, one of a million such stores. I stopped and gazed at the opposite side of the street: apartment buildings. Automatically I had started to cross at the corner, but the apartment buildings were all wrong. This was supposed to be a street of two-story, white frame houses with blue trim, green trim, with hedges and flowering trees, dogwoods and magnolia trees, tulip trees. I could almost smell the fragrance of vanished mock oranges.

Lissie was talking about the library, how close it was, such a short walk that she might even be able to go alone, and I was answering her chatter as we walked down the street on the wrong side, the dangerous side. Midway down it, I came to an abrupt stop again, and this time I must have tightened my grasp of her hand too hard.

"Mommy, don't," she said and pulled free.

"What? Oh, I'm sorry, honey. Let's hurry. I think it's going to storm."

It was the Waltham house, I realized, that had stopped me. There had always been something evil about that house; everyone had known it. All the children had known it. Every day I had passed it on my way to and from school, and I had always crossed the street at the corner and recrossed it at the next corner, and when I drew even with the house, I had averted my gaze. I had forgotten about the Waltham house. The yard was fenced, with a privet hedge that used to be too high to see over, but that now concealed nothing. The house was in good repair, two stories, white trimmed in tan. There was a deep, shadowed porch, and every window was closely curtained, shades drawn, probably against the western sun on this side. There was nothing to mark the house, nothing to indicate that it was evil.

I lay on the hot bed with nothing on and wished the gathering storm would come, wished it would cool the air, permit sleep finally. How long since I had slept through a whole night? Two weeks, three? It seemed a lifetime. How strange that there was no darkness, I thought. I had to leave the windows open, the shades up to catch what feeble breeze might stir before dawn; street light filled the room, cast grotesque shadows on the walls.

After I read to Lissie and kissed her good night, she had whispered, "And tomorrow we'll go home, won't we, Mommy?"

"Honey, remember our jobs? Daddy has a job in Alaska, you have to start first grade, and I have to go to school. That's our job now. Remember?"

"I don't like it here, Mommy. I'm too hot. There's nothing to do."

"Tomorrow we'll take a picnic to the park. I used to play

there all the time. You'll like it. There's a wading pool and swings and a slide."

She turned her face away.

I was a child, and he was a child and we thought we could play at being grown up, play at life, play at everything forever and ever. And suddenly we were parents and we were both twenty years old, and we thought we could keep playing, now with a child-doll. We lived in Vermont with many other people; then we lived in a van in Michigan, and we lived in a tent in the woods of California, and in a two-room apartment in Seattle for a winter . . . We played like children, and our lovemaking was passionate and innocent; our fights were like the summer storms that scream and wail and threaten, and leave without changing anything.

"You have to come with me," he said when it ended. "Where else can you go?" We lived outside Helena, Montana, then.

"I don't know. Judson, we can't keep on like this. Lissie has to go to school. She needs some stability. What if she got sick on the road? What if we had to hike for days to get help for the truck? Judson, please, don't do this."

"I have to," he said. "It's the chance of a lifetime. It's what I've been waiting for."

I shook my head and made no attempt to stop the tears or hide them. He was going to drive our truck to Alaska, get a job there, make a fortune, live happily ever after. I wept.

"Don't you love me anymore?" he asked then.

He was just like a child, I thought, exactly like a child, only now he was twenty-five years old with a five-year-old daughter.

I watched the unmoving shadows cast on my bedroom wall by the street lamp and willed them to life, willed the storm to start. Finally I got up and pulled on a thin cotton duster. How long could a human being go without sleep, I wondered. I started to go downstairs. Then I stopped. Lissie was talking.

I made no sound as I turned and went to her room, pushed the door open wide enough to enter. I had put a small fan in her room, aimed at the wall, to keep air moving. It hummed and blew hot air. Lissie was at the window, talking, her voice low; I could make out nothing of what she was saying.

"Lissie, what are you doing?"

She started violently and flung herself back into bed. I went to the window and looked; a man's figure was vanishing beyond the range of the streetlight.

"Lissie, who was that? Were you talking to that man?"

"He couldn't hear me," she said softly. "I was whispering, pretending it was Daddy."

I sat on her bed and reached for her; she pushed me away. "It's too hot."

"Do you want something? A glass of milk, a cookie?"

"No."

"Honey, you remember what we told you, Daddy and I both? About never talking to anyone you don't know? You remember?"

"Yes, Mommy."

Her Raggedy Ann doll and her stuffed dog were both on the floor. I picked them up and put them beside her. "I'm going to close your windows and pull your shades down now, honey. It's going to rain. If the storm wakes you up, come to my room, okay?"

She yawned. "Okay."

I took a long time to close her windows; I was searching the street in both directions as far as I could see. No one was on foot. Two or three cars went by, nothing else. When I could draw it out no longer, I kissed her, automatically feeling for a sign of fever, of anything wrong. Then I went back to my room where I stood at my windows looking up and down the street. He couldn't have seen her, couldn't have heard her whispers. She had been pretending it was Judson coming home, Daddy coming home.

Lissie slept through the storm that hit at two in the morning. When it was over, I fell asleep and dreamed that I was running toward Judson, into his outstretched arms. We were laughing, kissing, and then making love with a fierceness that was inhuman. I woke up aching with desire, hugged my knees to my chest and rocked back and forth, back and forth.

The park was unchanged. There was the concession stand where ice cream cones were oversized and the drinks were frosty. There was the bare dirt, hard-packed circle around the water fountain, and even what looked like the same mudholes. Lissie stepped in one cautiously, then with abandon, splashing us both with dirty water. The swings had the same squeak that I remembered, and the teeter-totters were as worn, but no more so, as they had always been. The wood was colorless, rounded at the edges, polished as if by design.

We wandered over to the amphitheater and walked down among the concrete seats. That was the first time I had known they were concrete. Here was where I saw *Pinocchio* performed, and *The Nutcracker Suite,* and decided I wanted to become a ballerina. I would get a program, I thought, and we would come for the first show that was suitable for a small child. I reined in my thoughts sharply. First I had to get a job. I had forty-eight dollars.

Lissie was running down the wide concrete stairs to see what it was like on the stage. She climbed the shorter flight of stairs up and turned to wave to me. I was only halfway down in the audience section. She looked past me and smiled happily. I whirled around to see the vague outlines of a man. The sun blinded me; he was no more than a silhouette against the bright sky. When I shaded my eyes with my hand, he was gone. I looked again at Lissie, but she was skipping across the stage, paying no attention now.

*   *   *

In the beginning Mother's anger with me extended to Lissie, not as anger, but as restraint and distance. Day by day that restraint eroded and on Friday she followed us into the kitchen when I started to clean up after dinner. Lissie and I played a story-telling game every evening while I washed dishes and she dried the silverware. In the game I started a story and she interrupted to add her own sequences from time to time. Her additions were always things like: *Piglet said let's go get an ice cream cone now,* or *Rumplestiltskin was so mad he jumped up and down.*

I was not aware of when Mother came into the kitchen. I first saw her when I turned to wipe off the stove. She was gazing at Lissie, her expression soft, her face defenseless. She said, "I'm going to the store, Lissie. Would you like to come with me?"

Lissie nodded and started to put down her dish towel.

"After you're done, dear," Mother said. "I'll wait for you. Finish your game first."

"Do you want to play with us?" Lissie asked.

"I think I'd better not, not just yet. Is it all right if I listen, to learn how to play it?"

Lissie nodded and looked at me. "Whose turn is it?"

And suddenly I felt awkward and foolish. She decided it must be her turn and she said, "Then the smallest Billy Goat Gruff jumped off the bridge."

Since the story was about the gingerbread man, that made for a strange twist, but I put something together, and she laughed with delight and the game went on. The next time I glanced at Mother, her eyes were moist, and I realized that the distance she had maintained with her grandchild had vanished completely. I was weak with relief; Lissie had been so used to having two people love her, maybe now she would stop begging to go home.

*   *   *

The next evening Mother asked me to stay in the living room with her after I put Lissie to bed. I had been going to my room every night.

"Beth, do you think you should see a doctor, get a prescription for something to help you sleep?"

"Have I disturbed you? I'm sorry."

She shook her head with a show of impatience. "I'm worried about you. You're so thin and I know you're up all hours every night, up early with Lissie. You have to get some sleep."

"I'm all right."

"It's not all right," she said sharply. "Beth, you know we sent your brother to school, even a year of graduate school before he dropped out. We wanted you to go on and finish. Your father was disappointed in you, and I was, too. But that's over and done with. I want to do for you what we did for Harry Lee. If you'll stay here and go back, I'll pay for your schooling. I won't charge you and Lissie for your housing or anything."

She said this in a rush, almost embarrassed looking, almost angry. Before I could respond, she went on, "I know you've found a day care center and that you have appointments next week with employment agencies. Cancel them, Beth. Get your loan and use that for your daily spending money. If you're in school at the same time as Lissie, you won't need to leave her with anyone, will you?"

I stared at her. Finally I said, "I didn't come here for charity, Mother. I didn't ask you for that. I wouldn't ask."

"Do you have any money?"

"A little." Then I shook my head. "Not really. Forty dollars. I got a job in the spring when I knew . . . I saved all I could, but the airfares were so high . . ."

"Did he leave you two? Or did you leave him?"

"We left each other. He wanted to go to Alaska this time. Every few months he wanted to go somewhere else and I couldn't keep doing that to Lissie. I said no and got a job and started saving a little money."

Mother stood up. "Well, think about it. I can afford this, you know. Your father had a lot of insurance, and the company made a settlement. I can afford it. If money is one of the things you're worried about, one of the things keeping you awake at night, forget it for now. You're depressed, I know, but that will pass. Thank God, people don't really die of broken hearts, but they sometimes do get sick from not sleeping." She started to leave the room, then paused at the door and after a moment turned around to regard me. "I'm worried about Lissie, too. I think you really should not put her in a day care center yet."

"What do you mean? What happened?"

"Nothing happened. When I had her out shopping, I drove past the elementary school and pointed it out to her. She said she won't be here to go to school. She seems to believe that her father is coming to take her home any day now. I think she needs you to be with her, not leave her with anyone else."

The days were cast in an inferno, molten days, endless days that stretched from dawn to eternity when I awakened each morning, and melted back into the day-material of darkness by two or later the next morning. I dreamed of Judson, of loving him, being loved, and woke up hurting, no longer weeping, but hurting again and again.

I dreamed: He was playing a game with me, hiding behind a tree, or a lamppost, almost visible. I ran toward him and he sped to the next hiding place. The tree trunks were too narrow to conceal him, but as soon as he ducked behind one, he vanished, his laughter floating on the still air of the dreamscape. I ran again. We played a game that only children can play and understand, laughing, happy, knowing that at the end of the play we would be together. He eluded me once more and we ran on, and then I stopped in terror. He had run into the Waltham yard, was hiding behind a sapling that was hardly thicker than a pencil. I tried to call him but the air had changed; it no longer was calm, summer air. It was a pressure, a substance that was too hot, that did not yield to my hands, outstretched, trying to push through it. The hot substance swallowed my words, there was not even an echo. It was like trying to walk on the bottom of a hot sea, burdened by the weight of the world. My legs ached with my efforts to move forward until finally I stopped trying, but continued to move, now in spite of myself, toward the porch of the Waltham house, deep in shadows that were somehow alive and full of motion. I tried to call him again, then again. When my hand closed on the stair rail, someone screamed.

"Mommy!"

"Mother!"

I sat up, soaking wet, my hair wet, the sheet clinging to my body. Lissie! I ran to her room only to find her sound asleep, arms spread wide, the doll on the floor, the stuffed dog at her feet. The fan hummed softly, her room was degrees cooler than mine. I went to the window to draw down the shades, hoping she would sleep late in the morning, let me sleep late, and I stopped with my hand on the shade pull. A man was standing across the street.

I moved back reflexively but even as I did I knew he could not see me. From outside, the windows were as dark as caves. I edged back to the side of the window and looked out.

Everything was in motion: the white lights of approaching cars, red lights receding, and beyond the traffic the streetlight flickered through the leaves as under the tree, deep shadows formed, grew, dissolved. He must have walked into the shadows, out of view.

Hurriedly I pulled down the shades and went to my own room to slip on a housecoat. I no longer was hot and sweat-

ing; I had become chilled and began to shiver before I got to
the window to look out again. Nothing.

I stood there for a long time, until my shivering stopped.
A car passed, another one, and a patrol car. I realized that
I should call the police, report that man, let them watch for
him.

I went downstairs to the family room telephone, but
stopped again with my hand on the receiver. What could I
say? Had he been standing there, or walking, on his way
home from a late stroll, from a late job? I couldn't even
describe him. Young? Old? Fair? Dark? I had nothing to tell
the police. Instead, I checked the doors on the first floor,
went down to the basement and checked the windows
there—they had burglar-proof bars on them. There was
nothing to see, nothing to say to the police, nothing I could
do. In the kitchen, holding a glass of water, I suddenly
thought, who screamed?

I put the water down and sat at the table, shivering again.
Not Lissie. It had been real, not a dream, I knew. It had
pulled me out of the dream, away from that frightening
house. Mother? I went to her door and listened. She had an
air conditioner on, the only one in the house; I could hear it,
nothing else. I went back upstairs and looked again at Lissie
who had turned over on her stomach. I put her dog and doll
on her bed and went to my room to sit at the window watching, until the sky started to brighten, and birds began their
sleepy chitterings. Who screamed?

All day I had been at the university, and the bank, arranging
for a student loan. It was three when I finished and went to
the day care center for Lissie.

"Such a charming child," Mrs. Stewart said, taking my
money, counting change. "She said her father might be the
one to call for her. I rather expected Superman, I'm afraid."
She laughed comfortably, a plump woman without any wor-

ries, pink and white, a woman who knew who she was, what she was doing, why. I felt an almost overwhelming dislike for her.

"Her father's in Alaska," I said and heard the stiffness in my voice. "Where is Lissie?"

"Out back on the swings, I think. Let's go see."

She led me through a large room with scattered playthings, blocks, tables with crayons, the usual toys for young children. Against the wall were rolled-up foam mats. Another room had small desks and a blackboard with clowns bordering it. Everything was bright and clean and inhuman, committee-planned, I thought. What does a child like? Get it. Get two. Be happy, children, don't scream in the night, don't whisper to your father who is in Alaska—I stumbled and caught the door frame for support.

"Are you all right, dear?" Mrs. Stewart asked, her hand on my elbow. Her hand startled me with its coolness.

"I'm not used to the heat," I said, and we went on through the building to the backyard. There were two wading pools, a large oak tree with deep shade, half a dozen swings and seesaws. Three young women were supervising what seemed a multitude of small children, all under eight, all laughing, screaming, chasing. Then I spotted Lissie sitting in the shade, her back to the tree trunk, watching the other children quietly.

"They often keep to themselves for the first time or two," Mrs. Stewart said. "Especially if they haven't had the opportunity to play with many other children." It was a gentle reproach.

"She's waiting for her father," I said under my breath. Then aloud, "Lissie, here I am."

We rode the bus and walked the four blocks from the stop to Mother's house, Lissie holding my hand, sometimes skipping, sometimes lagging. She answered my questions about

the center and offered no more than the question demanded.
Yes. No. Okay.

"Didn't you like playing with other kids?" I finally asked.

"They don't play right," she said, and suddenly she pulled
on my hand, started to run. I yanked back, stopped her.
"There he is!" she cried, tugging frantically.

I looked where she was staring and saw a man vanish into
the Waltham yard.

"Who, Lissie? Who is that?"

We had stopped on the sidewalk, the cars speeding by,
other pedestrians brushing past us. She looked at me and
shook her head. "Nobody. Did you get me a present? You
said you would."

"Yes. Let's go home and you can have it."

We were on the opposite side of the street from the Waltham house. We started to walk again, past the apartment
buildings, the cars parked at the curb. A boy on a bike
pedaled past us, a young woman in shorts and no shoes
. . . Lissie's hand was hot in mine, she was counting the lines
in the concrete sidewalk. Eight, nine, seven . . . I would not
look, would not, would not . . . When we drew even with the
house, I glanced across the street at the shadowed porch, the
blank windows hidden behind drapes, the neat yard. No one
was in sight. I had expected to see no one. "Twelve, thirteen,
seven . . ."

One time when Lissie counted Judson had laughed, and
said, "Honey, there are too many sevens," and she had said
seriously, "There can't be too many sevens. That's my favor-
ite number."

She did not look across the street, did not even glance at
the house.

"Are you sure you don't mind?" Mother asked that night.

"Of course. You need your vacation. You've been counting on it for months. I'd feel terrible if you called it off on our account."

"Well, you'll have the car," she said. She was to fly down to Atlanta to visit Harry Lee for a week, and then on to Florida for a second week. She was to meet an old friend there and they would do some gardens, a little sightseeing, a little relaxing on the beach. It sounded wonderful. I realized belatedly that the friend was male, and when the realization hit me, I had to look at her with different eyes. She was youthful, very attractive. Of course there should be a man in her life after all this time. I wished she had come out and said it directly, that she was interested in a man again.

That night I asked her about the old Waltham house. "I remember that I used to be scared to death of it," I said, fighting to keep the fear from my voice.

"Oh, that," she said. "Mr. Waltham was a cranky old man. He used to want to keep the kids completely away from his property, even his side of the street. He sprayed Harry Lee with a hose once. Your father went over and yelled at him over it."

Was that all? Had Harry Lee in turn frightened me about it? What insane things children drag from childhood to adulthood with them! My relief made me feel giddy. "Who lives there now?"

"His son, I guess. Do you remember him? I suppose you were too young. He was just like his father, mean and vindictive. He must be forty. He married one of the Garrison girls . . ." She rambled on. Bob Waltham was his name, and there were a couple of children, maybe three, she wasn't certain, but anyway his wife left him, took the kids and went to New York or someplace like that. He lived there alone now. Worked for the electric company, or the gas company, or was it the telephone?

And there was no mystery about it. A man going on middle age, living alone in a house that had been the symbol of all my childhood fears. This was how life's mysteries were resolved, I thought; they simply became banal chapters of a commonplace life.

Lissie played with the small wooden figures I had bought for her—a man, woman, two children, a car that they all fitted into. Actually she had already lost the wooden boy; he had been superfluous to begin with.

I sat on the back porch and watched her idly, a book on the table by my chair. A faint wind had come up, bringing in clouds, the oppressive feeling of another thunderstorm. They did not alleviate the heat, or turn the grass green, or replenish the water in the city reservoir apparently; there were stories about possible rationing in the daily papers. But I welcomed the storms. Temporarily they brought relief. And they were frenzied, wild, out of control.

"Now, Daddy, remember ice cream," Lissie ordered the man as she put him in the car and drove him away across the porch. "And Mommy said Daddy has a job now. Remember that."

She talked to the little people, told them about Grandma flying in a big airplane, about sleeping under a lot of trees in the woods, about the monkeys in their boxes. We had taken her to a carnival where she had seen monkeys in cages and asked why they didn't open the door and go home. She talked on; the breeze cooled my face, dried the sweat, and tomorrow I would take her for a ride out in the country, buy her something to eat in a restaurant, a cheap one, but something different, and if it got cooler, bake cookies, and she could help . . .

"No, Daddy, don't tickle." She laughed, and he laughed with her.

I jerked upright and looked for him. Lissie was at the side of the yard, at the fence. I screamed at her, and lightning split the sky at the same moment, followed almost instantly by a crash of thunder. I screamed again and this time she turned to look at me, a distant, preoccupied look that seemed not to register me in her consciousness, but rather to be directed at a minor nuisance that had disturbed her. I raced across the yard and caught her arm, yanked her away from the fence.

"Who are you talking to? Tell me! Who was there? Lissie, tell me!"

Then she was crying and I was shaking her by the shoulders, yelling at her, and the rain started in a frenzy of oversized drops mixed with hail. I picked her up and carried her inside the house; we were both crying.

That night after dinner we sat at the kitchen table and drew pictures and wrote letters to send to Judson. She drew her little people and their car and made a border of sevens around them, and then colored them all in with crayons. She had me print out a letter for her to copy, and while she was doing that, I said, trying to keep my voice casual, "When you talk to that man all the time, does he answer you?"

She shook her head.

"Lissie, you mustn't talk to him ever again. Okay? Little girls shouldn't talk to strange men. Remember what Daddy told you?"

"Okay," she said. She laboriously copied the message, concentrating, frowning at it intently.

"Lissie, look at me! I heard you talking to him! Promise me you won't do that again!"

She looked at me. "Okay."

And it was meaningless. I knew it was meaningless.

That night she took the little people to bed with her, and their car, as well as her doll and dog. The letter and pictures were in an envelope on her nightstand. I pulled her shades down, as I had been doing every night. I kissed her good night and sat on the side of her bed for another minute or two, and realized I was afraid to leave her alone. We had addressed the letter to Judson in care of General Delivery,

Juneau, Alaska. I had no other address for him yet, no way to get in touch with him.

"Tomorrow we'll go for a ride in the country," I said. "And we'll mail the letter. We'll eat dinner in a restaurant. You can have seven hamburgers. Okay?"

She giggled. "Then I'll be too fat."

"A little bit fat maybe. Six hamburgers."

"Seven," she said firmly and yawned.

I kissed her again and left her. There was a night-light in the hall outside her door, and another one in the upstairs bathroom, and my room was brilliant with the light from the street, but it seemed that the shadows were deeper than they should be, somehow thicker, and the house seemed noisier than I remembered. The wind from the storm had not died down altogether yet; the shadows of leaves danced on my walls, shifted, clumped, sprang apart. I sat at the window and stared out at the street, unwilling to go downstairs until I knew Lissie was sleeping.

Judson, I thought then, please call. At least call. She needs you, I thought at the street, at the distance, at Alaska. She needs you, I said under my breath. Alaska seemed too far away to comprehend, as if it belonged to another universe, existed, if it existed at all, across a void that swallowed all sound, all thought, and for the first time I allowed myself to consider that he might never come back, we might never see him again, he might even be dead. For the first time I wished that he was dead, that the waiting would end, and I knew I had been waiting just as much as Lissie was waiting, believing he would appear just as much as she believed. I wished he was dead and the notification would come and the waiting would end.

With the thought came the rejection of the thought. We just wanted him back. Lissie and I wanted him back.

I rested my head against the window frame, closed my eyes, and thought how much better it would be when the weather cooled off in the fall. I saw the maple tree in the progression of seasons: scarlet, flooding my room with rosy light; spidery against the lowering winter-bleached sky; how the tentative leaves swelled, then burst almost with explosive sound effects in the spring; the winged seeds riding the wind, spiraling, whirling in an ecstasy of fecundity, seeking the secrecy of the earth-bed.

And the summer tree standing alone, dancing alone, its leaves joining, springing apart, dipping and bowing with hardly a rustle.

I half-heard Lissie's soft voice: "Now Daddy and the little girl go for a ride far away. Good-bye, Mommy. We'll bring you a present." I jerked away from the window, searching the shadows under the tree; he was there, as I had known he would be.

I shook my head, whispered, "No!" I was on my feet, going out the door, not really touching the carpeting, the stairs, my fingers as insubstantial as air when I pulled the front door open, my bare feet gliding above the wood of the porch, the concrete of the walkway. I stopped at the fence gate. "No!" I said again, this time aloud. "No!"

He was there in the shadows; although everything moved around him, the shadows, light and dark, leaves, he was without motion, waiting, waiting. Up in her room Lissie was whispering to him, laughing, happy.

"Leave her alone!" I cried out to him. "You're in Alaska! Go back! Leave her alone!"

I looked up at the house, where the windows that should have been as black as caves were lighted; she was standing in her window, laughing, holding up the envelope with Judson's name, waving it back and forth, as if to say come and collect it, Daddy. I could feel him looking at me then, the way he used to do. We could be together again, something in me sang, the three of us together again forever and ever. The place that had been hard and clenched deep inside me dissolved. I pushed the gate open and took a step forward; he took a step toward me, and in her window Lissie waved the envelope and laughed.

We had been walking on a narrow ledge a thousand miles above the earth, Lissie and I, hand in hand, and my terror had filled us both, terror that the next step would plunge us down to our death. For I could not see the ledge, but had to trust my instincts, trust my feet, trust fate, and pretend all the while that I knew where I was taking us. I took another step and thought, how foolish I had been. There was no fall to death; letting go, yielding led only to freedom and happiness, safety in his arms again, the abandonment of the summer storms that blew wild and uncontrollable. Another step. He was matching my steps, coming closer, pacing me. I knew he was laughing softly, deep in his chest, the way he did.

Once, as we sat in the shade of a juniper tree at the edge of a meadow, he had said to Lissie, "You can make the deer come out. Magic girl, make them come."

And the deer had come, looking around warily.

Magic girl. She had made him come out of the shadows, but she couldn't hold him by herself; she needed help to keep him here. I had to help her. I took another step; he matched it. We were like the points of a triangle, drawing closer and closer together. Like a kaleidoscope pattern, shifting, always shifting to something new and wonderful, flowing to the center, only to explode into countless red and white fragments. I put my foot out and terror overwhelmed me; I didn't know where the edge was, where the fall began.

If I plunged, she would go down with me; her hand was so firmly in my own. And the fall was forever.

The maple leaves danced in the slight wind; the shadows merged, blended, sprang apart silently. He was in shadows, now seen, now hidden, waiting for me to move. My movement permitted his; waiting, waiting.

A thousand miles above the earth-bed, falling forever, caught in the magic forever.

"No!" I whispered then. "No!"

From a distant place, like an echo, I heard Lissie's agonized wail.

"No!"

A car passed me, inches away. A horn sounded loud and harsh, too close. I turned, ran back inside the house and locked the door. Gasping for air I raced upstairs, and then stood over Lissie for a long time, until my lungs stopped burning, my chest stopped heaving. She slept peacefully. The little people were scattered on the floor, the daddy, the mommy, the little girl. I picked them up and put them in their car, put it on the nightstand next to the envelope addressed to Judson.

No magic, I thought dully. You kill magic by denying it. Lissie and I were still on the ledge, but it had widened a little, and just ahead, just around the next curve, or the one after that, still out of sight, but reachable, I sensed that the ledge became level ground again. I felt that in the book of my life a chapter had ended; around the next curve a new one would start.

The Scream

The sea had turned to copper; it rose and fell gently, the motion starting so deep that no ripple broke the surface of the slow swells. The sky was darkening to a deep blue-violet, with rose streaks in the west and a high cirrocumulus formation in the east that was a dazzling white mountain crowned with brilliant reds and touches of green. No wind stirred. The irregular dark strip that was Miami Beach separated the metallic sea from the fiery sky. We were at anchor eight miles offshore aboard the catamaran *Loretta*. She was a forty-foot, single-masted, inboard motorboat.

Evinson wanted to go on in, but Trainor, whose boat it was, said no. Too dangerous: sand, silt, wrecks, God knew what we might hit. We waited until morning.

We had to go in at Biscayne Bay; the Bal Harbour inlet was clogged with the remains of the bridge on old A1A. Trainor put in at the Port of Miami. All the while J.P. kept taking his water samples, not once glancing at the ruined city; Delia kept a running check for radiation, and Bernard

154

took pictures. Corrie and I tried to keep out of the way, and
Evinson didn't. The ancient catamaran was clumsy, and
Trainor was kept busy until we were tied up, then he bowed
sarcastically to Evinson and went below.

Rusting ships were in the harbor, some of them on their
sides half in water, half out. Some of them seemed afloat, but
then we saw that without the constant dredging that had kept
the port open, silt and sand had entered, and the bottom was
no more than ten to fifteen feet down. The water was very
clear. Some catfish lay unmoving on the bottom, and a
school of big-eyed mullet circled at the surface, the first
marine life we had seen. The terns were diving here, and
sandpipers ran with the waves. J.P.'s eyes were shining as he
watched the birds. We all had been afraid that there would
be no life of any kind.

Our plan was to reconnoiter the first day, try to find transportation: bicycles, which none of us had ridden before,
skates, canoes, anything. Miami and the beaches covered a
lot of miles, and we had a lot of work; without transportation
the work would be less valuable—if it had any value to begin
with.

Bernard and Delia went ahead to find a place to set up our
base, and the rest of us started to unload the boat. In half an
hour we were drenched with sweat. At first glance the city
had seemed perfectly habitable, just empty of people, but as
we carried the boxes to the hotel that Bernard had found, the
ruins dominated the scene. Walls were down, streets vanished under sand and palmettos and sea grapes. The hotel
was five stories, the first floor covered with sand and junk:
shells, driftwood, an aluminum oar eaten through with cor-
rosion. Furniture was piled against walls haphazardly, like
heaps of rotting compost. The water had risen and fallen
more than once, rearranging floatables. It was hellishly hot,
and the hotel stank of ocean and decay and dry rot and heat.
No one talked much as we all worked, all but Trainor, who

had worked to get us here and who now guzzled beer with his feet up. Evinson cursed him monotonously. We carried our stuff to the hotel, then to the second floor, where we put mosquito netting at the windows of three connecting rooms that would be used jointly. We separated to select our private rooms and clear them and secure them against the mosquitoes that would appear by the millions as soon as the sun went down.

After a quick lunch of soy wafers and beer we went out singly to get the feel of the city and try to locate any transportation we could.

I started with a map in my hand, and the first thing I did was put it back inside my pack. Except for the general areas, the map was worthless. This had been a seawalled city, and the seawalls had gone: a little break here, a crack somewhere else, a trickle of water during high tide, a flood during a storm, the pressure building behind the walls, on the land side, and inevitably the surrender to the sea. The water had undermined the road system and eaten away at foundations of buildings, and hurricane winds had done the rest. Some streets were completely filled in with rubble; others were pitted and undercut until shelves of concrete had shifted and slid and now rested crazily tilted. The white sand had claimed some streets so thoroughly that growth had had a chance to naturalize, and there were strip-forests of palm trees, straggly bushes with pink and yellow flowers, and sea grapes. I saw a mangrove copse claiming the water's edge and stopped to stare at it for a long time, with curious thoughts flitting through my brain about the land and the sea in a survival struggle in which man was no more than an incidental observer, here, then gone. The afternoon storm broke abruptly, and I took shelter in a building that seemed to have been a warehouse.

The stench of mold and decay drove me out again as soon as the storm abated. Outside, the sun had baked everything, the sun and rain sterilizing, neutralizing, keeping the mold at bay, but inside the cavernous buildings the soggy air was a culture for mold spores, and thirty years, forty, had not been long enough to deplete the rich source of nutrients. There was food available on the shelves, the shelves were food, the wood construction materials, the glues and grouts, the tiles and vinyls, the papers neatly filed, the folders that held them, pencils, everything finally was food for the mold.

I entered two more buildings, same thing, except that one of them had become a bat cave. They were the large fruit bats, not dangerous, and I knew they were not, but I left them the building without contest.

At the end of the first day we had three bicycles and a flat-bottomed rowboat with two oars. I hadn't found anything of value. The boat was aluminum, and although badly corroded, it seemed intact enough. Trainor slouched in while J.P. was cooking dinner and the rest of us were planning our excursions for the next day.

"You folks want boats? Found a storehouse full of them."

He joined us for dinner and drew a map showing the warehouse he had found. His freehand map was more reliable than the printed ones we had brought with us. I suspected that he was salvaging what he could for his own boat. Unless he was a fool, that was what he was doing. When Evinson asked him what else he had seen that day, he simply shrugged.

"How's chances of a swim?" I asked Delia after we ate.

"No radiation. But you'd better wait for Corrie to run some analyses. Too much that we don't know to chance it yet."

"No swimming, damn it!" Evinson said sharply. "For God's sake, Sax." He issued orders rapidly for the next day, in effect telling everyone to do what he had come to do.

Strut and puff, you little bastard, I thought at him. No one protested.

* * *

The same ruins lay everywhere in the city. After the first hour
it was simply boring. My bicycle was more awkward than
going on foot, since I had to carry it over rubble as much as
I got to ride it. I abandoned it finally. I found the Miami
River and dutifully got a sample. It was the color of tea, very
clear. I followed the river a long time, stopped for my lunch,
and followed it some more. Ruins, sand, junk, palm trees.
Heat. Silence. Especially silence. I was not aware of when I
began to listen to the silence, but I caught myself walking
cautiously, trying to be as quiet as the city, not to intrude in
any way. The wind in the dry fronds was the only thing I
heard. It stopped, then started again, and I jerked around. I
went inside a building now and then, but they were worse
than the ruined streets. Rusty toys, appliances, moldering
furniture, or piles of dust where the termites had been, chairs
that crumbled when I touched them, and the heat and silence.

I got bored with the river and turned in to what had been
a garden park. Here the vegetation was different. A banyan
tree had spread unchecked and filled more than a city block.
A flock of blackbirds arose from it as I approached. The
suddenness of their flight startled me and I whirled around,
certain that someone was behind me. Nothing. Vines and
bushes had grown wild in the park and were competing with
trees for space—a minijungle. There were thousands of parakeets, emerald green, darting, making a cacophony that was
worse than the silence. I retraced my steps after a few minutes. There might have been water in there, but I didn't care.
I circled the park and kept walking.

The feeling that I was being followed grew stronger, and I
stopped as if to look more closely at a weed, listening for
steps. Nothing. The wind in some pampas grass, the louder
rustle of palm fronds, the return of the blackbirds. And in the
distance the raucous cries of gulls. The feeling didn't go
away, and I walked faster and sweated harder.

I got out my kit and finished the last of the beer in the shade of a live oak with branches eighty feet long spreading out sideways in all directions. Whatever had poisoned Miami and reduced its population to zero hadn't affected the flora. The wind started, the daily storm. I sat in the doorway of a stinking apartment building and watched sheets of water race down the street. After the storm passed I decided to go back and try to get Corrie to bed with me. It never occurred to me to snuggle up to Delia, who seemed totally asexual. Delia and J.P., I thought.

Corrie was alone, and she said no curtly. She was as hot as I was and as tired. But she had a working lab set up, complete with microscopes and test tubes and flasks of things over Bunsen burners. She glanced contemptuously at the collecting bottle that I handed her. They knew about me, all of them.

"What did I do wrong?"

"Label it, please. Location, depth, source, time of day. Anything else you can think of that might be helpful."

Her tone said, and leave me alone because I have real work to do. She turned back to her microscope.

"So I'm not a hydrologist. I'm a pamphlet writer for Health, Education and Welfare."

"I know." She glanced at me again. "But why didn't they send a real hydrologist?"

"Because we don't have one."

She stood up and walked to the window netting and looked out. Her shirt was wet under her sleeves and down her back, her hair clung to her cheeks and the nape of her neck. "Why?" she whispered. "Why? Why? Why?"

"If they knew that we wouldn't be here."

She walked back to her chair and sat down again, drawing the microscope toward her once more.

"Is the bay all right?"

"Yes." She adjusted the focus and forgot about me. I left.

The warehouse where Trainor had found the boats was half a dozen blocks up the waterfront. I walked and sweated. Trainor had dragged some small boats outside, and I chose the smallest of them and took it down to the water. I rowed out into the bay, undressed, and swam for half an hour; then I started to row, going no place in particular.

The water was marvelously calm, and I felt cooler and less tense after the swim. I stopped to dive a couple of times around a sunken yacht; it had been stripped. I stopped again, this time ashore at what looked like a copy of the Parthenon. It had been a museum. The water lapped about the foundation; marble stairs and massive fountains indicated that it had been a grandiose thing. A statue had toppled and I considered it. A female form—vaguely female, anyway. Rounded, curving, voluptuous-looking, roughly hewn out of granite, it was touching somehow. The eye-hollows were facing out to sea, waiting, watching the water, waiting. The essence of woman as childbearer, woman as nourisher, woman as man's sexual necessity. Her flesh would be warm and yielding. She would be passive, accept his seed, and let it come to life within her. Those great round arms would hold a child, let it suckle at the massive breasts. I wished I could stand the statue upright again. When it fell one of the arms had broken; it lay apart from the bulk of the work. I tried to lift it: too heavy. I ran my hand over the rough rock and I wanted to sit on the floor by the woman and talk to her, cry a little, rest my cheek against that breast. I began to feel suffocated suddenly and I turned and ran from the museum without looking for anything else. The sun was setting, the sky crimson and blue and green, incredible colors that looked like cheap art.

It was dark when I got back to headquarters. All the others were there already, even Trainor. Delia was cooking. I watched her as she added water to the dehydrated stew and stirred it over canned heat. She was angular, with firm muscles and hardly any breasts at all. Her hips were slim, boyish, her legs all muscle and bone. I wondered again about her sexuality. I had seen her studying Trainor speculatively once, but nothing had come of it, and I had seen almost the same expression on her face a time or two when she had been looking at Corrie.

I turned my attention to Corrie—a little better, but still not really woman, not as the statue had signified woman. Corrie was softer than Delia, her hips a bit rounder, her breasts bouncier, not much, but Delia's never moved at all. Corrie had more of a waistline. My thoughts were confusing to me, and I tried to think of something else, but that damn statue kept intruding. I should have talked to her, I found myself thinking. And, she would have looked at me with contempt. She would have looked at any of our men with contempt— except, possibly, Trainor.

I watched and listened to Trainor then, speaking with Bernard. Trainor was tall and broad shouldered, his hair white, face browned by the sun, very lean and very muscular.

"Have you ever seen any wild animals as far north as the cape?" Bernard asked, sketching. His fingers were swift and sure: that characterized him all the way, actually. He was soft looking, but he moved with a sureness always. A dilettante artist, photographer, in his mid-thirties, rich enough not to work. There had been a mild affair with Corrie, but nothing serious. I didn't know why he was here.

"Deer," Trainor said in answer to his question. "There's a lot of things up in the brush. Foxes, rabbits, muskrats, possum."

"Anything big? I heard that lions were let loose, or escaped around West Palm Beach. Did they live, multiply?"

"Can't say."

"Heard there were panthers."

"Can't say."

"How about Indians? You must know if any of them are

left in the swamps." Bernard's pencil stopped, but he didn't look at Trainor.

"Could be. Don't go inland much. No way to get inland, hard going by boat, hyacinths, thick enough to walk on. Too much stuff in the water everywhere. St. John's River used to be open, but not now."

"How about fish then? See any porpoises?"

"They come and go. Don't stay around long. Hear they're thick down around South America and in the Caribbean. Might be."

I watched Bernard for a long time. What was he after? And Trainor? I had a feeling that the seven people who had come to the city had seven different reasons, and that mine was the only simple one. Orders. When you work for the government and an undersecretary says go, you go. Why were the others here?

In bed later, I couldn't sleep. The odors all came back in triple strength after dark. I could feel the mold growing around me, on me, in my bedroll. The humidity was a weight on my chest. I finally got up again, drenched with sweat, my bed soaked through, and I went back to the second floor where I interrupted Delia and Bernard in a quiet conversation. I got a beer and sat down near the window, my back to them both. After a moment Delia yawned and got up.

At the doorway she paused and said, "Why don't you take him?"

I looked at her then. Bernard made a snorting sound and didn't answer. I turned back to the window. The silence was coming in along with the nighttime humidity, and I realized that I had chosen my room on the wrong side of the building. The night air blew from the land to the sea. There was a faint breeze at the window. The oil lamp was feeble against the pressure of the darkness beyond the netting.

"Night," Delia said at the door, and I looked at her again, nodded, and she started through, then stopped. A high, uncanny, inhuman scream sounded once, from a long way off. It echoed through the empty city. The silence that followed it made me understand that what I had thought to be quiet before had not been stillness. Now the silence was profound; no insect, no rustling, no whir of small wings, nothing. Then the night sounds began to return. The three of us had remained frozen; now Bernard moved. He turned to Delia.

"I knew it," he said. "I knew!"

She was very pale. "What was it?" she cried shrilly.

"Panther. Either in the city or awfully close."

Panther? It might have been. I had no idea what a panther sounded like. The others were coming down again, Evinson in the lead, Corrie and J.P. close behind him. Corrie looked less frightened than Delia, but rattled and pale.

"For heaven's sake, Bernard!" J.P. said. "Was that you?"

"Don't you know?" Corrie cried. At the same time Delia said, "It was a panther."

"No! Don't be a fool!" Corrie said.

Evinson interrupted them both. "Everyone, just be quiet. It was some sort of bird. We've seen birds for three days now. Some of them make cries like that."

"No bird ever made a sound like that," Corrie said. Her voice was too high and excited.

"It was a panther," Bernard repeated. "I heard one before. In Mexico I heard one just like that, twenty years ago. I've never forgotten." He nodded toward the net-covered window. "Out there. Maybe in one of the city parks. Think what it means, Evinson. I was right! Wildlife out there. Naturalized, probably." He took a breath. His hands were trembling, and he spoke with an intensity that was almost embarrassing. Corrie shook her head stubbornly, but Bernard went on. "I'm going to find it. Tomorrow. I'll take Sax with me, and our gear, and plan to stay out there for a day or two. We'll see if we can find a trace of it, get a shot. Proof of some kind."

Evinson started to protest. If it wasn't his plan, he hated it. "We need Sax to find water for us," he said. "It's too dangerous. We don't know what the beast is; it might attack on sight."

I was watching Bernard. His face tightened, became older, harsher. He was going. "Drop it, Evinson," I said. "They know about me. The only water I'll find is the river, which I already stumbled across, remember. And Bernard is right. If there's anything, we should go out and try to find it."

Evinson grumbled some more, but he couldn't really forbid it, since this was what the expedition was all about. Besides, he knew damn well there was no way on earth that he could enforce any silly edict. Sulkily he left us to plan our foray.

It was impossible to tell how the waterways had been laid out in many places. The water had spread, making marshes, and had changed its course, sometimes flowing down streets, again vanishing entirely, leaving dry beds as devoid of life as the Martian canals. Ruined concrete and sand lay there now. And the ruins went on and on. No frame houses remained; they had caved in, or had been blown down, or burned. A trailer court looked as if someone had taken one corner of the area and lifted it, tipping the chrome and gaudy-colored cans to one side. Creepers and shrubs were making a hill of greenery over them. We rowed and carried the boat and our stuff all day, stopped for the storms, then found shelter in a school building when it grew dark. The mosquitoes were worse the farther we went; their whining drowned out all other noises; we were both a mass of swollen bites that itched without letup. We saw nothing bigger than a squirrel. Bernard thought he glimpsed a manatee once, but it disappeared in the water plants and didn't show again. I didn't see it. There were many birds.

We were rowing late in the afternoon of the second day

when Bernard motioned me to stop. We drifted and I looked where he pointed. On the bank was a great gray heron, its head stretched upward in a strange but curiously graceful position. Its wings were spread slightly, and it looked like nothing so much as a ballerina, poised, holding out her tutu. With painful slowness it lifted one leg and flexed its toes, then took a dainty, almost mincing step. Bernard pointed again, and I saw the second bird, in the same pose, following a ritual that had been choreographed incalculable ages ago. We watched the dance of the birds in silence, until without warning Bernard shouted in a hoarse, strange voice, "Get out of here! You fucking birds! Get out of here!" He hit the water with his oar, making an explosive noise, and continued to scream at them as they lifted in panicked flight and vanished into the growth behind them, trailing their long legs, ungainly now and no longer beautiful.

"Bastard," I muttered, and started to row again. We were out of synch for a long time as he chopped at the water ineffectually.

We watched the rain later, not talking. We hadn't talked since seeing the birds' courtship dance. I had a sunburn that was painful and peeling; I was tired, and hungry for some real food. "Tomorrow morning we start back," I said. I didn't look at him. We were in a small house while the rain and wind howled and pounded and turned the world gray. Lightning flashed and thunder rocked us almost simultaneously. The house shook and I tensed, ready to run. Bernard laughed. He waited for the wind to let up before he spoke.

"Sax, we have until the end of the week, and then back to Washington for you, back to New York for me. When do you think you'll ever get out of the city again?"

"If I get back to it, what makes you think I'll ever want out again?"

"You will. This trip will haunt you. You'll begin to think

of those parakeets, the terns wheeling and diving for fish.
You'll dream of swimming in clean water. You'll dream of
the trees and the skies and the waves on the beach. And no
matter how much you want to get it back, there won't be any
way at all."

"There's a way if you want it bad enough."

"No way." He shook his head. "I tried. For years I tried.
No way. Unless you're willing to walk cross-country, and
take the risks. No one ever makes it to anywhere, you know."

I knew he was right. In Health and Education you learn
about things like public transportation: there isn't any. You
learn about travel: there isn't any, not that's safe. The people
who know how to salvage and make-do get more and more
desperate for parts to use, more and more deadly in the ways
they get those parts. Also, travel permits were about as plen-
tiful as unicorns.

"You wanted to go back to Mexico?" I asked.

"Yeah. For twenty years I wanted to go back. The women
there are different."

"You were younger. They were younger."

"No, it isn't just that. They were different. Something in
the air. You could feel it, sniff it, almost see it. The smells
were . . ." He stood up suddenly. "Anyway, I tried to get
back, and this is as close as I could get. Maybe I'll go ahead
and walk after all." He faced the west where the sky had
cleared and the low sun looked three times as big as it should
have.

"Look, Bernard, I could quote you statistics; that's my
job, you know. But I won't. Just take my word for it. That's
what I'm good at. What I read, I remember. The birth rate
has dropped to two per thousand there. As of six years ago.
It might be lower now. They're having a hell of a time with
communications. And they had plague."

"I don't believe that."

"What? The birth rate?"

"Plague." He looked at me with a strange smile.

I didn't know what he was driving at. I was the one with access to government records, while he was just a photographer. "Right," I said. "People just died of nothing."

"It's a lie, Sax! A goddamn fucking lie! No plague!" He stopped as suddenly as he had started, and sat down. "Forget it, Sax. Just forget it."

"If it wasn't the plague, what?"

"I said to let it drop."

"What was it, Bernard? You're crazy, you know that? You're talking crazy."

"Yeah, I'm crazy." He was looking westward again.

During the night I wakened to hear him walking back and forth. I hoped that if he decided to start that night, he'd leave me the canoe. I went back to sleep. He was still there in the morning.

"Look, Sax, you go back. I'll come along in a day or two."

"Bernard, you can't live off nothing. There won't be any food after tomorrow. We'll both go back, stock up, and come out again. I couldn't go off and leave you. How would you get back?"

"When I was a boy," he said, "my father and mother were rather famous photographers. They taught me. We traveled all over the world. Getting pictures of all the vanishing species, for one last glorious book." I nodded. They had produced two of the most beautiful books I had ever seen. "Then something happened," he said, after a slight hesitation. "You know all about that, I guess. Your department. They went away and left me in Mexico. I wasn't a kid, you see, but I'd always been with them. Then I wasn't with them anymore. No note. No letter. Nothing. They searched for them, of course. Rich gringos aren't—weren't—allowed to simply vanish. Nothing. Before that my father had taken me into the hills, for a hunt. This time with guns. We shot—God, we shot everything that moved! Deer. Rabbits. Birds. A couple of snakes. There was a troop of monkeys. I remember them most of all. Seven monkeys. He took the left side and I took the right and we wiped them out. Just like that. They shrieked and screamed and tried to run away, and tried to shield each other, and we got every last one. Then we went back to my mother and the next day they were gone. I was fifteen. I stayed there for five years. Me and the girls of Mexico. They sent me home just before the border was closed. All North Americans out. I got permission to go back to New York, and for seventeen years I never left again. Until now. I won't go back, Sax."

He leaned over and picked up a rifle. He had had it with his photographic equipment. "I have ammunition. I've had it for years. I'm pretty good with it. I'd demonstrate, but I don't want to waste the shell. Now, you just pick up your gear, and toss it in the boat, and get the hell out of here."

I suddenly remembered watching television as a child, when they had programs that went on around the clock—stories, movies. A man with a rifle stalking a deer. That's all I could remember of that program, but it was very clear and I didn't want to go away and let Bernard be that man. I stared at the rifle until it began to rise and I was looking down the barrel of it.

"I'll kill you, Sax. I really will," he said, and I knew he would.

I turned and tossed my pack into the boat and then climbed in. "How will you get back, if you decide to come back?" I felt only bitterness. I was going back and he was going to be the man with the rifle.

"I'll find a way. If I'm not there by Friday, don't wait. Tell Evinson I said that, Sax."

"Bernard . . ." I let it hang there as I pushed off and started to paddle. There wasn't a thing that I could say to him.

I heard a shot about an hour later, then another in the afternoon, after that nothing. I got back to headquarters during the night. No one was up, so I raided the food and beer and went to bed. The next morning Evinson was livid with rage.

"He wouldn't have stayed like that! You left him! You did something to him, didn't you? You'll be tried, Sax. I'll see you in prison for this." Color flooded back into his face, leaving him looking as unnaturally flushed as he had been pale only a moment before. His hand trembled as he wiped his forehead, which was flaky with peeling skin.

"Sax is telling the truth," Delia said. She had circles under her eyes and seemed depressed. "Bernard wanted me to go away with him to hunt. I refused. He needed someone to help him get as far away as possible."

Evinson turned his back on her. "You'll go back for him," he said to me, snapping the words. I shook my head. "I'll report you. I don't believe a word of what you've said. I'll report you. You did something, didn't you? All his work for this project! You go get him!"

"Oh, shut up." I turned to Corrie. "Anything new while I was gone?"

She looked tired too. Evinson must have applied the whip. "Not much. We've decided to take back samples of everything. We can't do much with the equipment we brought. Just not enough time. Not enough of us for the work."

"If you knew your business you could do it!" Evinson said. "Incompetents! All of you! This is treason! You know that, don't you? You're sabotaging this project. You don't want me to prove my theory. Obstacles every step of the way. That's all you've been good for. And now this! I'm warning you, Sax, if you don't bring Bernard back today, I'll press charges against you." His voice had been high pitched always, but it became shriller and shriller until he sounded like a hysterical woman.

I spun to face him. "What theory, you crazy old man? There is no theory! There are a hundred theories. You think those records weren't sifted a thousand times before they were abandoned? Everything there was microfilmed and studied again and again and again. You think you can poke about in this muck and filth and come up with something that hasn't been noted and discarded a dozen times? They don't give a damn about your theories, you bloody fool! They hope that Delia can come up with a radiation study they can use. That Bernard will find wildlife, plant life that will prove the pollution has abated here. That J.P. will report the marine life has reestablished itself. Who do you think will ever read your theories about what happened here? Who gives a damn? All they want now is to try to save the rest."

I was out of breath and more furious than I had been in years. I wanted to kill the bastard, and it didn't help at all to realize that it was Bernard that I really wanted to strangle. The man with the gun. Evinson backed away from me, and for the first time I saw that one of his hands had been bandaged.

Corrie caught my glance and shrugged. "Something bit him. He thinks I should be able to analyze his blood and come up with everything from what did it to a foolproof antidote. In fact, we have no idea what bit him."

"Isn't Trainor any help with something like that?"

"He might be if he were around. We haven't seen him since the night we heard the scream."

Evinson flung down his plastic cup. It bounced from the table to the floor. He stamped out.

"It's bad," Corrie said. "He's feverish, and his hand is infected. I've done what I can. I just don't have anything to work with."

Delia picked up the cup and put it back on the table. "This whole thing is an abysmal failure," she said dully. "None of us is able to get any real work done. We don't know enough, or we don't have the right equipment, or enough manpower, or time. I don't even know why we're here."

"The Turkey Point plant?"

"I don't know a damn thing about it, except that it isn't hot. The people who built that plant knew more than we're being taught today." She bit her lip hard enough to leave marks on it. Her voice was steady when she went on. "It's like that in every field. We're losing everything that we had twenty-five years ago, thirty years ago. I'm one of the best, and I don't understand that plant."

I looked at Corrie and she nodded. "I haven't seen a transplant in my life. No one is doing them now. I read about dialysis, but no one knows how to do it. In my books there are techniques and procedures that are as alien as acupuncture. Evinson is furious with us, and with himself. He can't come up with anything that he couldn't have presented as theory without ever leaving the city. It's a failure, and he's afraid he'll be blamed personally."

We sat in silence for several minutes until J.P. entered. He looked completely normal. His bald head was very red; the rest of his skin had tanned to a deep brown. He looked like he was wearing a gaudy skullcap.

"You're back." Not a word about Bernard, or to ask what we had done, what we had seen. "Delia, you coming with me again today? I'd like to get started soon."

Delia laughed and stood up. "Sure, J.P. All the way." They left together.

"Is he getting anything done?"

"Who knows? He works sixteen hours a day doing something. I don't know what." Corrie drummed her fingers on the table, watching them. Then she said, "Was that a panther the other night, Davidson? Did you see a panther, or anything else?"

"Nothing. And I don't know what it was. I never heard a panther."

"I don't think it was. I think it was a human being."

"A woman?"

"Yes. In childbirth."

I stared at her until she met my gaze. She nodded. "I've heard it before. I am a doctor, you know. I specialized in obstetrics until the field became obsolete."

I found that I couldn't stop shaking my head. "You're as crazy as Bernard."

"No. That's what I came for, Davidson. There has to be life out there in the Everglades. The Indians. They can stick it out, back in the swamps where they always lived. Probably nothing much has changed for them. Except that there's more game now. That has to be it."

"Have you talked to Evinson about this?"

"Yes, of course. He thinks it was Trainor who screamed. He thinks Trainor was killed by a snake, or something. After he got bitten himself, he became convinced of it."

"J.P.? Delia?"

"J.P. thinks it's a mystery. Since it has nothing to do with marine biology, he has no opinion, no interest. Delia thought Bernard was right, an animal, maybe a panther, maybe something else. She is afraid it's a mutated animal. She began to collect strange plants, and insects, things like that after you left. She even has a couple of fruit bats that she says are mutations."

I took a deep breath. "Corrie, why are we here? Why did the government send this expedition here?"

She shrugged. "What you told Evinson makes as much sense as anything else. The government didn't mount this expedition, you know. They simply permitted it. And sent an observer. It was Bernard's scheme from the start. He convinced Evinson that he could become famous through the proofs for his schoolboy theory. Bernard's money, Evinson's pull with those in power. And now we know why Bernard wanted to come. He's impotent." She looked thoughtful, then smiled faintly at me. "A lot of impotent men feel the need to go out and shoot things. And many, perhaps most men are impotent now. Don't look like that. At least you're all right."

I backed away from that. "What about Evinson? Does he believe a leak or an explosion brought all this about?"

"Bernard planted that in his mind," she said. "He doesn't really believe it now. But it leaves him with no alternative theory to fall back on. You can't tell anything by looking at these rotten buildings."

I shook my head. "I know that was the popular explanation, but they did investigate, you know. Didn't he get to any of the old reports? Why did he buy that particular theory?"

"All those reports are absolutely meaningless. Each new administration doctors them to fit its current platforms and promises." She shrugged again. "That's propaganda from another source, right? So what did happen, according to the official reports?"

"Plague, brought in by Haitian smugglers. And the water was going bad; salt intrusion destroyed the whole system. Four years of drought had aggravated everything. Then the biggest hurricane of the century hit and that was just too bloody much. Thirty thousand deaths. They never recovered."

She was shaking her head now. "You have the chronology all mixed up. First the drop in population, the exodus, then the plague. It was like that everywhere. First the population began to sag, and in industrialized nations that spelled disaster. Then flu strains that no one had ever seen before, and plague. There weren't enough doctors; plants had closed down because of a labor shortage. There was no defense. In the ten years before the epidemics, the population had dropped by twenty percent."

I didn't believe her, and she must have known it from my expression. She stood up. "I don't know what's in the water, Sax. It's crawling with things that I can't identify, but we pretend that they belong and that they're benign. And God help us, we're the ones teaching the new generation. Let's swim."

Lying on my back under the broiling sun, I tried again to replay the scene with my boss. Nothing came of it. He hadn't told me why he was sending me to Miami. Report back. On what? Everything you see and hear, everything they all do. For the record. Period.

Miami hadn't been the first city to be evacuated. It had been the largest up to that time. Throughout the Midwest, the far west, one town, one city after another had been left to the winds and rains and the transients. No one had thought it strange enough to investigate. The people were going to the big cities where they could find work. The young refused to work the land. Or agribusiness had bought them out. No mystery. Then larger cities had been emptied. But that was because of epidemics: plague, flu, hepatitis. Or because of government policies: busing or open housing; or the loss of government contracts for defense work. Always a logical explanation. Then Miami. And the revelation that population zero had been reached and passed. But that had to be because of the plagues. Nothing else made any sense at all. I looked at Corrie resentfully. She was dozing after our swim. Her body was gold-brown now, with highlights of red on her shoulders, her nose, her thighs. It was too easy to reject the official reasons, especially if you weren't responsible for coming up with alternative explanations.

"I think they sent you because they thought you would come back," Corrie said, without opening her eyes. "I think that's it." She rolled on her side and looked at me.

"You know with Trainor gone, maybe none of us will get back," I said.

"If we hug the shore we should make it, except that we have no gas."

I looked blank, I suppose. She laughed. "No one told you? He took the gas when he left. Or the snake that killed him drank it. I think he found a boat that would get him to the Bahamas, and he went. I suppose that's why he came, to get enough gas to cruise the islands. That's why he insisted on getting down by sail, to save what gas Evinson had requisitioned for this trip. There's no one left on the islands, of course."

I had said it lightly, that we might not get back, but with no gas, it became a statement of fact. None of us could operate the sail, and the boat was too unwieldy to paddle. The first storm would capsize us, or we would run aground. "Didn't Trainor say anything about coming back?"

"He didn't even say anything about leaving." She closed her eyes and repeated, "There's no one there at all."

"Maybe," I said. But I didn't believe there was, either. Suddenly, looking at Corrie, I wanted her, and I reached for her arm. She drew away, startled. They said that sun-spot activity had caused a decrease in sexual activity. Sporadically, with some of us. I grabbed Corrie's arm hard and pulled her toward me. She didn't fight, but her face became strained, almost haggard.

"Wait until tomorrow, Davidson. Please. I'll ovulate tomorrow. Maybe you and I . . ." I saw the desperation then, and the fear—worse, terror. I saw the void in her eyes, pupils the size of pinpricks in the brilliant light, the irises the color of the endless water beyond us. I pushed her away and stood up.

Don't bring me your fear, I wanted to say. All my life I had been avoiding the fear and now she would thrust it upon me. I left her lying on the beach.

Evinson was sick that night. He vomited repeatedly, and toward dawn he became delirious.

J.P. and I took turns sitting with him, because the women weren't strong enough to restrain him when he began to thrash about. He flung Corrie against the wall before we realized his strength and his dementia.

"He's dying, isn't he?" J.P. said, looking at him coolly. He was making a study of death, I thought.

"I don't know."

"He's dying. It might take a while, but this is the start of it." He looked at me fixedly for a long time. "None of us is going back, Sax. You realize that, don't you?"

"I don't know about the rest of you, but I'm going back. You're all a bunch of creepies, crazy as bedbugs, all of you. But I'm going back!"

"Don't yell." His voice remained mild, neutral, an androgynous voice without overtones of anything human at all.

I stamped from the room to get a beer, and when I got back, J.P. was writing in his notebook. He didn't look up again. Evinson got much worse, louder, more violent, then his strength began to ebb and he subsided, moaning fitfully now and then, murmuring unintelligibly. Corrie checked him from time to time. She changed the dressing on his hand; it was swollen to twice its normal size, the swelling extending to his shoulder. She looked at him as dispassionately as J.P. did.

"A few more hours," she said. "Do you want me to stay up with you?"

"What for?" I asked coldly. "I must say you're taking this well."

"Don't be sarcastic. What good would it do if I put on an act and wept for him?"

"You might care because he's a man who didn't deserve to die in this stinking city."

She shrugged. "I'll go on to bed. Call me if there's any change." At the doorway she turned and said, "I'll weep for myself, maybe even for you, Sax, but not for him. He knew what this would be like. We all did, except possibly you."

"You won't have to waste any tears for me. Go on to bed." She left and I said to J.P., "You all hate him, don't you? Why?"

J.P. picked up his pen again, but he hesitated. "I hadn't thought of it as hating him," he said thoughtfully. "I just never wanted to be near him. He's been trying to climb onto the glory train for years. Special adviser to presidents about urban affairs, that sort of thing. Absolutely no good at it, but very good at politics. He made them all think there was still hope. He lied and knew he lied. They used to say those that can do; those that can't teach. Now the saying goes, those that can't become sociologists." He put his pen down again and began to worry at a hangnail. His hands were very long and narrow, brown, bony with prominent knuckles. "A real scientist despises the pseudoscientist who passes. Something unclean about him, the fact that he could get permission for this when his part of it was certain to be negligible from the start."

"And yours was important from the start, I suppose?"

"For fifteen years I've wanted to get back into field research. Every year the funds dwindled more. People like me were put into classrooms, or let go. It really isn't fair to the students, you understand. I'm a rotten teacher. I hate them all without exception. I crammed and worked around the clock to get as good a background as I could, and when I was ready, I forced myself on Albert Lanier." He looked at me expectantly and I shook my head. Only later did I recall the name. Lanier had written many of the books on marine biology that were in the libraries. J.P.'s look became contemptuous. "He was a great man and a greater scientist. During his last years when he was crippled with rheumatoid arthritis, I was his eyes, his legs, his hands. When he died all field research died with him. Until now."

"So you're qualified for this work."

"Yes, I'm qualified. More than that fool." He glanced at Evinson, who was breathing very shallowly. "More than anyone here. If only my work is made known, this farce will be worth ten of him, of all of you."

"If?"

"If. Would any one of my own students know what I'm doing? My own students!" He bit the hangnail and a spot of blood appeared on his thumb. He started to scribble again.

At daybreak Evinson's fever started to climb, and it rose steadily until noon. We kept him in wet sheets, we fanned him, Corrie gave him cool enemas. Nothing helped. He died at one-thirty. I was alone with him. Corrie and Delia were both asleep.

J.P. knew when he looked at my face. He nodded. I saw his pack then. "Where the hell are you going?"

"Down the coast. Maybe down the Keys, as far as I can get. I'd like to see if the coral is coming back again."

"We leave here Saturday morning at dawn. I don't give a damn who's here and who isn't. At dawn."

He smiled mockingly and shook his head. He didn't say good-bye to anyone, just heaved his pack onto his back and walked away.

I rummaged on the *Loretta* and found a long-handled, small-bladed shovel, and I buried Evinson on the beach, above the high-water mark.

When I got back Corrie was up, eating a yellow fruit with a thick rind. I knocked it out of her hand reflexively. "Are you out of your mind! You know the local fruits might kill us." She had juice on her chin.

"I don't know anything anymore. That's a mango, and it's delicious. I've been eating the fruits for three days. A touch of diarrhea the first day, that's all." She spoke lightly, and didn't look at me. She began to cut another one.

"Evinson died. I buried him. J.P. left."

She didn't comment. The aromatic odor from the fruit seemed to fill the room. She handed me a slice and I threw it back at her.

Delia came down then looking better than she had in days. Her cheeks were pink and her eyes livelier than I had seen them. She looked at Corrie, and while she didn't smile, or do anything at all, I knew.

"Bitch," I said to Corrie bitterly. "Wait until tomorrow. Right. Bitch!"

"Take a walk, Sax," Delia said sharply.

"Let's not fight," Corrie said. "He's dead and J.P.'s gone." Delia shrugged and sat down at the table. Corrie handed her a piece of the mango. "Sax, you knew about me, about us. Whether or not you wanted to know, you did. Sometimes I tried to pretend that maybe I could conceive, but I won't. So forget it. What are you going to do?"

"Get the hell out of here. Go home."

"For what?" Delia asked. She tasted the slice of mango, then bit into it. She frowned critically. "I like the oranges better."

"These grow on you," Corrie said. "I've developed an absolute craving for them in the past three days. You'll see."

"I don't know about you," I said furiously, "but I'm leaving Saturday. I have things to do that I like doing. I like to read. To see a show now and then. I have friends."

"Are you married? Do you live with a woman? Or a man?" Delia asked.

I looked at Corrie. "We're in trouble. It'll take the three of us to manage the boat to get back. We have to make plans."

"We aren't going back," Corrie said softly. "We're going to the Seminoles."

"Corrie, listen to me. I've been out farther than either of you. There's nothing. Ruins. Rot. Decay. No roads. Nothing. Even if they existed, you'd never find them."

"There's the remains of the road. Enough for us to follow west."

"Why didn't you try a little bribery with me?" I yelled at her. "Maybe I would have changed my mind and gone with you."

"I didn't want you, Sax. I didn't think the Seminoles would want to take in a white man."

I left them alone for the rest of the day. I checked the *Loretta* again, swam, fished, gloomed. That night I pretended that nothing had been said about Seminoles. We ate silently.

Outside was the blackness and the silence, and somewhere in the silence a scream waited. The silence seemed to be sifting in through the mosquito netting. The wind had stopped completely. The air was close and very hot inside the building. "I'm going out," I said as soon as I finished eating.

Delia's question played through my mind as I walked. Did I live with a woman? Or a man? I stopped at the edge of the water. There were no waves on the bay, no sound except a gentle water murmur. Of all the people I knew, I could think of only three that I would like to see again, two of them because I had lived with them in the past, and our relationships had been exciting, or at least not abrasive, while they had lasted. And when they were finished, the ending hadn't been shattering. Two women, both gone from my life completely. One man, a coworker in my department. We did things together, bowled, swapped books, saw shows together. Not recently, I reminded myself. He had dropped out of sight.

A gust of wind shook me and I started back. A storm was coming up fast. The wind became erratic and strong, and as suddenly as the wind had started, the rain began. It was a deluge that blinded me, soaked me, and was ankle deep in the street almost instantly. Then, over the rain, I heard a roar that shook me through and through, that left me vibrating. A tornado, I knew, although I had never seen or heard one. The roar increased, like a plane bearing down on me. I threw myself flat, and the noise rocked the ground under me, and a building crashed to my left, then another, and another. It ended as abruptly as it had started.

I stumbled back to our building, shaking, chilled and very frightened. I was terrified that our building would be demolished, the women gone, dead, and that I would be alone with the silence and the black of the night.

Corrie opened the door on the first floor and I stumbled in. "Are you all right? It was a tornado, wasn't it?"

She and Delia were both afraid. That was reassuring. Maybe now they would be frightened enough to give up the nonsense about staying here. The storm abated and the silence returned. It didn't seem quite so ominous now.

"Corrie, don't you see how dangerous it would be to stay? There could be a hurricane. Storms every day. Come back with me."

"The cities will die, Sax. They'll run out of food. More epidemics. I can help the Seminoles."

Friday I got the *Loretta* ready for the return trip. I packed as much fruit as it would hold. Enough for three, I kept telling myself. Forbidden fruit. For three. I avoided Corrie and Delia as much as I could and they seemed to be keeping busy, but what they were doing I couldn't guess.

That night I came wide awake suddenly and sat up listening hard. Something had rattled or fallen. And now it was too quiet. It had been the outside door slamming, I realized, and jumped up from my bedroll and raced downstairs. No one was there, anywhere. They had left, taking with them Corrie's medical supplies, Delia's radiation kit, most of the food, most of the beer. I went outside, but it was hopeless. I hadn't expected this. I had thought they would try to talk me into going into the swamps with them, not that they would try it alone.

I cursed and threw things around, then another thought hit me. The *Loretta*! I ran to the dock in a frenzy of fear that they had scuttled her. But she was there, swaying and bobbing in the changing tide. I went aboard and decided not to leave her again. In the morning I saw that the sail was gone.

I stared at the mast and the empty deck. Why? Why for God's sake had they taken the sail?

They'll be back, I kept thinking all morning. And I'll kill them both. Gradually the thought changed. They would beg me to go with them inland, and I would say yes, and we would go into the first swamp and I would take their gear and leave them there. They would follow me out soon enough. They had needed the sail for a shelter, I thought dully. After noon I began to think that maybe I could go with them part of the way, just to help them out, prove to them that it was hopeless to go farther.

My fury returned, redoubled. All my life I had managed to live quietly, just doing my job, even though it was a stupid one, but getting paid and trying to live comfortably, keeping busy enough not to think. Keeping busy enough to keep the fear out. Because it was there all the time, pressing, just as the silence here pressed. It was a silent fear, but if it had had a voice, its voice would have been that scream we had heard. That was the voice of my fear. Loud, shrill, inhuman, hopeless. I felt clammy and chilled in the heat, and my stomach rejected the idea of food or drink.

Come back, I pleaded silently, willing the thought out, spreading the thought, trying to make contact with one of them. Come back for me. I'll go with you, do whatever you want to do. Please!

That passed. The storm came, and I shivered alone in the *Loretta* and listened to the wind and the pounding rain. I thought about my apartment, work, the pamphlets I wrote. The last one I had worked on was titled: "Methods of Deep Ploughing of Alluvial Soils in Strip Farming in Order to Provide a Nutritionally Adequate Diet in a Meatless Society." Who was it for? Who would read past the title? No one, I answered. No one would read it. They were planning for a future that I couldn't even imagine.

The silence was more profound than ever that evening. I sat on deck until I could bear the mosquitoes no longer. Below, it was sweltering, and the silence had followed me in. I would start back at first light, I decided. I would have to take a smaller boat. A flat-bottomed boat. I could row it up the waterway, stay out of the ocean. I could haul it where the water was too shallow or full of debris.

The silence pressed against me, equally on all sides, a force that I could feel now. I would need something for protection from the sun. And boiled water. The beer was nearly gone. They hadn't left me much food, either. I could do without food, but not without water and maps. Maybe I could make a small sail from discarded clothing. I planned and tried not to feel the silence. I lectured myself on synesthesia—I had done a pamphlet on the subject once. But the silence won. I began to run up the dock, screaming at Corrie and Delia, cursing them, screaming for them to come back. I stopped, exhausted finally, and the echo finished and the silence was back. I knew I wouldn't sleep; I built a fire and started to boil water.

I poured the water into the empty beer bottles and stacked them back in their original boxes. More water started to boil, and I dozed. In my near sleep, I heard the scream again. I jumped up shaking. It had been inhumanly high, piercing, with such agony and hopelessness that tears stood in my eyes. I had dreamed it, I told myself. And I couldn't be certain if I had or not.

Until dawn came I thought about the scream, and it seemed to me a thing uttered by no living throat. It had been my own scream, I thought, and I laughed out loud.

I loaded an aluminum rowboat the next day and rigged up a sail that might or might not fall apart when the wind blew. I made myself a poncho and a sun hat, and then, ready to go, I sat in the boat and watched some terns diving. They never had asked me what I had wanted to do, I thought bitterly.

Not one of them had asked me what I would have liked to have done.

J.P. had complained about being forced into teaching, while I would have traded everything I had for the chance to write, to teach—but worthless things, like literature, art appreciation, composition. A pelican began to dive with the terns, and several gulls appeared. They followed the pelican down, and one sat on his head and tried to snatch the fish from his mouth.

I thought again of all the pamphlets I had written, all the thousands of pages I had read in order to condense them. All wasted because in reducing them to so little, too much had been left out. I started to row finally.

When I left the mouth of the bay, I turned the small boat southward. The sea was very blue, the swells long and peaceful. Cuba, I thought. That many people, some of them had to be left. And they would need help. So much had been lost already, and I had it, all those thousands of pages, hundreds of books, all up there in my head.

I saw again the undersecretary's white, dry, dead face, the hurt there, the fear. He hadn't expected me to come back at all, I realized. I wished I could tell Corrie.

The wind freshened. If not Cuba, then Central America, or even South America. I put up my little sail, and the wind caught it and puffed it, and I felt only a great contentment.

Strangeness, Charm and Spin

*L*ate afternoon shadows striped the bright grass on the campus. Students in cutoffs, rolled-up jeans, sleeveless shirts, or no shirts lounged under the trees, or walked slowly, heads lowered. In the meadow by the duck pond other students were tossing frisbees lazily. Oblivious ducks glided, cutting points of arrows aimed at nothing in particular, in no hurry to arrive. Only the squirrels moved with energy and purpose on that unseasonably warm fall day; up trees, down, across swatches of lawn, vanishing among bushes, reappearing. Screening the parking lot from Hadley Hall was a row of shrublike filbert trees, convenience stores for generations of campus-bred-and-born squirrels that coexisted in fearless harmony with the students. The squirrels were plump, sleek, nourished by the same diet that fueled the young people; nuts, scraps of hamburgers, peanut butter sandwiches, apples, popcorn . . . The squirrels learned nothing; there was no need to scramble for the nuts, no need for the furious tail flicking as they competed for one among hundreds already on the ground, with thousands clinging to the trees, programmed to hang on until the first storm of the fall drove them to the soft earth, where the leaves would cover them swiftly and where, if nothing intervened, some would survive the winter, sprout, and eventually extend the row of filbert trees to a grove, then a forest, squirrel heaven.

Jeremy Seldon had arrived in class early enough to fill the blackboard with figures and diagrams, and then had watched the manic activity of the squirrels and had used the example of the filberts to start his lecture on waves of probability, the principle of indeterminacy. A good starting point, it had caught the attention of his class instantly. Now he found himself watching a squirrel race from branch to branch of a spruce tree outside the class window; it paused and gazed back at him, then whisked out of sight. Jeremy shook his head as he lost his chain of thought. The squirrel had looked directly at him, its cheeks so stuffed with nuts that it was like a caricature of itself. A child's concept of squirrel.

He turned again to his class, searching for the next word, unable to recall what his last word had been, his last thought. They waited unmoving; he glanced at his watch and felt a shock ripple through him, not unpleasantly, as if somewhere deep in his head a minute collision had taken place, two selves had merged, discharging energy. It was four-forty. The students continued to watch him, their expressions sharp with interest and concentration. Four-forty!

"I'm afraid I've run a little late," he said apologetically, and he had the impression that he had broken a spell. Now they began to shift, pick up books, look at their own watches, at each other, murmuring, chattering.

He walked home slowly, trying to remember his lecture, wondering if he had covered the material, knowing if he had not, a test would be unfair. Another essay test, he decided; make them tell him what he had said. He thought of the hours he would put in grading essays, and he scowled at the sidewalk, but found that he could not hold a scowl. His face kept coming apart in a silly grin. He knew his grins were silly; every snapshot Barbara took proved it over again. Lopsided, jack-o'-lantern toothy, he looked drunk when he smiled even a little, and a real grin made him look stoned to the limit. But hot damn, he kept thinking in elation, he had held the little bastards. English majors, art majors, history majors, today they had learned a little science.

He passed Lionel Hawley's house and wanted to thumb his nose. It had been a toss-up which of the two men would teach the new course, "Introduction to the Concepts of Physics," and in parentheses, the next phrase that made it a thankless task: "For nonscience majors." Ted Hawley and another boy were tossing a football back and forth in the driveway. He waved, and Ted heaved the ball to him; he dropped his briefcase, caught the ball and threw a good straight pass back to the boy, who missed.

At his own house he picked up Enid's bike in the middle of the drive and parked it against the garage. The front door was standing open, the screen door not quite closed.

"Hello, hello!" he yelled, closing both doors.

In the foyer there was a small table, where he deposited his briefcase; a closet, stairs down to the family room and his study, a doorway to the living room, and a hall entrance to the back of the house. Dust had collected on the table, and the parquet floor needed a good cleaning and waxing. Mail was in disarray on the table, Enid's backpack was leaning against it. The door to the living room was closed; that room was always ready for company, because no one ever went in there unless with company.

"Anybody home?" he yelled louder.

"Dad! Please, I'm on the phone." Enid appeared at the bottom of the stairs to the family room and scowled at him. She was thirteen, her hair was in strange rollers that stood out in all directions, and something terrible had happened to her eyes. They were smudged, as if she had two black eyes and enough time had elapsed since breakfast for the bruises to appear.

"She's experimenting with makeup," Barbara had explained. "Just pretend you don't notice."

He blinked and pretended hard. Enid vanished again into the family room and he went down the hallway to the kitchen. There were shoes on the stairs going to the bedrooms: his shoes and Enid's. Shoes in this house led a life of their own, appearing on stairs, under tables, by the sofa in the family room, sometimes even on the front porch. He thought it mysterious, without explanation. Actually many things tended to wander: tools never stayed put and scissors were more mobile than anything.

He made himself a drink in the kitchen and considered dinner. It was five-thirty; Barbara would have to work until eight, there was plenty of time. He moved the peanut butter and bread and jelly aside on the counter and began to assemble his own ingredients: jalapeños, onions, garlic, leftover pork roast . . .

"When's dinner?" Enid asked at the kitchen door.

"Eight-thirty."

"I won't be here."

He was on his knees searching for a can of tomatoes; he looked up at her. "Where are you going?"

"Skating with Patti and Doris."

"I thought you were grounded this weekend."

"Not for important things."

"That's not the way I remember it. All weekend, grounded."

"Why?"

"Ask your mother."

"You don't even know. It's so important you've forgotten."

"Anyway, you can't go out."

"But I already told them I could. And I washed my hair . . ."

He found the tomatoes and stood up. "Call back and tell them you can't."

"It isn't fair! You don't even know why!" She glared at him. "Whatever happened to making the punishment fit the crime?"

He found the salt and added it to the other things on the counter and started looking for the pepper mill.

"When you and Mother get divorced, I'm going to live with her!"

"That's a rotten thing to say."

"It's realistic. You're always telling me to be realistic, aren't you? Everybody gets divorced anymore. Women are tired of being slaves, second-class citizens. One day Mother will sashay right out of here, and I'll go with her!"

"Enid, let's fight later. Right now just tell me where is the goddamn pepper grinder."

"On the goddamn counter."

"This is what comes of treating brats like real people," he said coldly and saw the pepper mill behind the loaf of bread. "If all this gorp is yours, please put it away. I can't cook in such a mess."

"Everything in its place, all neat and orderly. Hah! Physicists! You built the atom bomb and now we'll go to war and use it and we'll all be put away all right."

"I wasn't even alive when they built the goddamn bomb!" He took a deep breath. "Besides I'm not a physicist in that sense. I don't *do* physics. I teach."

"Only because you couldn't get a job where they let you make bombs and things." She snatched up the bread and shoved it in the bread box, elbowed him out of the way, muttering, "Excuse me," in order to put the peanut butter in the cabinet and took the jelly to the refrigerator. Then she

went to the doorway and said, "You'd think a parent would
be glad his child wanted to do something physical, not just
lay around and smoke dope or something."

He was searching for the butcher knife and did not respond.

During the next half hour the phone rang three times and
each time Enid got it. He learned that he could not chop
vegetables, or mince the pork with a steak knife, or with a
serrated bread knife, and he found that they were out of
tortillas. He sat down with a second drink and stared at the
enchilada ingredients and wondered what else he could do
with them. The phone rang again.

He could browse through a cookbook; he eyed the wall
shelves where there were at least fifty, maybe sixty, cook-
books, not even counting the ones behind the glass doors, the
collectors' items. Barbara used all of them, from time to time,
but he always got bogged down and forgot a major ingredi-
ent, or was baffled by the methodology, or didn't have the
things called for, or something.

"Dad, Mother says I should go to the store and get milk
if you forgot it on your way home. Did you?"

"Yeah, guess I did. But I have to go anyway." He sipped
his bourbon and water.

"That's all right. I'll go. I called Patti and she'll go with
me. Anything besides milk?"

He looked at her without surprise at the mood change. It
was always like this with Enid. She had washed her face and
the curlers were gone. Her hair looked just the same as
always. He told her tortillas and gave her money and she
started out, then came back and said, "Anyway, if you really
wanted to work on bombs and stuff like that, you probably
could get a job doing it."

Alone again, he renewed his drink. She was in the cocoon
stage, he often thought. She had been a lovely pink worm,

soft and fuzzy and cuddly, and then one day she had come downstairs with strange machines in her hair and her eyes hideously made up and her mouth garish with near-purple lipstick—overnight she had metamorphosed. Sometimes she regressed and was the pretty little girl again, and sometimes he caught a glimpse of the woman she was turning into, but most of the time all that was visible were the layers of protective gadgets and paint.

Now, if only he had the goddamn knife, he brooded. His gaze landed on the blender and he pulled it out and started tossing jalapeños and onions into the container. He whirred them, added tomatoes, everything else except the meat. It turned into a lumpy, frothy, off-color glop. Just right, he decided, and dumped that into the skillet. He put in a chunk of meat and turned on the machine. It shredded the meat. He grinned and did the rest.

He had used the analogy of a thousand hunters with a thousand guns, he remembered suddenly. The waves of probability said that there would be a certain number of accidents even if the odds against any one hunter having an accident were very high. Any given class of one hundred students would probably lose from ten to eighteen percent by the end of the first quarter, even if no one had a method of selecting which ones would go. He had gone on to talk about radioactive decay and half-life.

"And we're not going to have another goddamn war!" he said and was surprised to hear his voice in the quiet kitchen.

His mishmash in the skillet had become very aromatic, and was bubbling furiously. He turned down the heat under it and put a lid on. Dessert, he thought. Something for dessert. He rummaged in the freezer and came out with a box of frozen strawberries and put it on the counter to thaw. Later he would make a salad, and that would be that.

He sat at the kitchen table to look over the evening paper and pushed it aside when he realized he was reading nothing.

He had to recreate the lecture, he thought with determination, in order to use it again. Not the same one, but the same kind of things he had gone into today. He would start taping his lectures, he decided, and remembered that he had made that decision before. Besides, he did not want them all, just the occasional ones when something clicked and it all came together like magic.

You can know where the particle is, or how fast it's moving, but not both. He scowled. That would hold them for a nanosecond. Enid had ears like a bat, he thought suddenly. Not a whisper escaped her, no matter how distant. How had she known he was thinking of applying for a job at Wendlow? She heard everything, knew everything, always had. Bratty kid. Her mouth was too big, too.

Enid came in with Patti, both talking at the same time, or so it seemed to his ears, but they always knew what the other was saying, and they knew how to interpret the giggles and the sighs and the wordless exclamations and the significant looks, all of which left him excluded.

"I got cream for the berries," Enid said, putting away the groceries. "And if I keep the change, then you'll only owe me four dollars and thirty cents for my allowance. We'll be watching television for a while. Okay?"

He didn't even bother to ask how she knew about the berries. She would simply give him one of her withering looks, inherited directly without alteration from her mother. The girls went out still talking.

You know it will fire, but never when, he thought; you know how much radioactivity a mass will lose, but not which atoms will decay. If you have a thousand silos and a thousand humans in charge, you know one of them will have an accident eventually . . .

He opened the newspaper to the comics and read them, then turned to the letters to the editor; some of his colleagues were in a running debate with an environmentalist group over the effects, or lack of effects, of low-level radiation. Nothing tonight. The letters were all about the possible registration of women into the armed services. A thousand women with a thousand guns . . . He closed the paper and went out to collect the mail from the foyer table. The girls were in the family room with the television and the stereo on, and they were talking. The front door was open.

Barbara had soft brown hair that fitted her head like a silky cap. Her eyes were brown, her skin tawny year round. He thought she was beautiful, more so now than when he had married her. That night when she came in, she was dirty, with dust in her hair, smudges on her arms, her nails dark with grime. "Hiram opened the Origami Room!" she exclaimed, washing at the kitchen sink. "It's like Aladdin's cave! You wouldn't believe the stuff in there that's been hidden away for fifty years or more. Hiram was ready to cry when he finally had to open the door. I think he said a prayer before he let any of us go in. Jack pretended he saw a silverfish and I thought Hiram would have a heart attack on the spot. I kicked Jack for it, probably bruised his leg. I hope so."

Barbara worked in the Special Collections department at the university library. Hiram was the department head. She went on talking about the newly opened room, Hiram, Jack's bruised leg, the new collection of original musical scores they were making room for, on and on, while Jeremy sprinkled cheese on the enchiladas and slid them under the broiler.

"No one even knew we had an origami collection, books, papers, folded objects, anything. Hiram never told anyone, I guess. When he dies what a field day it's going to be! He'll never retire. He's too afraid someone will try to get into one of those rooms, actually use one of the special collections. He was searching behind the books, under the windowsills, everywhere, hunting for silverfish . . ."

Jeremy called Enid to dinner. He asked if she had invited Patti.

"She ate hours ago," Enid said, bolting her food, "I told her I think it's romantic to wait this late, but she thinks it's dumb, and frankly so do I. We'll be in my room. She has to go home at eleven, in case we forget." Then, dramatically, she said, "We're discussing our plans for when they start drafting women. I think we'll go to Tahiti, or maybe Argentina. We're not sure which would be better."

"Whew! She's in a rare mood," Barbara said after Enid excused herself. "I was afraid she'd be in a snit."

"She's okay. Honey, were you terribly precocious when you were her age?"

"Of course. Weren't you?"

"No. I was backward, in fact. Not too bright, awkward, never sure of what I should say, so I usually didn't say much."

"Has she been picking on you again?" There was a glint of amusement in her eyes.

"She's only a kid," he said stiffly. "You want strawberries?"

"You bet, and lots of cream, and thick black coffee that will give me enough energy to get upstairs and into the tub. You wouldn't believe the dirt in those rooms that have been closed since year one. Today I breathed in the air that some great mastodon breathed out."

She helped him clear the table and load the dishwasher. If she saw the mess in the sink, on the counters, she did not show it. After she left to bathe, he cleaned up the rest of the kitchen. He did not turn on the dishwasher until she was finished with her bath, and he wished everyone else in the family remembered when he was the one in the shower or tub.

They sat in the family room watching a TV movie until Patti left at eleven to go across the street to her own house.

Enid came in to say good night; she kissed them both and gave Jeremy a little squeeze. She smelled like a perfume factory, and she had grown a bust since dinner. When she went up to bed, Barbara laughed.

"If you could see the expression on your face!"

"Falsies?"

"Size thirty-six, I'd say. I'll have a talk with her. I told Hiram I'd come in tomorrow at nine or a little later. You mind? We really do have to get those rooms straightened out and we can't do it during regular hours. An arsonist-student might get inside and play games, or something."

"Late again?"

"Oh no. We can go out to eat, if you'd like, or I can make something quick when I get home. About six probably, maybe a little before."

"I'll cook," he said. "No sweat."

"I'm going on to bed. You coming soon?"

"In a few minutes." He looked at her hopefully, but she was tired and he did not put much insistence in the look.

Presently he wandered to his study and sat down to make notes of the few things he had been able to remember about his lecture. Knowing the students were unfamiliar with the terms, probably had no math to speak of, and were terrified of math and science, he had hunted for similes they could grasp without trouble. Fleas, he thought in wonder. He had even talked about fleas.

They had secrets, they really did, he mused. Barbara understood Enid exactly and they shared something he could never know. He thought of Enid straining her robe with her size thirty-six falsies and he laughed out loud. Where had she found them? He didn't think they were being made any more. He moved the butcher knife that he had used to trim a linoleum block he was making, a stamp for his class of English majors dabbling in physics for the first time. The stamp was an atom—a miniature solar system with moons circling the planet, something they certainly were used to. He intended to use it on their final papers, and had already bought ink pads with different colors, red for excellence, blue for good, yellow for okay, green, so-so. Gray for dummy. He grinned and carved carefully, using his pocketknife. They'd like it, he thought; they'd get a kick out of it. As he carved, the rain began. He lifted his head, listening to it, his knife poised over the stamp. He hoped the campus squirrels were snug and dry. In his mind's eye he saw the filbert trees spreading their branches over new sprouts here and there.

The Dragon Seed

*B*ruce Enfield has a seat on the aisle and nowhere to put his elbows or his feet. Next to him is a woman with squatter's rights to the armrest, and in the aisle the stewardesses are hurrying back and forth, pushing their heavy carts, delivering drinks and peanuts. He huddles into himself hating it all, hating the rest of the day which will be just as bad with a two-hour wait in O'Hare, another cattle-car-in-the-sky to Portland, another two-hour delay, and finally the last lap, twenty minutes to Eugene, Oregon.

He is troubled because he is not certain why he is going back. Not to see *her,* he tells himself again, and he wishes he had taken the slim lucite piece from his pocket before he put his coat in the overhead bin. He will visit his parents, and an old friend or two, sleep and relax, and on Sunday afternoon make the rest of the trip to San Francisco, his actual destination. He will not see Cory. There is no reason to look her up; he is married, settled, rising in his world.

He twists and struggles to extract his wallet from his

197

pocket, gets a glare from his neighbor, and accepts his drink gratefully when the stewardess puts it before him. In his mind he is seeing Cory side by side with Beatrice, and that is embarrassing to him.

Cory in her jeans and heavy boots, caked with mud, a man's flannel shirt over a sweater, an unbuttoned, olive rain jacket over it all, her pale hair pulled back carelessly with a string or a rubber band. And Beatrice, elegant in a navy blue dressmaker suit, high heels, her nails and lips exactly the same shade of red, hair as soft and sweet as a baby's, kept in a style that flatters her delicate face and draws attention to her wonderfully made-up eyes. Beatrice has the loveliest eyes in the world, he thinks, and he finds he cannot summon an image of Cory's eyes. Pale lashes and brows, pale gray or blue eyes. The comparison of the two women is cruel, and again he feels embarrassed that he is making it. He gulps his scotch, and thinks of the lucite in his coat pocket, wishes he had it in his hand. He wants a cigarette although he has not smoked for almost a year. He thinks almost desperately that he has to have a cigarette, because in his head the comparison is continuing and he cannot stop it. Beatrice with her quick intelligence, her humor, her easy grasp of almost everything she reads or hears; and Cory, cowlike, if not clinically retarded, then so near that it makes little difference.

Whitman had put his ad in the paper on Sunday, and on Monday morning when he opened his door before seven to start work, she was there on the back doorstep. Whitman was a large muscular man in his late fifties, a widower for the last six years. To him Cory appeared an empty-faced child that bright morning.

"I've come for the job," she said.

"Worked in a nursery before?"

She shook her head. She was tall, strong enough, and the fact that she was there that early meant she wanted to work,

Whitman thought, studying her. "Where you live?" She told him, one of the subdivisions ten miles or more away. "How'd you get here?"

She pointed to a bicycle leaning against a tree, and he hired her. He would have to teach her everything, but then he always did, and come fall, they always left to go back to school and next year he had it to do over again.

He showed her how to take chrysanthemum cuttings and how to space and plant the pieces and mark them for a fall crop of blooming plants. She watched him silently, and then took over as if she had been doing it for years. He supervised for a short while before he went off to get his other tasks started; he came back from time to time to glance at her work. Neither of them spoke. At ten-thirty he told her she could have a break when she wanted it, that he didn't expect anyone to work straight through, he wasn't a slave driver. She listened as attentively as she had listened to his instructions about the cuttings and he realized that she could not distinguish between kidding and the straight goods. The tone he invariably took with his employees was either a brusque directive, or a banter that was meaningless; he knew no other way to address them. He stood looking at the girl kneeling in the bark mulch along the row of chrysanthemums, and he did not know how to speak to her. It was a mistake to hire her, he thought, and felt a stir of self-contempt as he realized he was shifting his own problem with communicating to her shoulders.

"When you get tired," he said, trying to soften his voice because she looked frightened, "go on over to the shed and get a drink, a coke or coffee. Rest a few minutes. Okay?"

She nodded and turned again to the chrysanthemums, began to cut fast.

"Cory, take it easy, girl. You're doing a fine job, the best of anyone I've hired starting as green as you. I don't expect you to finish all this in one day."

She looked at him again as if trying to measure his words, to test his truthfulness. And then she smiled, and he knew he had done right in hiring her. He walked away thinking about her smile, not that it made her pretty or anything like that, but it changed her. Her face was immobile, guarded, and then it began to soften a little, and very slowly, like the opening of a tight hard bud, the softening, relaxing continued until her whole face was transformed and was not protected at all.

During her lunch hour he saw her wandering over the nursery grounds, and he remembered that he had meant to show her around when he had time. There was always too much to do, not enough good people to get it done. Don, his brother and partner in the business, kept telling him to hire a full-time manager, but he resisted. He had tried that. No one else did anything his way, and his way was not the book way. He did things when they needed doing, not when the books said it was time. Only one man, Hank Valchak, might have worked out, but he had quit after a few years and opened his own nursery on the other side of Eugene. And meanwhile Whitman's Nursery was growing, business was expanding, and he, William Whitman, was a tired, over-worked man. At least he had nothing to do with the paper-work; that was Don's department; payroll, taxes, ordering, inventory, advertising, all that he cheerfully left to his brother, who in turn never set foot in one of the greenhouses, or the long rows of seedling trees and bushes and shrubs.

It was Don, filling in the employment records, who discovered that Cory had left home to go to school that day, and instead had come to the nursery. She had dropped out, he said, and only in the tenth grade.

Whitman tried to see Cory sitting quietly at a desk, immersed in history lessons, or math problems, and nothing came. He shrugged. "Her business," he said. But Don Whitman was concerned about it. He had three grown children and he knew teenagers sometimes did things their parents were ignorant of, until too late. He called Cory's mother that night and learned that Cory had a history of failing, and that the school counselor had advised a training school for her. The brothers dropped the subject and never referred again to it.

Cory's mother liked to go to her daughter's room on her day off from the bakery and just sit quietly a while. The room was not messy, the bed always neatly made; there was no scattering of books or records or clothes to offend the most fastidious housekeeper, but there were plants everywhere, in pots, coffee cans, milk cartons, rusty vegetable cans, Styrofoam cups . . . In here the light was soft and green, filtered through leaves at both windows.

A heavy rain was driving leaves from trees, marshaling them in untidy heaps. Mrs. Davenport had come in wet and cold from the weekly shopping and now sat drinking coffee, thinking nothing, content to smell the green smells of growing plants instead of cinnamon and vanilla and yeast. When the kitchen buzzer sounded, she got up and left the room and began to make supper. One day Raymond had come home to find her sitting in there and had raged all night at her, and, of course, at Cory. Sometimes when Mrs. Davenport came out of Cory's room she found that she had been weeping with no memory of the tears or the cause. Now that Cory had a good job and was doing well at it, there was no longer any reason to worry or cry over her, but still there were times when she wept.

If only Raymond could accept her, she thought at those times, that would make the difference, but he could not look at Cory without a shadow passing over his face, without his eyes narrowing, and a slight ridge forming along his cheek. Most times he avoided looking at her, and most times she stayed out of his way, out of his sight. Now that she was

working, they never even ate at the same time. He got home
at four-thirty and had his supper and Cory got in at six-
thirty, after he had settled in front of the television for the
rest of the evening.

Raymond was a good man, she thought as she peeled
carrots. He was a good man in all ways except with Cory.
From the start there had been something in her that drew out
the devil in him. Mrs. Davenport knew that one of those long
slow smiles from Cory was more important than hours of
giggles from other girls, but Raymond never had learned
that.

Tonight they would fight over their daughter, she knew,
stirring the meat and vegetables. Cory needed things, a new
sweater, new woolen socks, and he would act as if it were his
money. Each week Cory's check went to him, to be deposited
in the checking account where he guarded it jealously.

*How many years did we provide everything, ask nothing in
return?* he would yell, when her money was being argued. *Tell
me that! It's her turn to help. If she wants to keep her money,
let her move out! Once she's gone I don't give a damn what she
does.*

Sometimes Mrs. Davenport fantasized about moving out
with Cory, just the two of them sharing a small house with
a garden for Cory to work in. It was a pleasant reverie, but
it was frightening also, because she cared for Raymond; it
was only where Cory was concerned that he became a cruel
stranger. Sometimes Mrs. Davenport felt that on the day of
Cory's birth someone had planted a sharp knife in her skull
and day by day through the years had sliced downward a
little at a time, neatly dividing her into halves. She imagined
the knife was even with her heart by now, and that if she had
to make the decision about leaving with Cory, or driving
Cory away to be able to live with Raymond, the knife would
make the rest of the cut very fast.

*   *   *

Bruce Enfield has gone to the phone booth twice and each time has left it without placing the call to his friends in Chicago. He sits in a clattering coffee shop and stares out the window at fitful snow that looks dirty even before it hits the ground.

His friends would ask about Beatrice, and he does not want to talk about her, about his marriage. He sips his coffee, wishing he had gone to the bar; he hates coffee shops, the sights and smells of fried food and catsup, the foul coffee. The snow is stopping again; it is like the ash-fall they sometimes have in Savannah. He remembers standing at the glass wall of his house, close to Beatrice but not touching her as they watch the powdery ashes settle on the lawn, on the surface of the pool.

"Lovely," she says. "Your company?"

"No."

"Have you made an appointment with a doctor yet?" Still looking out the glass, pretending nonchalance, or actually feeling it—he no longer can tell which—she asks the question as if she were asking for the time.

"No."

A 747 rolls past the window and he watches until it is at home in its own bay and the caterpillar mouth has attached itself to the giant body.

He imagines the scene with the doctor: You say you have nightmares, Mr. Enfield. About what?

Dragons. They are chasing me, breathing flames, and I can feel the heat touching me, spreading, consuming me.

Dragons! Very interesting, Mr. Enfield.

He lights a cigarette and watches the tip, the smoke curling slightly at first, then ascending in a column until a draft hits it. He stubs out the cigarette and is mildly surprised to see four others already in the ashtray, all three-quarters intact.

Yesterday he changed his reservation, added this side trip to Eugene. Beatrice did not ask why. He wishes she would pretend to be interested, but understands that she won't play that game with him. From the start she refused games, then it did not matter because there was no game to play. But now . . . He hears again her indifference when she asked how long he would be gone. He can't remember if she acknowledged his answer, or even if he answered. It mattered so little, they both seemed to say.

Tell me about your mother, the doctor says, trying to hide a smile.

Not my mother. Not my father. It's Cory. And I can't tell you. Abruptly he stands up and snatches his check and hurries from the coffee shop. He can feel the hot breath on his back and he does not dare turn to look for fear he will see the dragon in daylight. He knows when that happens, he will be lost.

One morning Whitman woke up before daylight listening to sleet hit the roof. Drowsily he turned over, finding comfort in the steady pattering of icy feet while his own feet were warm. Then he sat up. Sleet. He switched on the radio before he reached for the light. They were already talking about the weather conditions: freezing rain throughout the valley, roads closed, schools closed . . .

He dressed, made coffee and eggs, and planned. He had to prune the two-year-old trees; he had it scheduled for early January as usual, but they would break under a load of ice. And cover the evergreens with plastic. And the balled and burlapped trees, and if he had time, get to the year old, dwarfed fruit trees . . . The radio was giving no comfort at all, not even trying to predict when the ice storm would pass, turn into ordinary rain, wash away the grief the ice always brought with it.

It was as dark as night when he was ready to go out and start what seemed to be a day of futile effort. The ice was already a quarter inch thick. For a moment he squinted in disbelief as he stared at the toolshed, brightly lighted. He hurried toward it; the gravel drive was already treacherous as ice smoothed out the irregularities.

"Cory! What the hell are you doing here?"

She ducked her head and mumbled and he drew closer to her.

"How'd you get here?"

Her mother had brought her, she said, on her way to work. She had heard the rain and knew it would turn to ice. He stared at Cory for another moment, and then they went to work. Together they pruned the trees and covered the evergreens and got to the grafted trees . . . By late afternoon they had it all done, everything they could do to protect the nursery stock. In exhaustion Whitman made his way to the house, motioning her to follow. He envied her young strong body, her stamina, but even she was tired by then, and hungry, and half frozen. Their outer coats were covered with ice; ice was an inch thick on everything in sight. It had stopped falling an hour earlier, but the temperature had dropped throughout the day; there would be no thaw until the wind changed. At the door of the house Cory stopped and looked at the magic world and she smiled her rare smile. Whitman nodded. It was truly beautiful, but he was too cold and tired to smile.

He made coffee and got steaks from the deep freeze and made a fire in the fireplace. They both sat very close to it, driven back gradually as the flames went from orange-yellow to blue. Neither talked. When Whitman felt himself drifting off in a doze he roused and went out to make their dinner. The telephone lines were down, and the radio was nothing but chatter about the ice storm and its consequences. Nothing was moving. Whitman sighed. She would have to spend the night, he thought gloomily, and there might be talk. No one else had been able to get to the nursery that day, and he had not talked to his brother, who probably was iced in. Who would ever know? He pushed the thought aside and went about making dinner methodically, the way he did everything.

And he wondered about Cory. She always knew about the weather; no matter what it did, she was dressed for it, or had clothes to change into. Today she had brought rain pants and heavy enough clothes to get by on an Arctic expedition. When they had come in, she had gone into the bathroom and stripped off a layer or two, and had come out dry and clean. She never lost plants to a drought or had them rot in a week of steady rain. She knew.

She could not handle money, or work the cash register, or take an order, or talk to a customer. She seldom talked to the other employees and never joked with them; she managed to take her lunch break after the others were back at work. Sometimes in good weather, she took her sack lunch out under one of the walnut trees and ate there alone, out of touch. She had not missed a day in a year and a half, never had a cold, an ache, a complaint. In fact, he had had to tell her she could not work seven days a week; it was the only thing he ever had to tell her more than once. And when he had tried to pin her down about her vacation, she had said sullenly that she had nowhere else to go, nothing else to do, and if she couldn't work, she would just sit under the trees and watch.

A few days later when everything was back to normal he told his brother he was raising Cory's salary.

"Why? You know her father gets her money."

"You been telling me for years I should hire myself another Hank Valchak, another manager. I been realizing more and more that she's it. She does more than Hank ever did. And we set up a trust and don't tell her daddy. When this goes," he said, motioning vaguely toward the grounds, the greenhouses, everything, "what's going to become of a girl like her? Set it up, Don."

Don Whitman was sixty-three and had begun to talk about training his own replacement one of these years. Whitman would be sixty in the fall of that year. Soberly they nodded at each other and it was done, the trust fund was established; Cory became the highest paid employee of the enterprise.

Bruce Enfield tries to remember if he ordered chicken or the seafood casserole. He cannot tell by tasting which one he has. He is on a DC-10 this time, seated by a window in the smoking section. The plane is two-thirds filled, service is prompt and efficient; already he has had two drinks, and after he finishes his meal, there will be plenty of time for several more. He wishes he had spaced out the drinks. High in the sky, he thinks, but his drunks are not highs, they are cellar-lows, tomb-lows, Dene hole-lows.

Beatrice travels more often than he does; she is an assistant buyer for a department store, and her trips are to New York, Paris, London, even Hong Kong. She will not consider a DC-10, and this is the first time in several years that he did not ask about his carrier, change his schedule, if necessary, to avoid this particular aircraft.

The food is taken away and presently a mellow voice suggests that the window seat passengers pull down their blinds in order to view the movie. He pulls down his blind and closes his eyes and remembers when he went to work for Whitman.

His master's degree was assured by the spring break, and in the fall he would report to MIT for the eighteen-month grind toward his Ph.D. That was already assured also; his project had been accepted, the execution would be a matter of putting in the time it took to do the designing, the drawings, the mockups . . . He was a chemical engineer specializing in plant design; there was a great need for him and the too

few others like him. Eighteen months from the day he
started, he would be finished, accepted, on his way.

What he wanted for that summer was an outdoor job that
required muscles and no mind. He found it at Whitman's.
The old man asked few questions, put him and Frank Fred-
rickson to work the day they applied.

"Cory, show these two fellows how to ball up the roses,"
Whitman called. Across the drive, near a shed, a girl nodded
and motioned to them to follow her. She was tall and could
have passed for a young man, bundled up as she was in jacket
and boots and gloves. It was a cold March day, misty, with
more rain threatened any minute.

Bruce and Frank exchanged a glance and followed her.
She went inside the shed and waited for them. Her directions
were terse, almost mumbled, and she did not look at them
directly.

Within a few minutes they all walked toward the rows of
roses, pulling long wagons. On hers there was a box with
labels, a stack of wooden flats, clipping shears, scissors;
Bruce's had a stack of burlap squares, a large box of wet
sawdust, a spool of wire, and wire cutters, and Frank's had
the spade and fork. The work was mindless enough, Bruce
decided quickly. Cory moved on ahead of them pruning the
roses that they then dug out and balled up in little bundles
with the roots packed in dirt and sawdust. The roses came
out easily; Bruce learned later that they had been root-
pruned twice to force them to make a compact root system,
easy to dig, easy to transplant, almost guaranteed to suffer no
shock when moved. He found himself watching the girl as she
left them behind. Her hands were so quick it was hard to
follow exactly what she was doing. First she seemed to feel
the rose bush, and then she clipped it so fast that he could not
tell what she looked for, how she determined what needed
cutting, what needed saving. Some of the cuttings fell around
the plants, to be cleaned up later by one of the younger boys;

some of them she kept until she had a bundle that she tied together and labeled. Her cuttings always grew, he learned that spring and summer. The more she cut, the more plant stock they seemed to have.

After a while she came back to Bruce and Frank to inspect their work. She shook her head over several of the burlaped roses and pointed to one she had done to demonstrate the procedure. It was a plump little package, neatly tied off with a wire. The ones she singled out were thin, scrawny. She told them to do theirs over and returned to her own task.

Frank watched her walk away. "And how did you spend your day? Balling roses." He laughed. "I'm going to be in her pants within two weeks, wanta bet?"

"Her? But she's a . . . ."

"A dummy? Sure, she is. They make the best lays. They're grateful, you know? And they don't tell. They do what you want them to do. Two weeks. I'll let you know how she is. A side bet. She's a virgin. Am I on?"

Bruce was revolted by the idea of taking a girl like her, revolted by Frank's easy appraisal, his experienced air. That winter Bruce had met Beatrice Langley, and although he looked at other girls, she was the one he always saw. The thought of groping a tall, frozen-faced, slow-witted girl like Cory was sickening.

Somehow Cory kept eluding Frank all spring. She was not where he expected to find her, or a third person entered when he thought he had her alone, or something else happened. He told Bruce that he had the place picked out, back behind the last greenhouse, the one they called Cory's trial greenhouse. A grove of holly trees had grown up behind it and Whitman had ordered them left alone; he liked them there. The holly trees hid the spot Frank had in mind, and no one ever bothered Cory when she went back to her own greenhouse. That was where she got strange grafts to take, where she hand-pollinated flowers to get new colors, new varieties. No one knew what all she did there because no one ever asked.

"Leave her alone," Bruce said sharply. "She doesn't bother anyone."

But he knew she did bother Frank. A frown from her was enough to make anyone have to do a day's work over again, and her a dummy, second in charge of a million dollar operation. Frank resented her; more, he feared her, because if a retard could go up like that in a couple of years, where did it leave someone like him? It wasn't right, he said; Whitman treated her like some kind of special royalty, excusing her from anything she didn't want to do, things she couldn't do that any normal eight-year-old could handle.

One day Frank grinned at Bruce and motioned for him to look at something. It was an envelope. Frank opened it carefully and showed Bruce.

"Seeds," he said triumphantly. "She can't talk about movies, or books, or television, anything. All she knows is plants. I have the ultimate weapon, my friend."

"What are they?"

"Damned if I know. My old man brought them back from Africa ten, fifteen years ago. They've been around the house ever since. Last night I remembered them and knew I had her."

Bruce thought so too. He had an impulse to knock the envelope out of Frank's hand, to grind the seeds into the earth, to yell out to Cory to hide, to run away. It was none of his business, he reminded himself, and went back to work.

It was late afternoon when Frank wandered over to Cory's greenhouse. Bruce watched him helplessly and slowly followed, knowing he would not interfere. He wished a storm would come up, lightning hit the greenhouse, set fire to the holly grove. At the screened door he stopped and listened.

"I knew you'd be the only one to plant them," Frank was saying. "See that black one? It's almost like a stone, isn't it?

And those little ones in the glassine envelope, they're more like grains of dust than seeds. And that red one. That must be the dragon seed."

Her voice did not carry enough for Bruce to make out her words.

Frank laughed. "Sure they did. Where do you think dragons came from? Two ways, seeds like that, and their own teeth. When you grow one, you save the teeth and plant them, too. They'll grow. You want to borrow my book about dragons?"

Bruce could no longer choose to move or not to move. He was as cold, as rigid as stone, without will as he listened to Frank's voice, then the wordless murmur that was her voice, Frank's voice again, like a snare drawing tighter and tighter before the victim ever had a chance to suspect its presence. He was moving her toward the back door, saying what a wonderful surprise she would have for Mr. Whitman when the seeds sprouted. Then he was talking about how much the seeds cost, how he had been willing to pay so much because he liked her, and wanted her to like him. Bruce could imagine his hands on her now, her bewilderment.

"When a man likes a girl, and she likes him, it's the most natural thing in the world to show each other."

Bruce never saw him coming, but suddenly Whitman was there, entering the greenhouse. "Cory, you run along home now." His voice was low and easy, the way he always spoke to her. She ran from the greenhouse clutching the envelope, ran to her bicycle and sped away. "You, you piece of shit! Get your gear and clear out and don't come back."

"You've got no right, Mr. Whitman. I wasn't going to hurt her."

"You say another word and I'm going to whip you. Get out!"

Frank came out blinking in the bright sunlight. He called

over his shoulder, "She's got free will, doesn't she? I was going to give her a good time, a little fun, that's all."

Bruce hurried back to the new greenhouse where he was supposed to be caulking windows. The next day when he met Whitman, he saw contempt on the old man's face.

Bruce opens his eyes in order to stop seeing that look. It is still there.

August heat lay over the land like someone opened the door to hell, Whitman thought, pulling up in the driveway of the Davenport house. He was not sure what he would say to Mrs. Davenport, but he had to say something, let her know Cory was vulnerable. All summer he had worried about this, pondered what he should do, what he could do, and finally he had got in his truck and started out to do something, but he still did not know what.

Mrs. Davenport was slightly built, pretty; she looked frightened, the same look that Cory got now and then. "Is anything wrong?" she asked.

"No, I didn't mean to scare you like that. I just dropped in to . . . make sure they did a good job with the greenhouse. Been meaning to check it out for months. Too busy."

She relaxed and admitted him to the house. It was cooler inside than out; the drapes were closed and a fan moved the air. Whitman had never been here before; he was surprised for a reason he could not put a name to. He had expected poverty, maybe, and this was middle-class nice. Cory dressed as if every penny had to be weighed. The house was clean without being antiseptic; there were bookshelves, and a stereo, and an oversized television. No plants, he noticed, with disappointment.

In Cory's room he nodded; this was what he had expected. The greenhouse had been built next to her room, a door led to it. A miniature rose in full bloom, each perfect yellow blossom smaller than a fingertip; half a dozen hanging orchids enclosed in plastic bags to conserve moisture during this hot dry weather; a bench covered with pots of blooming flowers—lobelias, begonias, a bronze-leaved geranium in bud . . .

He looked at the joints of the greenhouse, and peered at the lights, the heater, while Mrs. Davenport hovered in the doorway. There was room for only one in here.

"Looks fine," he said then. "Just fine. She's enjoying it, isn't she?"

"You've been awfully good to her," Mrs. Davenport said. "I've wanted to thank you, but . . ."

"She earned it," he said brusquely. "She saved my business last winter. She's a good worker, the best one I've got."

Mrs. Davenport nodded. "She's good with plants."

"With plants," he agreed, and now they looked at each other.

She knew he had come to tell her something, to ask her something, to warn her . . . She felt the knife in her chest come alive, waiting.

And he found he could not bring any more torment to this woman. He sighed. She had done the best she could. Maybe she had even talked to Cory about boys, about drugs, about sex. If she hadn't, and if he brought up any of it now, she would know something had happened, something that forced him to come here. He took a deep breath and smiled at her and, using the voice he used with Cory, he said, "She's a good girl, Mrs. Davenport. You've done a good job with her."

The next day he talked to Cory himself. What he said, quickly, almost roughly, was, "If any guy around here bothers you, you come tell me first thing. Understand?" It was all he could do.

For his sixtieth birthday that fall Cory gave him the bronze-leaved geranium; it had yellow flowers. "I'll be damned!" he said huskily. "I'll just be damned!" They would

have to name it, protect the seeds as if they were Christ's
tears, see if they came true . . . He looked from the plant to
Cory and her smile brought tears to his eyes.

A steady rain is falling in Portland. Bruce stands before a
glass wall and watches the water on the tarmac. Today is like
a repeat of his last trip home, it was raining that day too; he
had the same flights, stood in this same spot. That day, he
wanted to sing and dance all through the terminal, tell every
stranger that he had his Ph.D., and a job, and a fiancée
. . . The standing water has an oil swirl that twists and turns,
separates, recombines; it has a violet sheen that changes to
blue, green . . .

He drove to all the places he had known, hiked some
muddy trails, swilled beer at the old bars, saw a couple of his
old girlfriends—just for a drink, or lunch, nothing more. He
was too full of Beatrice for anything more. They were already
living together, and in one month they would be married and
move to Savannah.

He stands at the glass wall watching the rain, the uneasy
standing water, fingering the lucite piece in his pocket. If only
this could be that day, the intervening time a bad dream. He
remembers.

He had no intention of going into the greenhouses, or onto
the property, it was simply an act of finishing up the past that
took him to Whitman's that Saturday. He wanted to say
good-bye to all the past, the good and the bad. He drove by
slowly, waved, and left that part of his life for good.

A mile or two from the nursery he saw Cory pushing her
bicycle on the shoulder of the road. He knew it was she as
soon as the figure emerged from the rain and mist and became human, not just a shadow. He slowed down, passed
her, then stopped on the shoulder and got out.

"Hey, Cory, remember me? I used to work at Whitman's."

She stopped, then came on toward him, and said hello. She

was encased in a long green poncho with a hood pulled down nearly to her eyes.

"What happened? You have an accident?" The rain was cold and steady, already soaking through his sweater, into his shoes. He remembered the day she had taught them how to ball up the roses; it had rained that afternoon.

She shook her head and pointed to the front tire, which was flat.

"Let's put the bike in the station wagon and I'll give you a ride home."

As soon as he spoke, he was afraid she would remember that other day, connect him with Frank, but she did not hesitate. She nodded and wheeled the bicycle toward the station wagon. They put it in, she sat in the passenger seat, and he got in and started to drive, and he searched for something to talk about. "You'll have to direct me," he said, glancing at her. She looked ahead with no sign of unease.

She directed him, he assumed, the same way she rode her bike to work, through back streets, secondary roads with deep potholes, and no traffic. Because she waited until they were at the corners where he had to turn, he slowed down again and then again. The wagon grated sickeningly as the left rear wheel sank into a hole. Again he looked at Cory; she had not changed her position or expression. Damn her eyes, he thought, twisting the steering wheel hard, creeping along.

"You ever plant those funny seeds Frank gave you?" he asked.

She nodded.

He had to drag it out of her. One was a banana plant, there was a fuzzy bush that was too young to flower yet, maybe a tree, she didn't know. And one was a dragon plant, with a red dragon flower.

"You're kidding."

She remained silent until they had to turn again, and suddenly they were at her house. "You want to see it?" she asked.

He wanted to get away from her, never see her again, never think of her again, but he found himself nodding. She led him through the house; no one else was there, but lights were on, as if her parents would be back soon. She took him to her room, through it to the small greenhouse, and pointed to a bushy plant with a single red flower and many tiny buds.

He went closer and looked at it curiously, just a red flower. Pretty, and unusual, but no more than that. The air in the greenhouse, in her bedroom, was spicy, sharp, and clean. Beyond the glass walls, over his head against the glass ceiling, the rain was beating, running down crazily; the world was gray, and in here the light was green, there was a stillness. He turned abruptly from the greenhouse and looked at Cory who was standing inside the doorway in her room. He started to say it was just a flower, but he said nothing; he found he did not want to break the silence.

He reached out and touched her cheek, and a look of terror crossed her face. He wanted to shout, for God's sake, you don't have to be afraid of me! His hand left her cheek and went to her shoulder, and she was moving backward, he was following, now with his hands on both her shoulders, and he knew she was not going to stop him, and he was not going to stop himself. He fumbled with her clothes and his own and then he was atop her and she was moaning, then keening. And he heard a voice crying, "Oh, my God! Oh my God Oh my God . . ." and finally realized it was his own voice.

When it was over, he pushed himself away from her. She was staring dry eyed at the ceiling. He grabbed his jeans and ran to the bathroom he had seen on their way in. He slammed the door and leaned against it shaking, and again he heard his strange, thick voice: "Oh, my God! Oh, my God!"

When he returned to the bedroom she was not there. He looked in the greenhouse, but it was empty. He hesitated, then pulled the bloom from the dragon plant and left.

Sitting in the plane, waiting for take-off, he watches the rain running crazily down the window and he realizes at last what he has come back for. He has to give the dragon flower back to her. He has to face her and make her take it back. He looks at his hand and slowly opens it and stares at the lucite slab with a red flower embedded in it. She has to take it back, he says to himself.

Mrs. Davenport had to tell him; she couldn't make such a terrible decision by herself. For days she put it off, trying to think her way out of it, trying to will Cory back to normal, but it was no use, and finally she knew she had to tell him. They could take Cory away for a week or two, a vacation, they would say, and have it aborted. People did it every day.

He turned ashen and a low wordless cry came from his tightly clamped lips. He rushed to Cory's room and banged the door closed. Mrs. Davenport heard crashes, glass breaking. She sat rocking back and forth on a kitchen chair, clutching her head, her arms tight over her ears. When Cory came home, he pulled Mrs. Davenport away from the door and stormed out to meet Cory at the back of the house where she was parking her bicycle. He grabbed it in both hands and hurled it through the last standing wall of her greenhouse. Cory stared, then turned around and walked away. Raymond held Mrs. Davenport's arm and would not let her run after their daughter.

It was nearly ten when Cory knocked on Whitman's door. He opened it and stood back for her to come in.

"What is it, Cory? What happened?"

She told him and they looked at each other. Whitman nodded and motioned for her to go into the living room.

"You have anything to eat yet?" She shook her head, and now he could see the fatigue hunching her shoulders, drawing lines under her eyes. "Sit down, Cory. I'll get something hot for you." She followed him to the kitchen and sat at the table while he heated up leftover pot roast. She was waiting for him to tell her what to do, where to go. They would have it aborted, he thought, and he knew they must not do that, not to Cory.

It is only late afternoon when Bruce arrives at the nursery. It seems impossible for such a long day to go on and on and never turn into night, as this one has done. Everything looks exactly the same, as if this little pocket of the universe knows nothing of time and change.

He sees Whitman crossing the drive between the toolshed and the boiler house, and he starts to go to him. He has to see Cory alone, have a private talk with her, maybe in Whitman's house. He cannot talk to her while she's on her knees pruning roses, or potting up marigolds, or some damn thing. He draws nearer to Whitman who looks the same, maybe even more vigorous than before, less tired. Bruce starts to call him, then stops as a woman comes from around the potting shed, pulling one of the long wagons. A small boy is sitting on the wagon, trying to drag his feet on the ground. He is too short to reach.

"Cory!" he says; his voice is a whisper that no one can hear, but she stops and looks at him and her smile vanishes, leaving him feeling chilled.

The boy jumps from the wagon and runs across the drive to the boiler house, yelling, "Hey, Dad, we've got to go in now. Momma says it's going to rain real hard."

"You always knew," Bruce whispers, looking at her. She has not moved. His legs are heavy, his feet leaden, as he stumbles back to the rented car and gets in.

The rain starts as he drives back to his parents' house. It

is a hard, pounding rain that the windshield wipers cannot control. He is forced to pull off the road and wait for the rain to let up, he is driving blind. Only after he stops does he realize that he is weeping. He puts his forehead on the steering wheel and listens to the rain. His son, the son that Beatrice will never have. He hears her voice through the rain, "We can't go on like this, you know. If it isn't physical, it's psychological. It's that simple. You have to see a doctor."

I have nightmares, Doctor. About dragons. Always about dragons. And it isn't fair. It worked out for her, she's happy.

Mr. Enfield, now that you know she's happy, perhaps you won't need to torture yourself with guilt. Perhaps that is why you went back, to make amends, and you found none are needed.

He groans and starts the car. He won't see a doctor, he knows. There is no way he can ever explain.

"Bruce, what happened? It used to be so good with us. What happened?"

Cory happened, he thinks, and he feels the breath of the dragon on his back, in his chest, in his loins.

Forever Yours, Anna

nna entered his life on a spring afternoon, not invited, not even wanted. Gordon opened his office door that day to a client who was expected and found a second man also in the hallway. The second man brought him Anna, although Gordon did not yet know this. At the moment, he simply said, "Yes?"

"Gordon Sills? I don't have an appointment, but . . . May I wait?"

"Afraid I don't have a waiting room."

"Out here's fine."

He was about fifty, and he was prosperous. It showed in his charcoal-colored suit, a discreet blue-gray silk tie, a silk shirtfront. Gordon assumed the rest of the shirt was also silk. He also assumed the stone on his finger was a real emerald of at least three carats. Ostentatious touch, that.

"Sure," Gordon said and ushered his client inside. They passed through a foyer to his office-workroom. The office section was partitioned from the rest of the room by three rice-paper screens with beautiful Chinese calligraphy. In the office area were his desk and two chairs for visitors, his chair, and an overwhelmed bookcase, with books on the floor in front of it.

Their business only took half an hour; when the client left, the hall was empty. Gordon shrugged and returned to his office. He pulled his telephone across the desk and dialed his former wife's number, let it ring a dozen times, hung up.

He leaned back in his chair and rubbed his eyes. Late afternoon sunlight streamed through the slats in the venetian blinds, zebra light. He should go away for a while, he thought. Just close shop and walk away from it all until he started getting overdraft notices. Three weeks, he told himself, that was about as long as it would take.

Gordon Sills was thirty-five, a foremost expert in graphology, and could have been rich, his former wife had reminded him quite often. If you don't make it before forty, she had also said, too often, you simply won't make it, and he did not care, simply did not care about money, security, the future, the children's future . . .

Abruptly he pushed himself away from the desk and left the office, went into his living room. Like the office, it was messy, with several days' worth of newspapers, half a dozen books, magazines scattered haphazardly. To his eyes it was comfortable looking, comfort giving; he distrusted neatness in homes. Karen had most of the furniture; he had picked up only a chair, a couch, a single lamp, a scarred oak coffee table that he could put his feet on, a card table and several chairs for the kitchen. And a very good radio. It was sufficient. Some fine Japanese landscapes were on the walls.

The buzzer sounded. When he opened the door, the prosperous, uninvited client was there. He was carrying a brushed suede briefcase.

"Hi," Gordon said. "I thought you'd left."

"I did, and came back."

Gordon admitted him and led him through the foyer into

the office, where he motioned toward a chair and went behind his desk and sat down. The sunlight was gone, eclipsed
by the building across Amsterdam.

"I apologize for not making an appointment," his visitor
said. He withdrew a wallet from his breast pocket, took out
a card, and slid it across the desk. "I'm Avery Roda. On
behalf of my company I should like to consult with you
regarding some correspondence in our possession."

"That's my business," Gordon said. "And what is your
company, Mr. Roda?"

"Draper Fawcett."

Gordon nodded slowly. "And your position?"

Roda looked unhappy. "I am vice-president in charge of
research and development, but right now I am in charge of
an investigation we have undertaken. My first duty in con-
nection with this was to find someone with your expertise.
You come very highly recommended, Mr. Sills."

"Before we go on any further," Gordon said, "I should tell
you that there are a number of areas where I'm not interested
in working. I don't do paternity suits, for example. Or em-
ployer-employee pilferage cases."

Roda flushed.

"Or blackmail," Gordon finished equably. "That's why
I'm not rich, but that's how it is."

"The matter I want to discuss is none of the above," Roda
snapped. "Did you read about the explosion we had at our
plant on Long Island two months ago?" He did not wait for
Gordon's response. "We lost a very good scientist, one of the
best in the country. And we cannot locate some of his paper-
work, his notes. He was involved with a woman who may
have them in her possession. We want to find her, recover
them."

Gordon shook his head. "You need the police then, private detectives, your own security force."

"Mr. Sills, don't underestimate our resolve or our resources. We have set all that in operation, and no one has been able to locate the woman. Last week we had a conference during which we decided to try this route. What we want from you is as complete an analysis of the woman as you can give us, based on her handwriting. That may prove fruitful." His tone said he doubted it very much.

"I assume the text has not helped."

"You assume correctly," Roda said with some bitterness. He opened his briefcase and withdrew a sheaf of papers and laid them on the desk.

From the other side Gordon could see that they were not the originals, but photocopies. He let his gaze roam over the upside-down letters and then shook his head. "I have to have the actual letters to work with."

"That's impossible. They are being kept under lock and key."

"Would you offer a wine taster colored water?" Gordon's voice was bland, but he could not stop his gaze. He reached across the desk and turned the top letter right side up to study the signature. Anna. Beautifully written; even in the heavy black copy it was delicate, as artful as any of the Chinese calligraphy on his screens. He looked up to find Rode watching him intently. "I can tell you a few things from just this, but I have to have the originals. Let me show you my security system."

He led the way to the other side of the room. Here he had a long worktable, an oversized light table, a copy camera, enlarger, files. There was a computer and printer on a second desk. It was all fastidiously neat and clean.

"The files are fireproof," he said dryly, "and the safe is also. Mr. Roda, if you've investigated me, you know I've handled some priceless documents. And I've kept them right here in the shop. Leave the copies. I can start with them, but tomorrow I'll want the originals."

"Where's the safe?"

Gordon shrugged and went to the computer, keyed in his code, and then moved to the wall behind the worktable and pushed aside a panel to reveal a safe front. "I don't intend to open it for you. You can see enough without that."

"Computer security?"

"Yes."

"Very well. Tomorrow I'll send you the originals. You said you can already tell us something."

They returned to the office space. "First you," Gordon said, pointing to the top letter. "Who censored them?"

The letters had been cut off just above the greeting, and there were rectangles of white throughout.

"That's how they were when we found them," Roda said heavily. "Mercer must have done it himself. One of the detectives said the holes were cut with a razor blade."

Gordon nodded. "Curiouser and curiouser. Well, for what it's worth at this point, she's an artist more than likely. Painter would be my first guess."

"Are you sure?"

"Don't be a bloody fool. Of course I'm not sure, not with copies to work with. It's a guess. Everything I report will be a guess. Educated guesswork, Mr. Roda, that's all I can guarantee."

Roda sank down into his chair and expelled a long breath. "How long will it take?"

"How many letters?"

"Nine."

"Two, three weeks."

Very slowly Roda shook his head. "We are desperate, Mr. Sills. We will double your usual fee if you can give this your undivided attention."

"And how about your cooperation?"

"What do you mean?"

"His handwriting also. I want to see at least four pages of his writing."

Roda looked blank.

"It will help to know her if I know her correspondent."

"Very well," Roda said.

"How old was he?"

"Thirty."

"Okay. Anything else you can tell me?"

Roda seemed deep in thought, his eyes narrowed, a stillness about him that suggested concentration. With a visible start he looked up, nodded. "What you said about her could be important already. She mentions a show in one of the letters. We assumed a showgirl, a dancer, something like that. I'll put someone on it immediately. An artist. That could be right."

"Mr. Roda, can you tell me anything else? How important are those papers? Are they salable? Would anyone outside your company have an idea of their value?"

"They are quite valuable," he said with such a lack of tone that Gordon's ears almost pricked to attention. "If we don't recover them in a relatively short time, we will have to bring in the FBI. National security may be at stake. We want to handle it ourselves, obviously." He finished in the same monotone, "The Russians would pay millions for them, I'm certain. And we will pay whatever we have to. She has them. She says so in one of the letters. We have to find that woman."

For a moment Gordon considered turning down the job. Trouble, he thought. Real trouble. He glanced at the topmost letter again, the signature *Anna,* and he said, "Okay. I have a contract I use routinely . . ."

After Rode left he studied the one letter for several minutes, not reading it, in fact examining it upside down again, and he said softly, "Hello, Anna."

Then he gathered up all the letters and put them in a file which he deposited in his safe. He had no intention of starting until he had the originals. But it would comfort Roda to believe he was already at work.

Roda sent the originals and a few samples of Mercer's writing before noon the next day, and for three hours Gordon studied them all. He arranged hers on the worktable under the gooseneck lamp and turned them this way and that, not yet reading them, making notes now and then. As he had suspected, her script was fine, delicate, with beautiful shading. She used a real pen with real ink, not a felt-tip or a ballpoint. Each stroke was visually satisfying, artistic in itself. One letter was three pages long, four were two pages, the others were single sheets. None of them had a date, an address, a complete name. He cursed the person who had mutilated them. One by one he turned them over to examine the backs and jotted: "Pressure—light to medium." His other notes were equally brief: "Fluid, rapid, not conventional; proportions, 1:5." That was European and he did not think she was, but it would bear close examination. Each note was simply a direction marker, a first impression. He was whistling tunelessly as he worked and was startled when the telephone rang.

It was Karen, finally returning his many calls. The children would arrive by six, and he must return them by seven Sunday night. Her voice was cool, as if she were giving orders about laundry. He said okay and hung up, surprised at how little he felt about the matter. Before, it had given him a wrench each time they talked; he had asked questions: How was she? Was she working? Was the house all right? She had the house on Long Island, and that was fine with him, he had spent more and more time in town anyway over the past few years; but still, they had bought it together, he had repaired this and that, put up screens, taken them down, struggled with plumbing.

That night he took the two children to a Greek restaurant. Buster, eight years old, said it was yucky; Dana, ten, called him a baby and Gordon headed off the fight by saying he had bought a new Monopoly game. Dana said Buster was into winning. Dana looked very much like her mother, but Buster was her true genetic heir. Karen was into winning too.

They went to the Cloisters and fantasized medieval scenarios; they played Monopoly again, and on Sunday he took them to a puppet show at the Met and then drove them home. He was exhausted. When he got back he looked about, deeply depressed. There were dirty dishes in the sink, on the table, in the living room. Buster had slept on the couch and his bedclothes and covers were draped over it. Karen said they were getting too old to share a room any longer. Dana's bedroom was also a mess. She had left her pajamas and slippers. Swiftly he gathered up the bedding from the living room and tossed it all onto the bed in Dana's room and closed the door. He overfilled the dishwasher and turned it on and finally went into his workroom and opened the safe.

"Hello, Anna," he said softly, and tension seeped from him; the ache that had settled in behind his eyes vanished; he forgot the traffic jams coming home from Long Island, forgot the bickering his children seemed unable to stop.

He took the letters to the living room and sat down to read them through for the first time.

Love letters, passionate letters, humorous in places, perceptive, intelligent. Without dates it was hard to put them in chronological order, but the story emerged. She had met Mercer in the city; they had walked and talked and he had left. He had come back and this time they were together for a weekend and became lovers. She sent her letters to a post office box; he did not write to her, although he left papers covered with incomprehensible scribbles in her care. She was married to someone, whose name had been cut out with a razor blade every time she referred to him. Mercer knew him, visited him apparently. They were even friends, and had long serious talks from which she was excluded. She was afraid;

Mercer was involved in something very dangerous, and no one told her what it was, although her husband knew. She called Mercer her mystery man and speculated about his secret life, his family, his insane wife, or tyrannical father, or his own lapses into lycanthropy. Gordon smiled. Anna was not a whiner or a weeper, but she was hopelessly in love with Mercer and did not even know where he lived, where he worked, what danger threatened him, anything about him except that when he was with her, she was alive and happy. That was enough. Her husband understood and wanted only her happiness, and it was destroying her, knowing she was hurting him so much, but she was helpless.

He pursed his lips and reread one. "My darling, I can't stand it. I really can't stand it any longer. I dream of you, see you in every stranger on the street, hear your voice every time I answer the phone. My palms become wet and I tingle all over, thinking it's your footsteps I hear. You are my dreams. So, I told myself today, this is how it is? No way! Am I a silly schoolgirl mooning over a television star? At 26? I gathered all your papers and put them in a carton and addressed it, and as I wrote the box number, I found myself giggling. You can't send a Dear John to a post office box number. What if you failed to pick it up and an inspector opened it finally? I should entertain such a person? They're all gray and desiccated, you know, those inspectors. Let them find their own entertainment! What if they could read your mysterious squiggles and discover the secret of the universe? Do any of them deserve such enlightenment? No. I put everything back in [excised] safe—" Mercer was not the mystery man, Gordon thought then; the mystery was the other man, the nameless one whose safe hid Mercer's papers. Who was he? He shook his head over the arrangement of two men and a woman, and continued to read: "—and [excised] came in and let me cry on his shoulder. Then we went to dinner. I was starved."

Gordon laughed out loud and put the letters down on the coffee table, leaned back with his hands behind his head and contemplated the ceiling. It needed paint.

For the next two weeks he worked on the letters, and the few pages of Mercer's handwriting. He photographed everything, made enlargements, and searched for signs of weakness, illness. He keystroked the letters into his computer and ran the program he had developed, looking for usages, foreign or regional combinations, anything unusual or revealing. Mercer, he decided, had been born in a test tube and never left school and the laboratory until the day he met Anna. She was from the Midwest, not a big city, somewhere around one of the Great Lakes. The name that had been consistently cut out had six letters. She had gone to an opening and the artist's name had been cut out also. It had nine letters. Even without her testimony about the artist, it was apparent that she had been excited by his work. It showed in the writing. He measured the spaces between the words, the size of individual letters, the angle of her slant, the proportions of everything. Every movement she made was graceful, rhythmic. Her connections were garlands, open and trusting; that meant she was honest herself. Her threadlike connections that strung her words together indicated her speed in writing, her intuition, which she trusted.

As the work went on he made more complete notes, drawing conclusions more and more often. The picture of Anna was becoming real.

He paid less attention to Mercer's writing after making an initial assessment of him. A scientist, technologist, precise, angular, a genius, inhibited, excessively secretive, a loner. He was a familiar type.

When Roda returned, Gordon felt he could tell him more about those two people than their own mothers knew about them.

What he could not tell was what they looked like, or where Anna was now, or where the papers were that she had put in her husband's safe.

He watched Roda skim through the report on Anna. Today, rain was falling in gray curtains of water; the air felt thick and clammy.

"That's all?" Roda demanded when he finished.

"That's it."

"We checked every art show in the state," Roda said, scowling at him. "We didn't find her. And we have proof that Mercer couldn't have spent as much time with her as she claimed in the letters. We've been set up. You've been set up. You say that she's honest, ethical, and we say she's an agent or worse. She got her hooks in him and got those papers, and these letters are fakes, every one of them is a fake!"

Gordon shook his head. "There's not a lie in those letters."

"Then why didn't she come forward when he died? There was enough publicity at the time. We saw to that. I tell you he never spent any real time with her. We found him in a talent hunt when he was a graduate student, and he stayed in that damn lab ever since, seven days a week for four years. He never had time for a relationship of the sort she talks about. It's a lie through and through. A fantasy." He slumped in his chair. Today his face was almost as gray as his very good suit. He looked years older than he had the last time he had been in the office. "They're going to win," he said in a low voice. "The woman and her partner, they're probably out of the country already. Probably left the day after the accident, with the papers, their job done. Well done. That stupid, besotted fool!" He stared at the floor for several more seconds, then straightened. His voice was hard, clipped. "I was against consulting you from the start. A waste of time and money. Voodoo crap, that's all this is. Well, we've done what we can. Send in your bill. Where are her letters?"

Silently Gordon slid a folder across the desk. Roda went

through it carefully, then put it in his briefcase and stood up. "If I were you, I would not give our firm as reference in the future, Sills." He pushed Gordon's report away from him. "We can do without that. Good day."

It should have ended there, Gordon knew, but it did not end. Where are you, Anna? he thought, gazing at the world swamped in cold rain. Why hadn't she come forward, attended the funeral, turned in the papers? He had no answers. She was out there, painting, living with a man who loved her very much, enough to give her the freedom to fall in love with someone else. Take good care of her, he thought at that other man. Be gentle with her, be patient while she heals. She's very precious, you know. He leaned his head against the window, let the coolness soothe him. He said aloud, "She's very precious."

"Gordon, are you all right?" Karen asked on the phone. It was his weekend for the children again.

"Sure. Why?"

"I just wondered. You sound strange. Do you have a girlfriend?"

"What do you want, Karen?"

The ice returned to her voice, and they made arrangements for the children's arrival, when he was to return them. Library books, he thought distantly. Just like library books.

When he hung up he looked at the apartment and was dismayed by the dinginess, the disregard for the barest amenities. Another lamp, he thought. He needed a second lamp, at the very least. Maybe even two. Anna loved light. A girlfriend? He wanted to laugh, and to cry also. He had a signature, some love letters written to another man, a woman who came to his dreams and spoke to him in the phrases from her letters. A girlfriend! He closed his eyes and saw the name: Anna. The capital *A* was a flaring volcano, high up into the stratosphere, then the even, graceful *n*'s, the funny little final *a* that had trouble staying on the base line, that wanted to fly away. And a beautiful sweeping line that flew out from it, circled above the entire name, came down to cross the first letter, turn it into an *A,* and in doing so formed a perfect palette. A graphic representation of Anna, soaring into the heavens, painting, creating art with every breath, every motion. Forever yours, Anna. Forever yours.

He took a deep breath and tried to make plans for the children's weekend, for the rest of the month, the summer, the rest of his life.

The next day he bought a lamp, and on his way home stopped in a florist shop and bought half a dozen flowering plants. She had written that the sunlight turned the flowers on the sill into jewels. He put them on the sill and raised the blind; the sunlight turned the blossoms into jewels. His hands were clenched; abruptly he turned away.

He went back to work; spring became summer, hot and humid as only New York could be, and he found himself going from one art show to another. He mocked himself, and cursed himself for it, but he attended openings, examined new artists' work, signatures, again and again and again. If the investigators trained in this couldn't find her, he told himself firmly, and the FBI couldn't find her, he was a fool to think he had even a remote chance. But he went to the shows. He was lonely, he told himself, and tried to become interested in other women, any other woman, and continued to attend openings.

In the fall he went to the opening of yet another new artist, out of an art school, a teacher. And he cursed himself for not thinking of that before. She could be an art teacher. He made a list of schools and started down the list, perfecting a story as he worked down it one by one. He was collecting signatures of artists for an article he planned to write. It was a passable story. It got him nothing.

She might be ugly, he told himself. What kind of woman

would have fallen in love with Mercer? He had been inhibited, constricted, without grace, brilliant, eccentric, and full of wonder. It was the wonder that she had sensed, he knew. She had been attracted to that in Mercer, and had got through his many defenses, had found a boy-man who was truly appealing. And he had adored her. That was apparent from her letters; it had been mutual. Why had he lied to her? Why hadn't he simply told her who he was, what he was doing? The other man in her life had not been an obstacle, that had been made clear also. The two men had liked each other, and both loved her. Gordon brooded about her, about Mercer, the other man, and he haunted openings, became a recognized figure at the various studios and schools where he collected signatures. It was an obsession, he told himself, unhealthy, maybe even a sign of neurosis—or worse. It was insane to fall in love with someone's signature, love letters to another man.

And he could be wrong, he told himself. Maybe Roda had been right, after all. The doubts were always short-lived.

The cold October rains had come. Karen was engaged to a wealthy man. The children's visits had become easier because he no longer was trying to entertain them every minute; he had given in and bought a television and video games for them. He dropped by the Art Academy to meet Rick Henderson, who had become a friend over the past few months. Rick taught watercolors.

Gordon was in his office waiting for him to finish with a class critique session when he saw the *A,* Anna's capital *A.*

He felt his arms prickle, and sweat form on his hands, and a tightening in the pit of his stomach as he stared at an envelope on Rick's desk. Almost fearfully he turned it around to study the handwriting. The *A*'s in Art Academy were like volcanoes, reaching up into the stratosphere, crossed with a quirky, insouciant line, like a sombrero at a rakish angle. Anna's *A.* It did not soar and make a palette, but it wouldn't, not in an address. That was her personal sign.

He let himself sink into Rick's chair and drew in a deep breath. He did not touch the envelope again. When Rick finally joined him, he nodded toward it.

"Would you mind telling me who wrote that?" His voice sounded hoarse, but Rick seemed not to notice. He opened the envelope and scanned a note, then handed it over. Her handwriting. Not exactly the same, but it was hers. He was certain it was hers, even with the changes. The way the writing was positioned on the page, the sweep of the letters, the fluid grace . . . But it was not the same. The *A* in her name, Anna, was different. He felt bewildered by the differences, and knew it was hers in spite of them. Finally, he actually read the words. She would be out of class for a few days. It was dated four days ago.

"Just a kid," Rick said. "Fresh in from Ohio, thinks she has to be excused from class. I'm surprised it's not signed by her mother."

"Can I meet her?"

Now Rick looked interested. "Why?"

"I want her signature."

Rick laughed. "You're a real nut, you know. Sure. She's in the studio, making up for time off. Come on."

He stopped at the doorway and gazed at the young woman painting. She was no more than twenty, almost painfully thin, hungry looking. She wore scruffy sneakers, very old, faded blue jeans, a man's plaid shirt. Not the Anna of the letters. Not yet.

Gordon felt dizzy and held on to the door frame for a moment, and he knew what it was that Mercer had worked on, what he had discovered. He felt as if he had slipped out of time himself as his thoughts raced, explanations formed, his next few years shaped themselves in his mind. Understanding came the way a memory comes, a gestalt of the entire event or series of events, all accessible at once. Mercer's notes had shown him to be brilliant, obsessional, obsessed with time, secretive. Roda had assumed Mercer failed because he had blown himself up. Everyone must have assumed that. But he had not failed. He had gone forward five years, six at the most, to the time when Anna would be twenty-six. He had slipped out of time to the future.

Gordon knew with certainty that it was his own name that had been excised from Anna's letters. Phrases from her letters tumbled through his mind. She had mentioned a Japanese bridge, from his painting, the flowers on the sill, even the way the sun failed when it sank behind the building across the street. He thought of Roda and the hordes of agents searching for the papers that were to be hidden, had been hidden in the safest place in the world—the future. The safe Anna would put the papers in would be his, Gordon's, safe. He closed his eyes hard, already feeling the pain he knew would come when Mercer realized that he was to die, that he had died. For Mercer there could not be a love strong enough to make him abandon his work.

Gordon knew he would be with Anna, watch her mature, become the Anna of the letters, watch her soar into the stratosphere, and when Mercer walked through his time door, Gordon would still love her, and wait for her, help her heal afterward.

Rick cleared his throat and Gordon released his grasp of the door frame, took the next step into the studio. Anna's concentration was broken; she looked up at him. Her eyes were dark blue.

Hello, Anna.

And the Angels Sing

*E*ddie never left the office until one or even two in the
morning on Sundays, Tuesdays, and Thursdays. The
North Coast News came out three times a week, and
it seemed to him that no one could publish a paper unless
someone in charge was on hand until the press run. He knew
that the publisher, Stuart Winkle, didn't care particularly, as
long as the advertising was in place, but it wasn't right, Eddie
thought. What if something came up, something went
wrong? Even out here at the end of the world there could be
a late-breaking story that required someone to write it, to see
that it got placed. Actually, Eddie's hopes for that event,
high six years ago, had diminished to the point of needing
conscious effort to recall them even. In fact, he liked to see
his editorials before he packed it in.

This night, Thursday, he read his own words and then
bellowed, "Where is she?"

She was Ruthie Jenson, and *she* had spelled frequency with
one *e* and an *a*. Eddie stormed through the deserted outer
office looking for her, and caught her at the door just as she

236

was wrapping her vampire cloak about her thin shoulders. She was thin, her hair was cut too short, too close to her head, and she was too frightened of him. And, he thought with bitterness, she was crazy, or she would not wait around three nights a week for him to catch her at the door and give her hell.

"Why don't you use the goddamn dictionary? Why do you correct my copy? I told you I'd wring your neck if you touched my copy again!"

She made a whimpering noise and looked past him in terror, down the hallway, into the office. "I . . . I'm sorry. I didn't mean . . ." Fast as quicksilver then, she fled out into the storm that was still howling. He hoped the goddamn wind would carry her to Australia or beyond.

The wind screamed as it poured through the outer office, scattering a few papers, setting a light adance on a chain. Eddie slammed the door against it and surveyed the space around him, detesting every inch of it at the moment. Three desks, the fluttering papers that Mrs. Rondale would heave out because anything on the floor got heaved out. Except dirt; she seemed never to see quite all of it. Next door, the presses were running; people were doing things, but the staff that put the paper together had left now. Ruthie was always next to last to go, and then Eddie. He kicked a chair on his way back to his own cubicle, clutching the ink-wet paper in his hand, well aware that the ink was smearing onto his skin.

He knew that the door to the press room had opened and softly closed again. In there they would be saying Fat Eddie was in a rage. He knew they called him Fat Eddie, or even worse, behind his back, and he knew that no one on earth cared if the *North Coast News* was a mess except him. He sat at his desk scowling at the editorial, one of his better ones, he thought, and the word *frequancy* leaped off the page at him; nothing else registered. What he had written was "At this time of year the storms bear down on shore with such regularity, such frequency, that it's as if the sea and air are engaged in the final battle." It got better, but he put it aside and listened to the wind. All evening he had listened to reports from up and down the coast, expecting storm damage, light outages, wrecks, something. At midnight, he had decided it was just another Pacific storm and had wrapped up the paper. Just the usual: Highway 101 under water here and there, a tree down here and there, a head-on, no deaths . . .

The wind screamed and let up, caught its breath and screamed again. Like a kid having a tantrum. And up and down the coast the people were like parents who had seen too many kids having too many tantrums. Ignore it until it goes away and then get on about your business, that was their attitude. Eddie was from Indianapolis where a storm with eighty-mile-an-hour winds made news. Six years on the coast had not changed that. A storm like this, by God, should make news!

Still scowling, he pulled on his own raincoat, a great, black waterproof garment that covered him to the floor. He added his black, wide-brimmed hat, and was ready for the weather. He knew that behind his back they called him Mountain Man, when they weren't calling him Fat Eddie. He secretly thought he looked more like The Shadow than not.

He drove to Connally's Tavern and had a couple of drinks, sitting alone in glum silence, and then offered to drive Truman Cox home when the bar closed at two.

The town of Lewisburg was south of Astoria, north of Cannon Beach, population nine hundred eighty-four. And at two in the morning they were all sleeping, the town blackened out by rain. There were the flickering night lights at the drug store, and the lights from the newspaper building, and two traffic lights, although no other traffic moved. Rain pelted the windshield and made a river through Main Street, cascaded down the side streets on the left, came pouring off the mountain on the right. Eddie made the turn onto Third and hit the brakes hard when a figure darted across the street.

"Jesus!" he grunted as the car skidded, then caught and righted itself. "Who was that?"

Truman was peering out into the darkness, nodding. The figure had vanished down the alley behind Sal's Restaurant. "Bet it was the Boland girl, the young one. Not Norma. Following her sister's footsteps."

His tone was not condemnatory, even though everyone knew exactly where those footsteps would lead the kid.

"She sure earned whatever she got tonight," Eddie said with a grunt, and pulled up into the driveway of Truman's house. "See you around."

"Yep. Probably will. Thanks for the lift." He gathered himself together and made a dash for his porch.

But he would be soaked anyway, Eddie knew. All it took was a second out in that driving rain. That poor, stupid kid, he thought again, as he backed out of the drive, retraced his trail for a block or two, and headed toward his own little house. On impulse he turned back and went down Second Street to see if the kid was still scurrying around; at least he could offer her a lift home. He knew where the Bolands lived, the two sisters, their mother, all in the trade now, apparently. But, God, he thought, the little one couldn't be more than twelve.

The numbered streets were parallel to the coast line; the cross streets had become wind tunnels that rocked his car every time he came to one. Second Street was empty, black. He breathed a sigh of relief. He had not wanted to get involved anyway, in any manner, and now he could go on home, listen to music for an hour or two, have a drink or two, a sandwich, and get some sleep. If the wind ever let up. He slept very poorly when the wind blew this hard. What he most likely would do was finish the book he was reading, possibly start another one. The wind was good for another four or five hours.

Thinking this way, he made another turn or two, and then saw the kid again, this time sprawled on the side of the road.

If he had not already seen her once, if he had not been thinking about her, about her sister and mother, if he had been driving faster than five miles an hour, probably he would have missed her. She lay just off the road, face down. As soon as he stopped and got out of the car, the rain hit his face, streamed from his glasses, blinding him almost. He got his hands on the child and hauled her to the car, yanked open the back door and deposited her inside. Only then he got a glimpse of her face. Not the Boland girl. No one he had ever seen before. And as light as a shadow. He hurried around to the driver's side and got in, but he could no longer see her now from the front seat. Just the lumpish black raincoat that gleamed with water and covered her entirely. He wiped his face, cleaned his glasses, and twisted in the seat; he couldn't reach her, and she did not respond to his voice.

He cursed bitterly and considered his next move. She could be dead, or dying. Through the rain-streaked windshield the town appeared uninhabited. They didn't have a police station, a clinic or hospital, nothing. The nearest doctor was ten or twelve miles away, and in this weather . . . Finally he started the engine and headed for home. He would call the state police from there, he decided. Let them come and collect her.

He drove up Hammer Hill to his own house and parked in the driveway at the walk that led to the front door. He would open the door first, he had decided, then come back and get the kid; either way he would get soaked, but there was little he could do about that. He moved fairly fast for a large man, but his fastest was not good enough to keep the rain off his face again. If it would come straight down, the way God meant rain to fall, he thought, fumbling with the key in the lock, he would be able to see something. He got the door open, flicked on the light switch, and went back to the car to collect the girl. She was as limp as before, and seemed to weigh nothing at all. The slicker she wore was hard to grasp, and he did not want her head to loll about, for her to brain herself on the porch rail or the door frame, but she was not easy to carry, and he grunted although her weight was insignificant. Finally he got her inside and kicked the door shut and made his way to the bedroom where he dumped her on the bed. Then he took off his hat that had been useless, and his glasses that had blinded him with running water, and the streaming raincoat that was leaving a trail of water with every step. He backed off the Navajo rug and out to the kitchen to put the wet coat on a chair, let it drip on the linoleum. He grabbed a handful of paper toweling and wiped his glasses, then returned to the bedroom.

He reached down to remove the kid's raincoat and jerked his hand away again.

"Jesus Christ!" he whispered, and backed away from her. He heard himself saying it again, and then again, and stopped. He had backed up to the wall, was pressed hard against it. Even from there he could see her clearly. Her face was smooth, without eyebrows, without eyelashes, her nose too small, her lips too narrow, hardly lips at all. What he had thought was a coat was part of her. It started on her head, where hair should have been, down the sides of her head where ears should have been, down her narrow shoulders, the backs of her arms that seemed too long and thin, almost boneless.

She was on her side, one long leg stretched out, the other doubled up under her. Where there should have been genitalia, there was too much skin, folds of skin.

Eddie felt his stomach spasm, a shudder passed over him. Before, he had wanted to shake her, wake her up, ask questions; now he thought that if she opened her eyes, he might pass out. And he was shivering with cold. Moving very cautiously, making no noise, he edged his way around the room to the door, then out, back to the kitchen where he pulled a bottle of bourbon from a cabinet and poured half a glass that he drank as fast as he could. He stared at his hand. It was shaking.

Very quietly he took off his shoes, sodden, and placed them at the back door next to his waterproof boots that he invariably forgot to wear. As soundlessly as possible he crept to the bedroom door and looked at her again. She had moved, was now drawn up in a huddle, as if she was as cold as he was. He took a deep breath and began to inch around the wall of the room toward the closet where he pulled out his slippers with one foot, and eased them on, and then tugged on a blanket on a shelf. He had to let his breath out then; it sounded explosive to his ears. The girl shuddered and made herself into a tighter ball. He moved toward her slowly, ready to turn and run, and finally was close enough to lay the blanket over her. She was shivering hard.

He backed away from her again and this time went to the living room, leaving the door open so that he could see her, just in case. He turned up the thermostat, retrieved his drink from the kitchen, and again and again went to the door to peer inside.

He should call the state police, he knew, and made no motion toward the phone. A doctor? He nearly laughed. He wished he had a camera. If they took her away, and they would, there would be nothing to show, nothing to prove she had existed. He thought of her picture on the front page of the *North Coast News,* and snorted. *The National Enquirer?* This time he muttered a curse. But she was news. She certainly was news.

Mary Beth, he decided. He had to call someone with a camera, someone who could write a decent story. He dialed

Mary Beth's number, got her answering machine and hung up, dialed it again. At the fifth call her voice came on.

"Who the hell is this, and do you know that it's three in the fucking morning?"

"Eddie Delacort. Mary Beth, get up, get over here, my place, and bring your camera."

"Fat Eddie? What the hell—"

"Right now, and bring plenty of film." He hung up.

A few seconds later his phone rang; he took it off the receiver and laid it down on the table. While he waited for Mary Beth he surveyed the room. The house was small, with two bedrooms, one that he used for an office, on the far side of the living room. In the living room there were two easy chairs covered with fine, dark green leather, no couch, a couple of tables, and many bookshelves, all filled. A long cabinet held his sound equipment, a stereo, hundreds of albums. Everything was neat, arranged for a large man to move about easily, nothing extraneous anywhere. Underfoot was another Navajo rug. He knew the back door was securely locked; the bedroom windows were closed, screens in place. Through the living room was the only way the kid on his bed could get out, and he knew she would not get past him if she woke up and tried to make a run. He nodded, then moved his two easy chairs so that they faced the bedroom; he pulled an end table between them, got another glass, and brought the bottle of bourbon. He sat down to wait for Mary Beth, brooding over the girl in his bed. From time to time the blanket shook hard; a slight movement that was nearly constant suggested that she had not yet warmed up. His other blanket was under her and he had no intention of touching her again in order to get to it.

Mary Beth arrived as furious as he had expected. She was his age, about forty, graying, with suspicious blue eyes, and no makeup. He had never seen her with lipstick on, or jewelry of any kind except for a watch, or in a skirt or dress.

That night she was in jeans and a sweatshirt, and a bright red hooded raincoat that brought the rainstorm inside as she entered, cursing him. He noted with satisfaction that she had her camera gear.

She cursed him expertly as she yanked off her raincoat, and was still calling him names when he finally put his hand over her mouth and took her by the shoulder, propelled her toward the bedroom door.

"Shut up and look," he muttered. She was stronger than he had realized, and now twisted out of his grasp and swung a fist at him. Then she faced the bedroom.

She looked, then turned back to him red faced and sputtering. "You . . . you got me out . . . a floozy in your bed . . . So you really do know what that thing you've got is used for! And you want pictures! Jesus God!"

"Shut up!"

This time she did. She peered at his face for a second, turned and looked again, took a step forward, then another. He knew her reaction was to his expression, not the lump on the bed. Nothing of that girl was visible, just the unquiet blanket, and a bit of darkness that was not hair but should have been. He stayed at Mary Beth's side, and his caution was communicated to her; she was as quiet now as he was.

At the bed he reached out and gently pulled back the blanket. One of *her* hands clutched it spasmodically. The hand had four apparently boneless fingers, long and tapered, very pale. Mary Beth exhaled too long and neither of them moved for what seemed minutes. Finally she reached out and touched the darkness at the girl's shoulder, touched her arm, then her face. Abruptly she pulled back her hand. The girl on the bed was shivering harder than ever, in a tighter ball that hid the many folds of skin at her groin.

"It's cold," Mary Beth whispered.

"Yeah." He put the blanket back over the girl.

Mary Beth went to the other side of the bed, squeezed

between it and the wall and carefully pulled the bedspread and blanket free, and put them over the girl also. Eddie took Mary Beth's arm and they backed out of the bedroom. She sank into one of the chairs he had arranged and automatically held out her hand for the drink he was pouring.

"My God," Mary Beth said softly after taking a large swallow, "what is it? Where did it come from?"

He told her as much as he knew and they regarded the sleeping figure. He thought the shivering had subsided, but maybe she was just too weak to move so many covers.

"You keep saying it's a she," Mary Beth said. "You know that thing isn't human, don't you?"

Reluctantly he described the rest of the girl, and this time Mary Beth finished her drink. She glanced at her camera bag, but made no motion toward it yet. "It's our story," she said. "We can't let them have it until we're ready. Okay?"

"Yeah. There's a lot to consider before we do anything."

Silently they considered. He refilled their glasses, and they sat watching the sleeping creature on his bed. When the lump flattened out a bit, Mary Beth went in and lifted the covers and examined her, but she did not touch her again. She returned to her chair, very pale, and sipped bourbon. Outside, the wind moaned, but the howling had subsided, and the rain was no longer a driving presence against the front of the house, the side that faced the sea.

From time to time one or the other made a brief suggestion.

"Not radio," Eddie said.

"Right." said Mary Beth. She was a stringer for NPR.

"Not newsprint," she said later.

Eddie was a stringer for AP. He nodded.

"It could be dangerous when it wakes up," she said.

"I know. Six rows of alligator teeth, or poison fangs, or mind rays."

She giggled. "Maybe right now there's a hidden camera taking in all this. Remember that old TV show?"

"Maybe *they* sent her to test us, our reaction to *them.*"

Mary Beth sat up straight. "My God, more of them?"

"No species can have only one member," he said very seriously. "A counterproductive trait." He realized that he was quite drunk. "Coffee," he said, and pulled himself out of the chair, made his way unsteadily to the kitchen.

When he had the coffee ready, and tuna sandwiches, and sliced onions and tomatoes, he found Mary Beth leaning against the bedroom door contemplating the girl.

"Maybe it's dying," she said in a low voice. "We can't just let it die, Eddie."

"We won't," he said. "Let's eat something. It's almost daylight."

She followed him to the kitchen and looked around it. "I've never been in your house before. You realize that? All the years I've known you, I've never been invited here before."

"Five years," he said.

"That's what I mean. All those years. It's a nice house. It looks like your house should look, you know?"

He glanced around the kitchen. Just a kitchen, stove, refrigerator, table, counters. There were books on the counter, and piled on the table. He pushed the pile to one side and put down plates. Mary Beth lifted one and turned it over. Russet colored, gracefully shaped, pottery from North Carolina, signed by Sara. She nodded, as if in confirmation.

"You picked out every single item individually, didn't you?"

"Sure. I have to live with the stuff."

"What are you doing here, Eddie? Why here?"

"The end of the world, you mean? I like it."

"Well, I want the hell out. You've been out and chose to

be here. I choose to be out. That thing on your bed will get me out." She bit into a sandwich.

From the University of Indiana to a small paper in Evanston, on to Philadelphia, New York. He felt he had been out plenty, and now he simply wanted a place where people lived in individual houses and chose the pottery they drank their coffee from. Six years ago he had left New York, on vacation, he had said; he had come to the end of the world and stayed.

"Why haven't you gone already?" he asked Mary Beth.

She smiled her crooked smile and shook her head. "I was married, you know that? To a fisherman. That's what girls on the coast do, marry fishermen, or lumbermen, or policemen. Me, Miss Original No-talent, herself. Married, playing house forever. He's out there somewhere. Went out one day and never came home again. So I got a job with the paper, this and that. Only one thing could be worse than staying here at the end of the world, and that's being in the world broke. Not my style."

She finished her sandwich and coffee, and now seemed too restless to sit still. She went to the window over the sink and gazed out. The light was gray. "You don't belong here any more than I do. What happened? Some woman tell you to get lost? Couldn't get the job you wanted? Some young slim punk worm in in front of you? You're dodging just like me."

All the above, he thought silently, and said, "Look, I've been thinking. I can't go to the office without raising suspicion, in case anyone's looking for her, I mean. I haven't been in the office before one or two in the afternoon for more than five years. But you can. See if anything's come over the wires, if there's a search on, if there was a wreck of any sort. You know. If the FBI's nosing around, or the military. Anything at all."

Mary Beth rejoined him at the table and poured more coffee, her restlessness gone, an intent look on her face. Her business face, he thought.

"Okay. First some pictures, though. And we'll have to have a story about my car. It's been out front all night," she added crisply. "So, if anyone brings it up, I'll have to say I keep you company now and then. Okay?"

He nodded, and thought without bitterness that that would give them a laugh at Connally's Tavern. That reminded him of Truman Cox. "They'll get around to him eventually, and he might remember seeing her. Of course, he assumed it was the Boland girl. But they'll know we saw someone. Even if no one asks him directly, he knows if a flea farts in this town."

Mary Beth shrugged. "So you saw the Boland girl and got to thinking about her and her trade, and gave me a call. No problem."

He looked at her curiously. "You really don't care if they start that scuttlebutt around town, about you and me?"

"Eddie," she said almost too sweetly, "I'd admit to fucking a pig if it would get me the hell out of here. I'll go on home for a shower, and by then maybe it'll be time enough to get on my horse and go to the office. But first some pictures."

At the bedroom door he asked in a hushed voice, "Can you get them without using the flash? That might send her into shock or something."

She gave him a dark look. "Will you for Christ sake stop calling it a her!" She scowled at the figure on the bed. "Let's bring in a lamp, at least. You know I have to uncover it."

He knew. He brought in a floor lamp and turned on the bedside light and watched Mary Beth go to work. She was a good photographer, and in this instance she had an immobile subject; she could use timed exposures. She took a roll of film, and started a second one, then drew back. The girl on the bed was shivering hard again, drawing up her legs, curling into a tight ball.

"Okay. I'll finish in daylight, maybe when it's awake."

Mary Beth was right, Eddie had to admit; the creature was not a girl, not a female probably. She was elongated, without any angles anywhere, no elbows or sharp knees or jutting hipbones. Just a smooth long body without breasts, without a navel, without genitalia. And with that dark growth that started high on her head and went down the backs of her arms, covered her back entirely. Like a mantle, he thought, and was repelled by the idea. Her skin was not human, either. It was pale, with yellow rather than pink undertones. She obviously was very cold; the yellow was fading to a grayish hue. Tentatively he touched her arm. It felt wrong, not yielding the way human flesh covered with skin should yield. It felt like cool silk over something firmer than human flesh.

Mary Beth replaced the covers, and they backed from the room as the creature shivered. "Jesus," Mary Beth whispered. "You'd think it would have warmed up by now. This place is like an oven, and all those covers." A shudder passed through her.

In the living room again, Mary Beth began to fiddle with her camera. She took out the second roll of film, and held both rolls in indecision. "If anyone's nosing around, and if they learn that you might have seen it, and that we've been together, they might accidentally snitch my film. Where's a good place to stash it for a while?"

He took the film rolls and she shook her head. "Don't tell me. Just keep it safe." She looked at her watch. "I won't be back until ten or later. I'll find out what I can, make a couple of calls. Keep an eye on it. See you later."

He watched her pull on her red raincoat and went to the porch with her where he stood until she was in her car and out of sight. Daylight had come; the rain had ended although the sky was still overcast and low. The fir trees in his front yard glistened and shook off water with the slightest breeze. The wind had turned into no more than that, a slight breeze. The air was not very cold, and it felt good after the heat

inside. It smelled good, of leaf mold and sea and earth and
fish and fir trees . . . He took several deep breaths and then
went back in.

The house really was like an oven, he thought, momentarily refreshed by the cool morning and now once again feeling
logy. Why didn't she warm up? He stood in the doorway to
the bedroom and looked at the huddled figure. Why didn't
she warm up?

He thought of victims of hypothermia; the first step, he
had read, was to get their temperature back up to normal,
any way possible. Hot water bottle? He didn't own one. Hot
bath? He went to the girl and shook his head slightly. Water
might even be toxic to her. And that was the problem, he
knew; she was an alien with unknown needs, unknown dan-
gers. And she was freezing.

With reluctance he touched her arm, still cool in spite of all
the covering over her. Like a hothouse plant, he thought
then, brought into a frigid climate, destined to die of cold.
Moving slowly, with even greater reluctance than before, he
began to pull off his trousers, his shirt, and when he was
down to undershirt and shorts, he gently shifted the sleeping
girl and lay down beside her, drew her to the warmth of his
body.

The house temperature by then was close to eighty-five,
much too warm for a man with all the fat that Eddie had on
his body; she felt good next to him, cooling, even soothing.
For a time she made no response to his presence, but gradually her shivering lessened, and she seemed to change subtly,
lose her rigidity; her legs curved to make contact with his
legs; her torso shifted, relaxed, flowed into the shape of his
body; one of her arms moved over his chest, her hand at his
shoulder, her other arm bent and fitted itself against him. Her
cool cheek pressed against the pillows of flesh over his ribs.
Carefully he wrapped his arms about her and drew her
closer.

He dozed, came awake with a start, dozed again. At nine he woke up completely and began to disengage himself. She made a soft sound, like a child in protest, and he stroked her arm and whispered nonsense. At last he was untangled from her arms and legs and stood up, and pulled on his clothes again. The next time he looked at the girl, her eyes were open, and he felt entranced momentarily. Large, round, golden eyes, like pools of molten gold, unblinking, inhuman. He took a step away from her.

"Can you talk?"

There was no response. Her eyes closed again and she drew the covers high up onto her face, buried her head in them.

Wearily Eddie went to the kitchen and poured coffee. It was hot and tasted like tar. He emptied the coffeemaker and started a fresh brew. Soon Mary Beth would return and they would make the plans that had gone nowhere during the night. He felt more tired than he could remember and thought ruefully of what it was really like to be forty-two and a hundred pounds overweight, and miss a night's sleep.

"You look like hell," Mary Beth said in greeting at ten. She looked fine, excited, a flush of her cheeks, her eyes sparkling. "Is it okay? Has it moved? Come awake yet?" She charged past him and stood in the doorway to the bedroom. "Good. I got hold of Homer Carpenter, over in Portland. He's coming over with a video camera, around two or three. I didn't tell him what we have, but I had to tell him something to get him over. I said we have a coelacanth."

Eddie stared at her. "He's coming over for that? I don't believe it."

She left the doorway and swept past him on her way to the kitchen. "Okay, he doesn't believe me, but he knows it's something big, something hot, or I wouldn't have called him. He knows me that well, anyway."

Eddie thought about it for a second or two, then shrugged. "What else did you find out?"

Mary Beth got coffee and held the cup in both hands, surveying him over the top of it. "Boy oh boy, Eddie! I don't know who knows what, or what it is they know, but there's a hunt on. They're saying some guys escaped from the pen over at Salem, but that's bull. Roadblocks and everything. I don't think they're telling anyone anything yet. The poor cops out there don't know what the hell they're supposed to be looking for, just anything suspicious, until the proper authorities get here."

"Here? They know she's here?"

"Not here here. But somewhere on the coast. They're closing in from north and south. And that's why Homer decided to get his ass over here, too."

Eddie remembered the stories that had appeared on the wire services over the past few weeks about an erratic comet that was being tracked. Stuart Winkle, the publisher and editor in chief, had not chosen to print them in his paper, but Eddie had seen them. And more recently the story about a possible burnout in space of a Russian capsule. Nothing to worry about, no radiation, but there might be bright lights in the skies, the stories had said. Right, he thought. Right.

Mary Beth was at the bedroom door again, sipping her coffee. "I'll owe you for this, Eddie. No way can I pay for what you're giving me."

He made a growly noise, and she turned to regard him, suddenly very serious.

"Maybe there is something," she said softly. "A little piece of the truth. You know you're not the most popular man in town, Eddie. You're always doing little things for people, and yet, do they like you for it? Tell me, Eddie. Do they?"

"Let's not do any psychoanalysis right now," he said coldly. "Later."

She shook her head. "Later I won't be around. Remember?" Her voice took on a mocking tone. "Why do you suppose you don't get treated better? Why no one comes to visit? Or invites you to the clambakes, except for office parties, anyway? It's all those little things you keep doing, Eddie. Overdoing maybe. And you won't let anyone pay you back for anything. You turn everyone into a poor relation, Eddie, and they begin to resent it."

Abruptly he laughed. For a minute he had been afraid of her, what she might reveal about him. "Right," he said. "Tell that to Ruthie Jenson."

Mary Beth shrugged. "You give poor little Ruthie exactly what she craves—mistreatment. She takes it home and nurtures it. And then she feels guilty. The Boland kid you intended to rescue last night. You would have had her, her sister, and their mother all feeling guilty. Truman Cox. How many free drinks you let him give you, Eddie? Not even one, I bet. Stuart Winkle? You run his paper for him. You ever use that key to his cabin? He really wanted you to use it, Eddie. A token repayment. George Allmann, Harriet Davies ... It's a long list, Eddie, the people you've done little things for. The people who go through life owing you, feeling guilty about not liking you, not sure why they don't. I was on that list, too, Eddie, but not now. I just paid you in full."

"Okay," he said heavily. "Now that we've cleared up the mystery about me, what about her?" He pointed past Mary Beth at the girl on his bed.

"It, Eddie. It. First the video, and make some copies, get them into a safe place, and then announce. How does that sound?"

He shrugged. "Okay. Whatever you want."

She grinned her crooked smile and shook her head at him. "Forget it, Eddie. I'm paid up for years to come. Look, I've got to get back to the office. I'll keep my eyes on the wires, anything coming in, and as soon as Homer shows, we'll be back. Are you okay? Can you hold out for the next few hours?"

"Yeah, I'm okay." He watched her pull on her coat and walked to the porch with her. Before she left, he said, "One thing, Mary Beth. Did it even occur to you that some people like to help out? No ulterior motive or anything, but a little human regard for others?"

She laughed. "I'll give it some thought, Eddie. And you give some thought to having perfected a method to make sure people leave you alone, keep their distance. Okay? See you later."

He stood on the porch taking deep breaths. The air was mild; maybe the sun would come out later on. Right now the world smelled good, scoured clean, fresh. No other house was visible from his porch. He had let the trees and shrubbery grow wild, screening everything from view. It was like being the last man on earth, he thought suddenly. The heavy growth even screened out the noise from the little town. If he listened intently, he could make out engine sounds, but no voices, no one else's music that he usually detested, no one else's cries or laughter.

Mary Beth never had been ugly, he thought then. She was good looking in her own way even now, going on middle age. She must have been a real looker as a younger woman. Besides, he thought, if anyone ever mocked her, called her names, she would slug the guy. That would be her way. And he had found his way, he added, then turned brusquely and went inside and locked the door after him.

He took a kitchen chair to the bedroom and sat down by her. She was shivering again. He reached over to pull the covers more tightly about her, then stopped his motion and stared. The black mantle thing did not cover her head as completely as it had before. He was sure it now started farther back. And more of her cheeks was exposed. Slowly he drew away the cover and then turned her over. The mantle was looser, with folds where it had been taut before. She reacted violently to being uncovered, shuddering long spasm-like movements. He replaced the cover.

"What the hell are you?" he whispered. "What's happening to you?"

He rubbed his eyes hard and sat down, regarding her with a frown. "You know what's going to happen, don't you? They'll take you somewhere and study you, try to make you talk, if you can, find out where you're from, what you want here, where there are others . . . They might hurt you. Even kill you."

He thought again of the great golden pools that were her eyes, of how her skin felt like silk over a firm substance, of the insubstantiality of her body, the lightness when he carried her.

"What do you want here?" he whispered. "Why did you come?"

After a few minutes of silent watching, he got up and found his dry shoes in the closet and pulled them on. He put on a plaid shirt that was very warm, and then he wrapped the sleeping girl in the blanket and carried her to his car and placed her on the backseat. He went back inside for another blanket and put that over her, too.

He drove up his street, avoiding the town, using a back road that wound higher and higher up the mountain. Stuart Winkle's cabin, he thought. An open invitation to use it any time he wanted. He drove carefully, taking the curves slowly, not wanting to jar her, to roll her off the backseat. The woods pressed in closer when he left the road for a logging road. From time to time he could see the ocean, then he turned and lost it again. The road clung to the steep mountainside, climbing, always climbing; there was no other traffic on it. The loggers had finished with this area; this was state land, untouchable, for now anyway. He stopped at one of the places where the ocean spread out below him and watched the waves rolling in forever and ever, unchanging, unknowable. Then he drove on.

The cabin was high on the mountain. Up here the trees were mature growth, mammoth and silent, with deep shadows beneath them, little understory growth in the dense shade. The cabin was redwood, rough, heated with a wood stove, no running water, no electricity. There was oil for a lamp, and plenty of dry wood stacked under a shed, and a store of food that Stuart had said he should consider his own. There were twin beds in the single bedroom, and a couch that opened to a double bed in the living room. Those two rooms and the kitchen made up the cabin.

He carried the girl inside and put her on one of the beds; she was entirely enclosed in blankets, like a cocoon. Hurriedly he made a fire in the stove, and brought in a good supply of logs. Like a hothouse orchid, he thought, she needed plenty of heat.

After the cabin started to heat up, he took off his outer clothing and lay down beside her, the way he had done before, and as before, she conformed to his body, melted into him, absorbed his warmth.

Sometimes he dozed, then he lay quietly thinking of his childhood, of the heat that descended on Indiana like a physical substance, of the tornadoes that sometimes came, murderous funnels that sucked life away, shredded everything. He dozed and dreamed, and awakened and dreamed in that state, also.

He got up to feed the fire, and tossed in the film Mary Beth had given him to guard. He got a drink of water at the pump in the kitchen, and lay down by her again. His fatigue increased, but pleasurably. His weariness was without pain, a floating sensation that was between sleep and wakefulness. Sometimes he talked quietly to her, but not much, and what he said he forgot as soon as the words formed. It was better to lie without sound, without motion. Now and then she shook convulsively, and then subsided again. Twilight came, darkness, then twilight again. Several times he aroused enough to build up the fire.

When it was daylight once more, he got up, reeling as if drunken; he pulled on his clothes and went to the kitchen to make instant coffee. He sensed her presence behind him. She was standing up, nearly as tall as he was, but incredibly insubstantial, not thin, but as slender as a straw. Her golden eyes were wide open. He could not read the expression on her face.

"Can you eat anything?" he asked. "Drink water?"

She looked at him. The black mantle was gone from her head; he could not see it anywhere on her as she stood facing him. The strange folds of skin at her groin, the boneless appearance of her body, the lack of hair, breasts, the very color of her skin looked right now, not alien, not repellent. The skin was like cool silk, he knew. He also knew this was not a woman, not a she, but something that should not be here, a creature, an it.

"Can you speak? Can you understand me at all?"

Her expression was as unreadable as that of a wild creature, a forest animal, aware, intelligent, unknowable.

Helplessly he said, "Please, if you can understand me, nod. Like this." He showed her, and in a moment she nodded. "And like this for no," he said. She mimicked him again.

"Do you understand that people are looking for you?"

She nodded slowly. Then, very deliberately, she turned around, and instead of the black mantle that had grown on her head, down her back, there was an iridescence, a rainbow of pastel colors that shimmered and gleamed. Eddie sucked in his breath as the new growth moved, opened slightly, more.

There wasn't enough room in the cabin for her to open the wings all the way. She stretched them from wall to wall. They looked like gauze, filmy, filled with light that was alive. Not realizing he was moving, Eddie was drawn to one of the wings, reached out to touch it. It was as hard as steel, and cool. She turned her golden liquid eyes to him, and drew her wings in again.

"We'll go someplace where it's warm," Eddie said hoarsely. "I'll hide you. I'll smuggle you somehow. They can't have you!"

She walked through the living room to the door and studied the handle for a moment. As she reached for it, he lumbered after her, lunged toward her, but already she was opening the door, slipping out.

"Stop! You'll freeze. You'll die!"

In the clearing of the forest, with sunlight slanting through the giant trees, she spun around, lifted her face upward, and then opened her wings all the way. As effortlessly as a butterfly, or a bird, she drew herself up into the air, her wings flashing light, now gleaming, now appearing to vanish as the light reflected one way and another.

"Stop!" Eddie cried again. "Please! Oh, God, stop! Come back!"

She rose higher, and looked down at him with her golden eyes. Suddenly the air seemed to tremble with sound, trills and arpeggios and flutings. Her mouth did not open as the sounds increased until Eddie fell to his knees and clapped his hands over his ears moaning. When he looked again, she was still rising, shining, invisible, shining again. Then she was gone.

Eddie pitched forward into the thick layer of fir needles and forest humus and lay still.

He felt a tugging on his arm, and heard Mary Beth's furious curses, but as if from a great distance. He moaned and tried to go to sleep again. She would not let him.

"You goddamn bastard! You filthy son of a bitch! You let it go! Didn't you? You turned it loose!"

He tried to push her hands away, moaning.

"You scum! Get up! You hear me? Get up! Don't think for a minute, buster, that I'll let you die out here! That's too good for you, you lousy tub of lard. Get up!"

Against his will he was crawling, then stumbling, leaning on her, being steadied by her. She kept cursing all the way back inside the cabin, until he was on the couch, and she stood over him, arms akimbo, glaring at him.

"Why? Just tell me why? For God's sake, Eddie, why?" Then she screamed at him, "Don't you dare pass out on me again. Open those damn eyes and keep them open!"

She savaged him and nagged him, made him drink whiskey that she had brought along, then made him drink coffee. She got him to his feet and made him walk around the cabin a little, let him sit down again, drink again. She did not let him go to sleep, or even lie down, and the night passed.

A fine rain had started to fall by dawn. Eddie felt as if he had been away a long time, to a very distant place that had left few memories. He listened to the soft rain and at first thought he was in his own small house, but then he realized he was in a strange cabin, and that Mary Beth was there, asleep in a chair. He regarded her curiously and shook his head, trying to clear it. His movement brought her sharply awake.

"Eddie, are you awake?"

"I think so. Where is this place?"

"Don't you remember?"

He started to say no, checked himself, and suddenly he was remembering. He stood up and looked about almost wildly.

"It's gone, Eddie. It went away and left you to die. You would have died out there if I hadn't come, Eddie. Do you understand what I'm saying? You would have died."

He sat down again and lowered his head into his hands. He knew she was telling the truth.

"It's going to be light soon," she said. "I'll make us something to eat, and then we'll go back to town. I'll drive you. We'll come back in a day or so to pick up your car." She stood up and groaned. "My God, I feel like I've been wrestling bears all night. I hurt all over."

She passed close enough to put her hand on his shoulder briefly. "What the hell, Eddie. Just what the hell."

In a minute he got up also, and went to the bedroom, looked at the bed where he had lain with *her* all through the night. He approached it slowly and saw the remains of the mantle. When he tried to pick it up, it crumbled to dust in his hand.